DREAM BOY

MARY CROCKETT *and* MADELYN ROSENBERG

sourcebooks
fire

Published by Sourcebooks Fire, an imprint of Sourcebooks, Inc.
P.O. Box 4410, Naperville, Illinois 60567-4410
(630) 961-3900
Fax: (630) 961-2168
www.sourcebooks.com

Library of Congress Cataloging-in-Publication data is on file with the publisher.

Printed and bound in the United States of America.
WOZ 10 9 8 7 6 5 4 3 2 1

In memory of my mother,

Nedra May Wade Crockett,

an exceptional dreamer

—Mary Crockett

For The Girls

—Madelyn Rosenberg

I've always been a dreamer. Daydreams. Night dreams. Dreams of grandeur and dreams of escape. If I were an onion and you peeled back the papery outside, you'd find layer after layer of eye-watering dreams. And in the center, where there's that little curlicue of onion heart? There'd be a puff of smoke from the dreams that burned away.

It was all just brain waves, I thought—disconnected, like the notebook that my friend Talon keeps. She draws a line down the middle of the page; on the right she writes everything she remembers about a dream, and on the left she puts notes about the stuff that's happening in real life, things that might trigger her subconscious. Reality on one side, dreams on the other—a clear line between the two.

But it turns out there are no clear lines, just a jumble of what is and what might be. And all of it is real.

Chapter 1

Will found me by the river.

It's not like it took a rocket scientist to figure out where I'd be—though it wouldn't surprise me if Will ended up *being* a rocket scientist. He's that smart. And nothing about him surprised me anymore.

I'm guessing not much about me could surprise him, either. He knew all of my usual reasons for sitting on my usual mossy rock, the water rushing by like it had someplace better to be.

But this time I wasn't on my rock for the usual reasons, which include but are not limited to Mom having one of her Marathon Bathrobe Days, my prepubescent brother Nick playing too much air guitar, and my great-aunt Caroline calling long-distance to see how Mom is faring since that no-good husband (meaning my dad) left her stranded with those kids (meaning my brother and me).

No, today I was here for Josh. I wanted to see him again. And for that, I needed the kind of noisy quiet that only the river can offer.

I watched the water and tried to remember. His face came to

me in outline at first. So handsome it was almost embarrassing. A dash of golden brown hair across his forehead. High cheekbones. Full lips. Eyes that were the electric blue of windshield wiper fluid, which is something I'd never thought could be sexy until now.

I'd brought my sketchbook and box of charcoals, so when his face appeared in my mind, I was ready.

Sometimes drawing seemed to be almost another way of dreaming. Not that they're exactly the same, of course. I'm awake when I draw, so there's that. But with either—drawing or dreaming—anything might appear, no matter how random. And it's not like I exactly get to choose what happens next.

Yeah, I can say "I will draw a house. I will draw a tree." Or "I will dream about marshmallows." But what actually occurs when I sit down to draw or I drift off to sleep has always seemed to me to be entirely out of my control. Like my art teacher says, sometimes the sketch has a mind of its own. For example, there was an intensity to Josh's face that made me feel—even while I sat drawing it—as if I were made of the most delicate glass.

"That your latest masterpiece?"

I knew Will's voice before I looked up.

He was wearing his holey jeans, the ones with last week's chemistry homework scribbled in ballpoint pen on the left knee, and a too-big ash-gray T-shirt that read "I listen to bands that don't exist yet." His smile was, as always, lopsided, and his dark brown hair had that just-woke-up messiness that generally lasted all day.

Flipping the sketchbook closed, I scooted over and patted the moss beside me. "Pull up a rock."

He gave me a dubious look. The rock was really only big enough for one, maybe one and a half. "Come on." I took his hand to tug him down beside me. It was close, but we fit. With any other boy I might be a little weirded out by the contact, but with Will it felt comfortable.

"So do I get to see?" He gestured to the sketchbook.

"I'm not done yet," I said, which was a total dodge. Will knew I didn't like showing my pictures to anyone until I was finished, but I never intended to show him this. I felt way too awkward about the whole thing, though I'm not sure why. Will had been my best friend since preschool and he already knew the most awkward parts of me. He was the guy who taught me how to flip my eyelids backward, the guy who talked me through being dumped by Daniel Kowalski *and* my parents' divorce. He'd seen me crying so hard I had snot bubbles in my nose, and laughing so uncontrollably I started to gag on my tongue. Not a pretty sight, either one. So why couldn't I tell him about Josh?

"Anyway, it's just a sketch," I said. "I'll probably never finish."

As I started to put my charcoal back in its box, my hand wavered, and the stick slipped from my fingers. Just before the charcoal tumbled to the mud at the edge of the river, Will's hand shot out and nabbed it.

He sat back up, examining the stick in his palm. "You know, people used to burn sticks and smear the charred part on cave walls—and forty thousand years later, here you are," he tucked the charcoal back in my box and closed the lid, "doing pretty much the same thing."

"I thought charcoal was just a charcoal-and-paper thing," I said.

"Paper as we know it didn't come around until around the second century in China."

"So, what? People just drew on cave walls with burned sticks until the second century?"

Will looked at me as if he really couldn't believe I'd actually said that. "Well...there were all sorts of other things in between. Like bone."

"Bone?" I shuddered, thinking of etching Josh's face on the femur of...what? A buffalo?

"Papyrus, bamboo, silk..."

"I'll take the silk," I said, dusting my smudged fingertips on the legs of my jeans. "Where do you even come up with this stuff?"

"Internet? I don't know. I just sort of collect it."

"I'm ignoring the Internet this week," I said.

"Bold move."

"I keep expecting to not get a note from my dad," I said.

"So if you're not on the Internet you can pretend that maybe you *did* get one?" he said. It seemed so simple, the way Will said it. And it was true: if I avoided getting online (which I was usually only able to do for about two hours at a time), I might have a dozen emails from my dad waiting for me, saying how much he missed us, that he was flying me and Nick to Alaska so we could see his new place, that skipping school for a week wasn't a problem because Alaska itself was "educational."

Except.

Except that even if I wasn't online, I knew the truth.

I scowled. "Remind me to never get married."

"Why would I do that?"

"Because then you'd also be reminding me to never get divorced," I said. "Or how about this? *You* marry me. Like in that movie, you know. If we haven't married anyone else by the time we're thirty—"

"Didn't that movie end badly?"

"I don't know. I never saw it." But it had to end better than my parents' marriage. "Okay, forget marriage; save me from the other stuff."

"Like what?"

"Like…homecoming," I said, remembering last year when Daniel Kowalski spent half the night looking at other girls' butts and half the next morning telling me I was delusional. "If neither one of us is seeing anybody by then, we go to homecoming."

"That's like, what…ten days from now? I think I'll still be free."

I tapped out G-O-O-D in Morse code on his knee.

A-N-Y-T-I-M-E he tapped back.

It was something we'd learned during our secret agent phase. I like to think of it as "pre-texting."

Will grinned down at me. There were times his eyes seemed to say things without him saying them out loud. And right now was one of those times. But I wasn't totally sure what he wasn't saying. It was almost like in his mind, he was just saying my name. *Annabelle.*

"Anyway, I'm just asking you as, you know, as friends. Like this," I said, feeling my mouth go dry.

"Of course," he said.

It looked like poor Will was going to have to wear a tie instead of a T-shirt. Because the chances of me dating someone else by homecoming were less than slim.

There was Josh, of course. Only there wasn't. Because he wasn't just out of my league. He was out of my universe.

On paper—or papyrus or bone or whatever—it might seem like he was the perfect guy to whisk me away for a fairy-tale homecoming. But Will had one slight edge that made him the more viable candidate: Will was a real person. And Josh?

Josh was a dream.

Chapter 2

I'm sailing on a lake the exact color of a blueberry jelly bean. Josh is on the other side of the little boat, singing something that sounds Gaelic, and while I don't understand the words, I know in the way you know things in dreams that he's telling me I'm beautiful.

A pair of dolphins jumps through the water, even though it's a lake and there wouldn't be dolphins. Josh stands up and his eyes catch the light.

"Let's go swimming," he says.

We strip down to our underwear. Luckily I'm wearing my best bra, the one with little daisies, and my underwear is, if boring, clean. I'm not even feeling embarrassed about showing my body in the middle of the day to a near-stranger, because he's not a stranger. It's as if Josh were made just for me.

He dives in, and I'm about to follow when I feel someone watching. I can just make out on the bank the figure of a girl in a white tea-party dress. She's like something from the Impressionistic paintings we studied in art, all exaggerated bows. Behind her is an old brick pump house, like the one by the river back home. Something about the girl creeps me out. It bothers me that she seems so alone. No, not just alone…abandoned. What is she doing out here by herself?

I don't want her to see me in my underwear, and I don't want Josh to know she's there, so I jump feetfirst into the water. Only the water doesn't feel like water; it feels like cloth, not wet at all.

"This way." Josh motions me after him, and starts swimming toward the shore, straight for the girl.

"You have to catch me first!" I swim in the opposite direction. When a dolphin passes, I clasp onto its fin and the dolphin pulls me to the opposite side of the lake, where he drops me off, like some kind of taxi.

I'm in the shallows now. I feel sandy grit and rocks beneath my feet. It's real water again, and as I walk toward the empty shore, minnows swirl around my legs.

When I look up, Josh is beside me. We're only knee-deep now.

"You're perfect," he says. His eyes look sort of watery, but I don't know if it's from emotion or the fact that we're soaking wet.

Either way, what he says makes me want to cry, because anyone who knows me knows I'm the furthest thing from perfect. Josh looks deep into my eyes and says it again, "Perfect."

And in that moment, I can believe nothing bad will ever happen, and no one will ever make me feel like that awkward little girl at the Halloween party where I knocked an entire cauldron of fake-intestine spaghetti onto the Beasleys' living room carpet. Josh's words wipe out every time I felt stupid or clumsy or ugly or wrong. It makes it somehow okay that my dad is on the other side of the earth and my brother is a pest and my mom works too hard and comes home late to eat ravioli cold out of the can.

Then he leans down and puts his hands on my shoulders and kisses me.

It's the most perfect kiss you can imagine, the kind of kiss poets write about and rock stars sing about, the kind with just the right amount of tongue and skyrockets when you close your eyes.

When he pulls away, the look on his face is unlike any expression I've ever seen—a heartfelt pain and intense relief. He's looking right at me with his impossibly blue eyes.

"You know what this means, Annabelle," he starts to say, only he doesn't move his lips; he's in my head. "This means—"

"Yo, yo, yo—"

My bedside radio honked to life, jerking me awake with the musical equivalent of a car wreck. A car wreck with a heavy bass line.

> *Love is patient so they say in Corinthians*
> *I say it too, can't find another synonym*
> *They call me Mac Z but it's just a little pseudonym*
> *I'm waiting for you; you know it's time to be through with him*

I hit the snooze, hard. It wasn't just that Mac Z wrote bad songs—it was that he wrote bad songs about *love*, as if he knew anything about it. In his videos, he always has these superhot women plastered against him with their boobs popping out of black leather. I mean, no cow should have to sacrifice her life for that.

Still, I would've hated Mac Z this morning even if he wrote songs about rainbows and buttercups because this morning his rapping *woke me up when I was dreaming*. And okay, it was Friday, and I did need to get to school. But I also needed to be back in that lake.

I closed my eyes, trying to conjure the water, the dolphins, that look in Josh's eyes. Wasn't he trying to tell me something just as I was waking? I squeezed shut my eyes and willed myself back.

The radio alarm went off again. Not Mac Z, this time, though the sentiments were the same.

I see you walking in the club, wearing that tight sweater
Make me lose my mind, girl, we got to be together

No go. Dream over. It was time to haul myself up and prepare to face another day in Chilton, Virginia, where there is no perfect guy, no perfect kiss, and nothing halfway resembling a dolphin. Where the town's only lake (which was more like a pond to begin with) dried up completely about five years back, leaving behind fissured earth and, swear to God, the skeleton of some guy who fell out of a rowboat during the Great Depression.

I pulled my hair out of my face and sighed. Sometimes I don't think I'll ever get out of this place. I'll end up stuck here like my mom, playing board games with old people all day.

Will says I just have to be patient, like the song. (He claims he doesn't like Mac Z, either, only I caught him singing "Patient Love" by his locker once and he knew almost every word.) Two more years of high school, he says, might as well enjoy it. But two years is one eighth of my life so far.

And time goes slower in Chilton than anywhere else on earth. It should be the town motto: Two years in Chilton is eternity.

Because isn't that what eternity is? It's your own high school. Where the good girls are always good, the stupid boys are always stupid, the marching band always plays some lame tribute to whatever Broadway musical was big twenty-five years ago, and the hands of the hallway clock just keep plodding the same tired loop day after day. That sort of sameness has pretty much ruled my whole life so far. I keep waiting for eternity to be over, to wake up one day and suddenly I'm in control of my own life and everything is different. The sky isn't gray, and my parents aren't divorced, and my brother Nick is a rock star, and Will is at Harvard or someplace, and I'm majoring in art at VCU *and* in the middle of a passionate love affair at the very same time.

I'm not convinced it'll ever happen, not in two years, not ever. Will says sometimes you don't have to wait for two whole years; sometimes, if you're patient, you could just open your eyes and see everything in a whole new way.

But so far I only see those things when I'm sleeping.

Chapter 3

The Chilton High School cafeteria is ruled by a social order that is, to be fair, no more ruthless than any other culture that engages in slavery and human sacrifice. We're not cutting off our enemies' heads and displaying them on fence posts, exactly. But there are other ways to claim ownership of human flesh and to torment those who resist.

There is, for example, Stephanie Gonzales.

Captain of the Cheerleading Squad, a member of the Model UN, French Club, and Devils Are Angels, our high school's team of ostentatious do-gooders, Stephanie is the undisputed queen bee. With her sleek black hair and almond eyes, she looks like Cleopatra, accessorized with pompoms instead of an asp. She moved here at the beginning of last year, and she's ruled our class with a golden fist ever since.

There are some advantages to being noticed by Stephanie Gonzales, but there are *more* advantages to being ignored. Luckily my friends and I are, for the most part, invisible.

Stephanie sits in the center of the room with the Beautiful People. Her BFF Trina Myers sits on one side and her jock-du-jour (actually, for many jours) Billy Stubbs sits on the other. To either side of them is a roster of the best looking and most athletic people at the school.

Beside the Beautiful People sit the Preps and Second Tier Jocks, including the late, great Daniel Kowalski, whom I rarely see because I sit intentionally facing the opposite direction. Not that seeing him is such a big deal anymore—in the same way it's no big deal to pluck my heart out of my chest daily so it can be trampled on by a boy who never really got me, even when he had me, and never really wanted what he got.

But on the up side, Daniel has apparently decided his new look involves both a sparse goatee and an excessive amount of hair gel, so looking away is smarter all around.

Orbiting out from the Beautiful-Preppy-Jocky center of our high school universe are tables for the Wannabes, the Geek Squad, the Band, the WWJDs, and the Unredeemables.

I sit at a self-proclaimed table of Nobodies with Will, my other best friends, Talon Fischer and Serena Mendez, and Will's other best friend, Paolo Langit. Paolo moved to Chilton last year from the Philippines. He and Will immediately bonded because they both owned T-shirts with a bastardized quote from Jack Kerouac: *"Great things are not accomplished by those who yield to trends... like this shirt."* Our spot is on the far end of the cafeteria, next to the station where people dump their trays. We talk, eat, and have attacks of major angst while we watch the hormones and humanity that swirl around us.

Will, who *never* has angst, just likes people watching. It's some kind of anthropological study for him. But this particular Friday, he wasn't people watching. This Friday, he was watching me.

My cell phone beeped.

Are we on? It was Will.

On what? I sent back.

Talon and Serena were talking about some trig equation they couldn't figure out and Will took a bite of burrito instead of typing. I had to resist the urge to reach over and wipe the refried beans from the corner of his mouth, but he caught it and went back to his phone.

Homecoming, he typed.

Oh, right. Yikes.

My phone beeped again. Remember?

!! I wrote back. I was stalling, I knew. But I needed to have a rethink. I'd made clear that this wasn't a date-date. We were going as friends, Will knew that. But what if, after an evening under crepe-paper streamers and cardboard stars, I ended up *like*-liking him and he still only *friend*-liked me…or what if he *like*-liked me and I only *friend*-liked him? I didn't want to bring any weirdness into what I had with Will. It was too important for that.

We can laugh at the DJ, he wrote.

Ha, I wrote, at the exact same time Will asked Serena, out loud, "Are you going to homecoming?"

"I'm going camping with my parents," she said.

"You're not staying in that rat-infested cabin again?" asked Talon.

"They weren't rats. They were mice."

Talon and I had accompanied the Mendezes on their last camping trip, and Serena's dad found some traps in a wooden storage box. He set them up, after reading in the cabin guest book that it was "ABSOLUTELY VITAL." The traps snapped all night. In the morning, the cabin was full of dead mice and before breakfast, Serena insisted that we wrap the small, furred bodies in toilet paper and bury them. Part of me was surprised she hadn't sewn them little suits first. She led us into the woods, looking for a place with enough solemnity for a mouse funeral.

What we found in those woods, though, was more strange than solemn—possibly the strangest place I'd ever been. At the end of a random trail, we came to a grassy clearing, almost perfectly round and edged with moss. In the very middle of the opening stood a single tree, maybe fifty feet high, with wild branches that sprawled toward the sky.

It reminded me of something Salvador Dalí would have painted, only without the eyeballs and melting stopwatches. But in their place was something equally peculiar—bottles, dozens of them, in different sizes and colors. Some had been tied to the tree with cords; others had been jammed mouth-first on the nubby ends of branches.

Serena took it as a sign. She buried the mice at the base of the tree, as the bottles above our heads clinked in the wind.

"Same cabin," Serena told us. "I'm making my dad bring the Havahart traps from home this time."

We all rolled our eyes and said things like "that sucks." But in a way Serena didn't mind camping with her parents and a bunch of mice because she didn't have a date to the dance. And in a way the rest of us were jealous. Will's dad was too busy for camping. Paolo's mother had malaria as a child and harbored an irrational fear of mosquitoes. Talon's parents were divorced like mine, but unlike my parents they were trying to one-up each other, so she spent nearly every weekend doing cultivated things like going to the opera in Roanoke. My mom didn't have the energy for much more than watching old movies on cable. And my dad, well. Anyway.

"You got any homecoming offers—you know, since yesterday?" Will asked me.

"I think Ronny Lobman was checking me out in French," I said.

"And English, too," added Talon.

Will smiled. "Yeah, that's only because you look like Queen Amidala when you wear your hair up." Ronny Lobman is obsessed with *Star Wars*.

"She really does." Talon tilted her head, examining me. "If we dyed your hair black and slabbed on some face paint, you could rule entire galaxies."

I knew Talon, whose dark hair didn't have to be dyed, looked ten times more Amidala than I ever could, even with her asymmetrical bob and fishing-lure earrings. But I also knew that she got snarky whenever I complimented her looks. So I just gave a solemn half-bow and quoted, "My place is with my people."

My phone beeped again. I was no good at having two conversations at once. When I looked at the screen, all it said was: Stph alert.

"Stph?" I asked Will. "What's Stph?"

He didn't have time to answer. Stephanie Gonzales, the queen bee herself, buzzed by our table with her tray. At first I thought she was going to stop and I tried to think of a comeback before she even said anything. But she just murmured, "poor creatures," and walked on.

I yawned. The big, embarrassing kind of yawn that takes over your whole body and ends with an audible sigh.

"What's with you?" Talon asked.

"Just spent," I said.

"Let me guess: Your mom kept you up watching *Gone with the Wind* again."

"No such luck."

Talon gave a fake shudder. "What you southerners see in that movie I will never understand. The whole hoopskirt and magnolia thing is so…hoopskirt and magnolia."

Talon said "you southerners" but she'd been born in Chilton like pretty much everyone else. Her dad, though, was from New Jersey. Apparently, that was enough for Talon to consider herself on the other side of the Mason-Dixon line—in spirit, if not in body.

"Fiddle-dee-dee," I said, fanning myself.

"You really do look tired, Annabelle," Serena said. "I can see little moons under your eyes again. My mom says almond oil works, and cucumber slices."

"Thanks for the tip." I loved how she said "moons" and not "bags." Leave it to Serena to make total exhaustion seem somehow romantic.

"Well, if that doesn't work, there is this new thing called sleep you might try," Will said. "People lie down on stuffed mattresses and close their eyes. It's all the rage in Europe. Spain has even started a national competition for afternoon napping."

"Sign me up!" said Talon. "I could totally go for a nap during P.E."

"It's not sleep that's the problem," I said. "I keep having these crazy dreams. I can't even remember half of them. One minute I'm running down the hallways in an abandoned hotel, looking for lightning. The other..."

"What?" Will asked.

"Uh, more...stuff," I finished, lamely. The other I'd been on that boat with Josh.

I yawned again, crumpled up my bagged lunch, and tossed it from my seat into the nearby trash can.

It seemed sometimes like sleeping had become my real job, and the waking hours—school, homework, family—well, that was just me resting up for my dreams. Which maybe wasn't so bad, in the grand scheme of things. At least my dreams got me out of Chilton, if only for the night.

———

I was still yawning through pre calc...U.S. history...chemistry.

"X-ray crystallography captures the distinct lattice pattern of the crystal, so we can see how the electrons that surround the atoms interact with the incoming X-ray photons…"

Mr. Ernshaw might as well have been speaking Xhosa, which is the only language I know of that begins with an X. It wasn't that I didn't like chemistry, or even that chemistry didn't like me. It was just…Friday. And last period. And COME ON, MR. ERNSHAW CAN'T YOU GIVE US A BREAK?

To keep myself awake, I opened my dream dictionary app and read once again the entry for "lake." According to dream guru Cynthia Rêve, a lake meant either I was unable to express my emotions freely or I had serenity and peace of mind. *So which is it, Ms. Rêve?* I thought. *Because repressed emotion doesn't exactly scream "serenity."*

There was nothing for "blue eyes," but under "blue" was "birth and unavoidable change," while "eye" was (duh) "vision."

"Annabelle?" said Mr. Ernshaw. "Are you with us?"

I put the phone away, and to make it look like I was taking notes, I sketched a stinkbug that was dead on the windowsill. Then I copied a list of the ingredients in diet soda. Mr. Ernshaw was great about letting us bring drinks into the classroom, as long as it wasn't a lab day; plus, the list looked chemical-y, so I figured that was *like* paying attention.

Caffeine

Aspartame

Citric Acid

The lab door opened then and I looked up and promptly stopped breathing. There *he* was, standing right by the door of the classroom, smiling, talking to Mr. Ernshaw, like an ordinary person.

Only he wasn't ordinary. He wasn't even a person.

He was Josh.

My Josh.

The guy from my dream.

Chapter 4

But it wasn't my dream. It was chemistry, and Josh was *here*. The light—from a window? just the fluorescents?—made him seem golden. I glanced around to see if anyone else was looking at the door, because it was possible I was hallucinating. Other students were staring, too. Then Mr. Ernshaw said something and picked up a paper from his desk and handed it to Josh, who nodded. "Fine," Mr. Ernshaw said. "I'll see you Monday."

Josh smiled his amazing smile and looked in my direction. Before I remembered how to exhale, he was gone.

For a moment, the world was utterly still. It was as if I'd landed on another planet; I didn't know the language or if my lungs could handle the atmosphere.

The afternoon bell rang, and everything started moving again. The classroom was full of the shuffle of backpacks being shouldered, cell phones being turned on again, and the garble of conversation.

I jumped up too quickly, knocking my notebook onto the floor. As I crouched down to get it, I told myself to keep breathing.

In. Then out. I must have just dreamed it up. My restlessness and boredom and overactive imagination had simply combined to create a very realistic waking dream. Right, Ms. Rêve?

Josh wasn't real. He was *Josh*—which meant he was by his very nature a figment of my imagination.

But he'd looked real. In fact, it seemed entirely possible that right now somewhere beyond my classroom door stood the boy of my dreams.

I grabbed my backpack and started pushing my way through the bottleneck of students. I could at least look, right? But looking wasn't so easy.

The school was built fifty years ago when the student population was half its current size, so even on a normal afternoon the hallways were as packed as a cattle chute on market day. But this was *Friday* afternoon—and what's more, it was the Friday afternoon before the football game with our archrivals, the Pulaski Cougars. So the hallways were not only packed, they were packed with hyped-up, pompom-wielding nut jobs.

Some guy had dressed up as a mangy cougar and was being led around on a leash by our mascot, the Chilton Blue Devil. Scattered pep band trumpet players were blaring the fight song. In the middle of it all stood Stephanie Gonzales, decked out in the wardrobe of the privileged class, aka her cheerleader uniform. She was handing out little gold footballs.

"Want one?" she asked in a voice that was very diet soda.

I wouldn't have answered at all but I was stuck going two miles an hour behind some guy in a letter jacket who was as broad as he was slow. If there was time for pleasantries, I figured there was time for unpleasantries.

"No thanks," I said, just as sweetly. "I'm avoiding unnecessary plastics. But you just go right on killing the planet by increasing your environmental footprint."

"Whatever."

Okay, maybe it was rude, but I've had what my mother would call "uncharitable feelings" toward Stephanie ever since she moved here because (1) she always asks me where I get my clothes in this super-fake "what a cute sweater" way, even when she knows that half of the stuff I wear comes from Goodwill; (2) on a particularly bad hair day last month, she told me the cosmetology students always needed to practice on "extreme cases"; and (3) she was clogging up the hallway with little plastic footballs at the exact moment I needed to MOVE.

Stephanie turned to offer a football to Macy White, an exchange that went better than it had with me. They put their heads together in a friendly way that suggested Macy wasn't issuing an environmental impact statement.

Guh! How was I ever going to find anyone in this chaos? Much less someone who probably didn't exist in the first place.

When I made it to the main hall, it was Will, not Josh, that I found—or rather he found me, since I was looking so hard for Josh that at first I didn't see Will at all.

"Annabelle!" He shouted over the noise. "Hey, you okay?"

He and Paolo were walking together in the opposite direction of the general traffic flow, probably headed to the photo lab, where they spent most of their time after school.

"I guess," I said, scooting into a nook outside the teachers' lounge, away from the press of bodies. "Look, have you seen this guy? He's about your height, gold-brown hair—"

"Tim Linkous?" Paolo asked. Tim Linkous ate ants when we were in sixth grade, not even on a dare.

"Good God no!" I said. "This guy is new."

"New how?" Paolo said. "New to Chilton High or new life-form?"

"Guess," I said.

"I saw a new guy heading for Coach Masterson's office a few minutes ago," Will said.

"Wavy hair?" I asked. "Really, really blue eyes?"

"I didn't see his eyes," Will said.

"What was he wearing?"

"Jeans. Maybe a blue shirt, you know like a T-shirt, but with a few buttons and a collar," Will said.

"That could be him," I said. My pulse quickened, I could feel it.

"For someone who is so smart," Paolo said to Will, "how can you possibly *not* know that that's called a polo shirt?"

"Guess I know now," Will said.

"But I bet you know what they call the padded shirt a knight wears under his chain mail," Paolo said.

"That'd be a gambeson."

"Bet you know—"

"So, thanks," I interrupted, already heading toward the Athletics Department.

"Wait, Annabelle," Will called. I didn't.

The halls cleared out as I turned toward the wing that held the gym. By the time I got to the coach's office, I couldn't find life-forms of any sort. Just me and a deserted hallway. Cue the tumbleweed.

The five-minute bell for the buses sounded. I hadn't bummed a ride with anyone, and since Lucifer, the '73 Dodge Dart my grandma left me in her will, needed a new starter that I couldn't afford, that bell meant I had to haul my butt all the way back to the front of the school to catch my bus. Fast.

It was humiliating. Not only did I have to ride the bus, which is bad enough since I'm a junior, but Miss Pat had to reopen the doors for me. Plus, I was panting. The only open seat was next to Ronny Lobman's little brother Dale, a freshman who was as crazy about *Star Wars* as Ronny. They were both nice enough, but I wasn't up to hearing a thirty-minute monologue about the potential mechanical problems of Darth Maul's Sith Infiltrator.

As the bus threaded the narrow streets of Chilton's river neighborhoods, I tried to untangle my thoughts.

I'd seen a guy who looked exactly like the guy from my dreams. But that, of course, was insane. People from dreams didn't just pop up in a person's chemistry lab. At least not in Chilton, Virginia.

Things like that didn't happen in real life. Did they?

Chapter 5

We're Chilton born
and Chilton bred,
and when we die
we'll be Chilton dead!
So go-go Chilton!
Devils rule!

Talon glowered down the line of blue and gold pompoms. "Did they really just say they'll be 'Chilton dead'?"

I shrugged. "Maybe it's some kind of zombie thing?"

"Idiot zombies." She shifted on the bleacher like she was propped on a bed of nails. "And we're idiots for watching them. Why are we here again?"

"Yeah." Serena took a long sip from a forty-two-ounce diet soda she'd bought before I could tell her the ingredient list. "I thought you hated football."

"I did, I mean I *do*, it's just I'm…" I trailed off, craning my neck so I could see beyond a row of blue-and-gold shoulders and hats.

"A little preoccupied?" Serena offered. "Annabelle, who are you looking for?"

"What do you mean?"

"Let me translate," interjected Talon. "First you insist we come *here*—which totally screws up our standing as Chilton's All-Time Least Spirited—when you *know* the Pacers are playing a gig at the Crow's Nest tonight; next you want Serena to drive down every side street and back alley on our way to Pulaski; then you can hardly stand still while we're in line at the concession stand; and now you're rubbernecking like a demented bobble head and we can't get a coherent word out of you. So, yeah, that's what we mean."

"Really?" I asked, defeated.

Serena gently brushed back a lock of my hair from where it had fallen in front of my eyes. "Are you all right, honey?" she asked. "You've been acting kind of loony."

"It's nothing, really." I looked up. "I'm just—hey, is that Macy?" I pointed to a bleach-blond head up in the stands.

"Yeah, I think so," said Serena.

"So?" said Talon.

So this was Macy White, from my *chemistry* class. "Look, I, uh, I'll be right back," I said as I started climbing up the bleachers.

"Case in point!" Talon called after me.

I knew she and Serena were giving each other WTF looks, but I could explain stuff to them later—or at least make up something that would pass for an explanation. Right now I had to talk to Macy.

"Macy, hey," I said, sitting down in an empty seat in front of her.

"Hey." She looked a little confused as to why I was talking to her. We probably hadn't said more than ten words to each other since she moved here last January. It wasn't that I hated Macy. At least, not exactly. It's just that she had started dating Daniel Kowalksi the week *before* he dumped me, so I *had* hated her. Then. When I was Crazy Annabelle, I'd given her a fair share of stink eye and said some things that I hope never got back to her. Now that I was calmer and knew I was better off without Daniel (right?) the hate had mostly passed. Plus, Macy had dumped him, which sort of helped. He was sitting even farther up in the stands, not looking at either one of us.

"Um, so like, this is my first football game," I told Macy, turning around in my seat.

"Your first?" Her tone was kind of "so what?"

Maybe if I brought up the class, she'd just magically start talking about Josh...? "You have Ernshaw for seventh period, right?" I asked.

"Yeah." Her eyes flickered, registering my face for a second, then went back to the field.

Or maybe not.

"He's okay, but kind of boring," I added, trying to keep the conversation—or what I hoped would become a conversation— moving. "Ernshaw."

"Yeah," she said.

"Um, Macy..." I suppose it would be too weird just to ask *Did*

30

an amazingly hot guy happen to walk in at the end of class today or was I just hallucinating?

Yep, definitely too weird.

"Did you get that crystal thing Ernshaw was talking about?"

"Not really." She was watching the pep band, which was playing an especially horrid rendition of Go-Fight-Win.

"Me neither." I tried again. "You know, um, at the end of class, that guy…" I trailed off, hoping she'd finish my sentence for me. When she didn't, I rambled on.

"I was kind of dozing at the end of class, but some girls were talking about a guy, you know, who just sort of showed up."

Macy turned her eyes full on me now, like she was seeing me for the first time. "You mean Martin?"

"Martin?" *So there WAS a guy in Ernshaw's class? And his name was—*

"Martin Zirkle. You know him?" The question seemed loaded, an overfull washing machine. I suspected there were all sorts of other questions in there, swishing around with the socks and underwear.

"No," I said. "I mean, not personally." The guy I knew was named Josh, wasn't he? Not Martin. Josh.

Macy looked at me harder, like she was trying to see something in my eyes. Now I was the one to look away as I said, in what I hoped was a casual tone, "He seemed nice, though. I mean, he seemed like he would be nice."

She angled herself so she could study my face. "He's been to Egypt."

31

"Wild," I said.

"He's really—"

"Join me in welcoming to Cougar Stadium the Chilton Blue Devils!!" an absurdly loud announcer blasted over a speaker, drowning out Macy's words.

As the team ran on the field, Macy got to her feet and started clapping. "Let's go, Devils!" she screamed.

"That's him!" Macy pointed. "Number twenty-three!"

It didn't seem possible. But I guess if someone from a dream can just show up in real life, there's nothing stopping him from joining the football team.

I looked to where a few dozen helmeted football players were running down the middle of the field. From this distance, they were interchangeable, like the guys on a foosball table.

Across the field, the Pulaski drum line started pounding out a cadence.

"Now, the moment we've all been waiting for," the announcer boomed, "the Pulaski Cougars!" As the Cougars ran across the field, a thunderous flushing sound filled the stadium.

"What was that?" I asked Macy, straining to be heard above the general pandemonium in the background.

"It's the cougar's roar," she yelled.

"Oh," I yelled back.

"Sounds like the Cosmic Toilet, if you ask me." It was Talon. She and Serena had climbed up into the stands and were in the aisle beside us. "So, can we bolt?"

"Not yet," I said, scooting over to make room for them. "I want to see this."

They sat down. "You know, if we leave now, we could still catch the Pacers," Talon said.

"Soon, I promise," I said. "Let's just see a little of the game. I mean, we're here, right?"

Not that it made a difference. All I saw of Number 23 for a long time was the back of his uniform as he sat on the sidelines. And when he was out on the field, the little cage-thing at the front of the helmet pretty much obscured his face. He ran and caught the ball and *moved* like Josh would have. But it could have been anyone in there.

And then, before I knew it, the whole team jogged into a little concrete building at the end of stadium, and the marching band took the field. Halftime. Talon, who was never known for her patience, looked ready to blow. "Have you seen enough?" As the band started in on the "Circle of Life," she stood, tapping her foot like somebody's mother.

"I guess," I said. "See you in chemistry," I said to Macy.

"See you," she said.

I followed Talon and Serena the way I'd seen kids follow their parents out of the park. "Just five more minutes?"

"No."

We walked along the fence and past the concession stand. I stopped.

"You guys go on to the car," I said to Talon and Serena. "I have to go pee. I'll catch up with you."

I sprinted off before they could argue. But I wasn't headed toward the bathroom.

Chapter 6

As soon as Talon and Serena passed the gates to the stadium parking lot, I ran back toward the field and darted through the door of the concrete building that had just swallowed the football team. I didn't think about the relative sanity of what I was doing; I just did it, a walking, talking Nike commercial.

The front room was empty. The hallway was empty, too. I followed it to the end and found two doors. One was marked with a mural of a cougar, fangs exposed. The second door had "VISITORS" stenciled on it in chipped, black paint. I put my hand on Door Number Two. It creaked.

Peeking in, I saw Coach Masterson scrawling on a chalkboard on the far side of the room, his team huddled around him. No one was looking at the door. As silently as possible, I slid in and edged myself in a corner beside a row of lockers. At the end was an open locker door. I inched behind it and peered through the space where it was hinged, unseen.

They seemed to be talking strategy. I could make out words like "defensive line," "fake out," and "grapevine." Number 23 still had his back to me. Then he turned his head.

I wanted to shout and scream and hurl myself into his arms. Maybe I would've, if I weren't scared out of my wits.

He looked over his shoulder, toward the corner where I was hiding, and smiled. I got jelly knees and wondered if I would fall.

"Zirkle!" Coach Masterson barked. "Get your head in the game."

Josh—because it *was* Josh, my Josh—turned back. "Yes, sir."

After a final pep talk, the team got up, did that hand-tower thing, yelled "Devils!" and jogged out of the room. As Josh passed me, he slowed down.

He didn't look at me, but I swear he said my name. "Annabelle."

"You talking to me?" Billy Stubbs asked him.

"I said 'Give 'em hell,'" Josh said.

"GIVE 'EM HELL!" Billy Stubbs shouted. His voice ricocheted off the lockers. Then they were gone, and I was alone. And crap. I was going to be totally alone if I didn't find Serena and Talon. I ran out of the locker room and up the hill to where we'd parked. They were both sitting on the hood of Serena's pink VW Beetle with their arms folded across their chests to keep warm.

"Sorry," I said. *He knew my name.*

"Where was the bathroom? Roanoke?" Talon asked.

"No." *Of course he knew my name. If it were him he would know my name.*

"New York then?" she suggested.

"I just had a hard time finding it," I said. "I'm not exactly a regular here. Give me a break." *But why was his name Martin? I definitely hadn't dreamed about anyone named Martin Zirkle.*

I climbed into the backseat of the Bug, thinking that if I gave Talon shotgun she would go easy on me. Wrong.

She shifted sideways so she could face both Serena in the driver's seat and me in the back at the same time. Maybe it was just Talon's edgy profile, but I started to feel a little twitchy, like prey. "Come on, Annabelle. Football? *Macy White?*"

"She's in my chem class," I said, stalling. Assessing.

"Yeah," Talon said. She opened her mouth but she didn't want to remind me about Daniel; nobody did. "Look. *We're* your friends," she said. "We'd be a lot more cooperative if you'd just tell us why you're acting crazy."

Normally Will served as the landfill for most of the garbage clogging up my brain. But he wasn't here and he was, after all, a guy, which meant that there were certain things that were beyond his understanding. My head felt like Mount Vesuvius. I had to tell someone.

Serena reached into the backseat and put her hand on my forehead. "No fever," she said.

I gave her a thin smile. She put the key in the ignition, and pulled off the grass and onto the road. Her headlights caught a path of cougar paw prints, painted in white.

"Spill it," Talon said, turning the radio down to nothing as Serena turned onto 114.

"Okay…so there's this guy," I began.

Serena burst out laughing. "That can explain all kinds of crazy."

36

"You *like* someone?" Talon said. "Around here?" Now she reached back and put a hand on my forehead, too. "Raging," she said.

"Just tell me he's not a Cougar," Serena said. School rivalries run deep, even if we pretend not to care.

"He's not a Cougar," I said. "He's new. I thought I saw him in chem class last period and then Will said he saw him talking to Coach Masterson."

"So you thought he might be at the game," Talon finished.

"He *is* at the game," I said. "He's playing."

"Football?" Talon spat out the word like a piece of phlegm.

"Why didn't you just tell us?" Serena said. "We would have stuck around."

"Speak for yourself," Talon said.

"I wasn't sure he was here at first and I didn't want to drag you on a wild goose chase," I said.

"Hello? You did drag us on a wild goose chase," Talon pointed out.

"But she caught the goose," Serena said. "Honestly, we would have helped you find him, Annabelle. And no fair. Now we have to wait until Monday to get a look at him."

"You couldn't have seen him anyway," I said. "Not with those helmets on. I didn't catch the goose. I just saw the back of his uniform."

"So what's his name?" Serena asked.

I almost said Josh, but remembered in time. "Martin...Zirkle."

"That's not something you hear every day," Talon said. As a girl who was named after a bird claw, Talon usually went pretty easy on people with unusual names.

"I don't know any Zirkles," Serena said. "His family must not be from around here."

We were quiet for a minute, as Serena tried to decide whether or not to pass a red pickup that was in front of us. She decided not to. Our car slowed and I let the other shoe drop.

"The thing is," I said, lowering my voice even though it was just us, "I saw him someplace before today."

"What, like downtown?" Talon asked.

"No."

"Like on TV? YouTube?" Serena asked.

My own private channel, maybe. "No," I said. They waited for me to finish. "I think I had a dream about him. Do you think that's nuts?"

Serena didn't swerve the car and drive us off the road.

"That makes sense, actually," she said.

"It does?"

"Sure. You probably saw him someplace but didn't realize it, and then you *did* have a dream about him. After. I mean if he's that good looking—he's good looking, right?"

"He's amazing looking," I said.

"It's easy for amazing-looking guys to creep into your subconscious," she said.

"It wasn't just one dream," I said. "It was more than one."

Talon still hadn't weighed in. I hit her on the back of the head. "Well? Say something."

"Is this the first time that's ever happened to you?"

"What?"

"The first time you've ever dreamed something and then, you know, *seen it*."

"Yes. I mean, I get that déjà vu thing sometimes. Like I remember thinking Stephanie Gonzales looked familiar when I first saw her, but then I figured out she just looks like a young Elizabeth Taylor," I said. "My mom had watched a marathon on the classic movie channel that weekend and it must have gone to my head. But this—this was totally different. I'm sure I've never seen this guy before. In real life. But he was in my dream."

"Of course he was." Talon had that eerie look she gets sometimes, like when she wants to pull her tarot cards out from under her bed.

"Why?" I asked. "Has it happened to you?"

"Twice."

"No way."

"The first time was when my grandfather died," she said. "I dreamed about it, and when I woke up in the morning we got a phone call saying he died. I was the only one who wasn't surprised. For a long time I thought it was my fault. For dreaming it, I mean. The other dream was about Spice."

Spice was Talon's dog, a spotted mutt that was part beagle, part Chihuahua, a seriously strange-looking beast.

"You dreamed about a dog?" Serena asked.

"I dreamed about *my* dog. I dreamed her name and everything. We were all playing with her at the mall, calling her Spice. You were there, Annabelle, and let's see…Will, and some girl with long black hair. Come to think of it, she might have looked like Stephanie Gonzales, too. Oh, and the guy who works at the library was there. In the dream, I mean."

"I was there with Spice?"

"Yep."

"Which library guy?" I asked.

"The young one. Lennon glasses, soul patch, always reading Faulkner."

"Robert?"

"Maybe," she said. It was the "maybe" that means *I don't know his name*, not the one that means *maybe yes, maybe no*.

I'd majorly crushed on Robert the spring of my freshman year. He was wiry, but the cute kind of wiry, not the scary, malnourished kind. I kept checking out *As I Lay Dying* in hopes he would talk to me, which of course he never did. At least he worked at the library instead of a bookstore, so there was no financial investment, just time and brain cells and, since it was Faulkner, suffering.

"My mom went to the shelter to drop off some dog food that people at her work had collected as a charity thing," Talon resumed the story. "She saw this little dog there and, I mean, who could resist Spice? So she brought her in the house, like it was supposed to be a big surprise, but I just said, 'Here, Spice,' and she came right to me."

"Weird."

I didn't say it out loud, because Talon doted on that dog, but I

40

could totally see why Spice was at the animal shelter. She brown snaggletooth that made her lip curl up, and when she sat in your lap, licking the back of her paws, the stink went straight to your brain. She wasn't the kind of dog you'd make up in a dream unless you were a seriously disturbed individual.

"How do you even remember all that stuff?" Serena asked. "I mean, I can hardly remember what happens in *real* life and—"

"Dream journal," Talon interrupted. "I keep it by my bed and write everything out before I even get up."

"You keep a dream journal?" Serena asked. I could almost hear her eyes widen.

"It's just a notebook," Talon said. "Something The Doctor made me do." Since her parents' divorce, Talon and her dad went to counseling with a woman who, as far as I could tell, was some sort of new age therapist, not a medical professional, but was neverthe-less always and only referred to as "The Doctor."

"Anyway," she went on. "I could show you the dream about Spice. My grandfather died before I started keeping track."

"I'm sure there's a logical explanation," Serena said. If there was a contest among the three of us, Serena would have been voted Most Likely to Believe in Fairies, but here she was quoting Mr. Spock. "Like, you heard your mom talking about collecting dog food, and the idea sort of slipped in there. Or maybe you'd heard your parents talking about your grandfather being sick."

"But how would I know what Spice looked like?" Talon said. "And my grandfather hadn't been sick; he had a heart attack."

"Maybe you were afraid he'd die because you'd just heard about someone else's grandfather dying. And with Spice, I don't know. It could have been déjà vu, like with Annabelle." We were almost back in Chilton now. Serena turned onto Fast Food Row where seven of the town's twelve restaurants sat side by side next to the highway off-ramp. Mostly crappy chain stuff. Burgers, burgers everywhere and not a place to eat. In the relative darkness of ten fifteen in Chilton, the Row glowed like a landing strip. "Maybe that happened with your dream guy," Serena said. "Your brain processed everything superfast and you just thought you'd seen him before."

"That's not what happened," Talon and I said at the exact same time. Then we started laughing like lunatics because we were totally, totally serious.

Chapter 7

Talon and Serena wanted to catch the final set of the Pacers, but I asked them to drop me at home first.

Now that they knew why I was acting certifiable, they were gentler with me.

"Call us if anything happens," Serena said.

"*Anything.*" Talon nodded.

"I love you guys," I said.

"Back atcha."

"And don't, you know, don't tell anyone." It was one of those things that seemed unnecessary to say, but I said it anyway.

"Not even Will?" Talon raised one eyebrow without raising the other.

"Not anyone."

I slipped out of the car and Serena backed slowly down my driveway.

I'd never kept secrets from Will, not on purpose. I told him whatever, no matter how weird it was—like my nightmare where

MARY CROCKETT AND MADELYN ROSENBERG

the Pigeon Lady tried to kidnap me in her helicopter. (Cynthia Rêve says helicopters represent transformation. I forget what she says about pigeons.) But I wasn't quite ready to open myself up to Will's questions. Josh, or Martin—I suppose if he was a real boy with real flesh I would have to start calling him that—was just for me.

The front door wasn't locked, so I didn't have to use my key.

"I'm home," I yelled.

"Up here," called my mom, but I already knew that. She was lying against the pillows, wearing a flannel nightgown that made her look like Old Mother Hubbard. "You're home early," she said.

I shrugged.

"You look flushed." She reached out and felt my forehead. There was a lot of that going around. "How was the game?"

"We only saw part of it. Mostly I just drove around with Talon and Serena."

"I don't like you guys just driving around," she said. "You need a destination."

"Where's Nick?"

"He went to a movie with Jeremy. He'll be home soon."

"Whatcha watching?"

"*Bride of Frankenstein*," she said. "The old one with Boris Karloff. Spooky…You want to watch the end with me?"

What I wanted, for the first time in American teenhood, was to go to sleep early. Because if I couldn't talk to the boy of my dreams at the football game, maybe he'd be waiting for me there. In my

44

head. But as much as I *wanted* to go to sleep, I was too wired, and if I went into my room I would just stare at the ceiling, which I had painted with lavender unicorns in the seventh grade, and which I hadn't gotten around to repainting even though they were god-awful. Plus, we were reading *Frankenstein* for English; maybe this would count as SparkNotes.

"Come on," Mom said. "It's a good one."

She was right. It was good. Lots of crazy hair, heartbreak, and fire. Nick came home during the storm scene and added some extra sound effects. Will texted me as the credits rolled.

I faked a yawn and gave my mother a kiss on her forehead. "I'm going to bed," I said.

"You sure you're not coming down with something?"

"Growing pains," I told her.

"I thought you looked taller. Sleep tight, sweetie."

"I will."

"Sleep tight, sweetie," Nick echoed.

"You, too, brother dearest," I said. I looked at my phone on my way to my room and read Will's message: Where are you?

I sat down on my bed. Bed, I texted back.

Why not HERE? Will wrote.

He must have gone to the Pacers show, too. The fact that he was asking meant Talon and Serena hadn't said anything. Good.

Tired, I wrote.

Oh. I don't think Will understood what the word "tired" even meant. He's one of those people, like Thomas Edison, who only needs three hours of sleep a night. A second later, he wrote: Good night then.

Night, I wrote back.

They're playing Kerosene! he wrote a minute later. "Kerosene" was my favorite Pacers song ever.

See you tomorrow? he wrote.

Night, he sent again.

My phone stopped vibrating. I got into a T-shirt, flicked off the light switch, and tried to jump into my bed before the room got dark, which was something my grandma taught me when I was little. She said it took a second or so for darkness to come after you turned off the light, and that sometimes you could beat it to bed. I spent two years trying before I realized it was just a trick to get me into bed faster. But I never stopped racing the light switch.

I lay in bed a long time, thinking about J—Martin. He had said my name. He knew me.

I squeezed my eyes tight and willed myself to dream. But my heart was pumping too hard for sleep. The game had to be over by now. Martin was probably in the shower. Had he looked for me?

Oh my God. What if he saw Stephanie Gonzales in her cheer-leading uniform? "Give me a Z-I-R-K-L-E."

What if he saw Macy, who already knew he'd been to Egypt and who knows what else?

What if—

———

"Annabelle. Hey, Annabelle."

The sun was breathing a white-hot glare through my window as Nick yelled into my closed door. "Annnabelllle!"

"What?"

"Mom says, 'Do you want French toast?'"

"Mom's making French toast?" It had been a while since my mother had cooked anything.

"You want some?"

Even though I knew that French toast was just my mother's way of dealing with stale bread, it was still a treat. "Tell her yes," I said.

"I was only supposed to deliver one message," Nick said. "You tell her."

I opened the door to my room. My brother was already dressed in his soccer uniform. He didn't have sweats on, even though it was cold out. He was the type of kid who wore shorts even when it was snowing.

"MOM," I yelled, right in Nick's face. "I WANT FRENCH TOAST, TOO."

"Okay!" she shouted back.

I stopped in the bathroom and looked in the mirror. I had little raccoon eyes and the imprint of a ring on my right cheek. I rubbed the spot and went downstairs. My mother was at the stove, humming.

"Sleep well?" she asked.

I could lie and say "yes," but as soon as she looked at me she'd know the truth.

"Same as always," I said.

"Sorry, honey."

"Girl hungry," Nick said, pointing at me. He put his hand to his mouth and made eating motions. "You eat? Me eat!" Then he pulled up his shirt and squeezed his belly button so it talked. "Me like food!"

"Shut up," I said.

"Don't say 'shut up' at the breakfast table," said my mother.

"But—" I said.

"Eat your French toast."

"Brother, darling?" I said, in my sweetest voice. "Will you please pass the syrup if it's not too much trouble?"

Nick picked up the bottle of syrup and waved it over his head. "Uga uga!" He was still in caveman mode. Sometimes he's like a *Saturday Night Live* skit. He just doesn't know when to stop.

"Mom!" I said.

"Pass her the syrup, Nicholas."

"I was gonna."

My mom smiled and took her own plate to the table. "There," she said.

Nick looked past her out the window.

"What are you looking at?" she said.

"Some guy," he said.

"Where?" my mother turned and looked over her shoulder.

"The dude on the bike," Nick said. "He's gone, but he'll be back. He's ridden by our house like a dozen times this morning."

48

My insides went all electric, like someone had plugged me in.

"Maybe he's in training," my mother said. "The Ridge Top Bike Race is soon."

But I had another idea. I shoveled in my French toast but I kept my eyes on the street.

"There he is," Nick said.

He had on a helmet again, but this time I could see his face. Martin. He slowed down a little as he passed in front of our house, and raised his head from where it had been bent low over the handlebars. I slumped down in my chair and hoped he couldn't see me.

"Maybe he's lost," my mother said.

Martin sped up then, like he had someplace to be.

"I'm going to get dressed," I said, finishing the last of the French toast in two bites.

"You just sat down. Don't you want another piece?"

"Later." I sprinted upstairs, pulled on my favorite jeans and a brown T-shirt, then changed to a blue one with little buttons. What was I wearing in that dream (at least for the clothes-wearing portion of it)? I couldn't remember. No, wait. White. I changed into a long-sleeved white V-neck with a little lepre-chaun on the pocket and the words "Erin Go Bragh" on a pot of gold. It was six months until St. Patty's day, but that was the only white shirt I could dig up other than one of my dad's old undershirts, which I still wore sometimes when Mom was at work. Anyway, the leprechaun shirt made my boobs look bigger than usual, which wasn't much, but was something. I ran to the bathroom and brushed my teeth until my mouth smelled like a candy cane. Then I combed my hair back into a ponytail—pulling out a couple wisps to make it more romantic. There was nothing I could do about the dark circles without some sort of miracle cream. Besides, I didn't have time.

I ran downstairs again. "I'm going outside for a minute," I said.

"Bring in the garbage can while you're out there," my mother called. "I forgot to do it last night."

I slammed the front door without answering. There was no sign of Martin. Not up the street. Not down.

I sat on the porch step for a minute, hoping he'd circle back around. Then I moved to the swing. I should have worn a sweater. It wasn't arctic, but it was chilly, and the air made my neck feel longer than usual, more exposed.

How much time did it take to go around the block? Five minutes later he still hadn't shown up. My mom rapped once on the kitchen window. "Gar-bage," she mouthed.

"O-K," I mouthed back, and walked toward the curb to get it. I grabbed the can by the handle and pulled it back on its rollers so I could drag it up the driveway. My back was to the street when I heard the sound of the air moving, and the slight buzz of bicycle brakes. I stopped walking and let go of the can, but I didn't turn around. Not yet. Not until I heard his voice.

"Hey."

That was it. I turned.

Chapter 8

I wanted to touch him, to see if he was real. Instead I jammed my hands into my pockets and willed them to stay there.

He got off his bike and set it in the grass like it was a piece of china. Then he took off his helmet.

"Hey," he said again.

I didn't know how to start. *I was looking for you*, I thought.

"Same here," he said. His smile shifted into a sort of grin.

Wait. Did he—? I started over. "Do I know you?"

"You tell me."

We were like dogs in the park, sniffing each other.

"You're in my chemistry class," I began. "Or you will be."

He nodded.

"You're...Martin?"

"You're Annabelle."

Now it was my turn to nod.

"You've been to Egypt," I said.

"Word gets around fast at your school." He took a step toward me.

"It's your school, too, right? Don't you play football?"

Another step. "It appears so."

He was right next to me. If I'd leaned in just a little, my head could have been on his shoulder, but I stayed upright. He reached toward me and I stood stock-still. Then his hand went past me. "I've got this," he said, as he grabbed the garbage can. "Where does it go?"

I pointed up the driveway, toward the carport, and followed him as he put the can near the wall. He dusted off his hands.

"Are you real?" I froze when I realized I actually said the words out loud.

"It appears so," he repeated, as if he couldn't quite believe it himself. He looked me right in the eyes. My stomach flipped. "Here." He reached for my wrist and pulled me closer, laying my palm flat against his chest. I could feel his heart beating, *ta-dum, ta-dum, ta-dum.*

I jerked my hand away as if it burned. Seeing and hearing him was one thing. That could all be explained away. Some sort of super vivid daydream. A total psychotic break that would have my mother on the phone to the mental hospital. But touch was different. The part of me still convinced that none of this could be happening couldn't argue with the feel of his heartbeat.

"It's okay," he said, holding out his hand, palm up. But his eyes were saying more than just *it's okay*; they were saying, *it's me.*

I took his wrist, then let out a nervous laugh. It *was* more than okay. It was what I'd been dreaming about.

For a second, I stood in the driveway, holding his outstretched hand. Talon had gotten seriously into palmistry the summer after seventh grade, when her parents were going through their divorce and she planned to run away with the gypsies or the hippies or, at the very least, the carnies, so I knew which lines were which. I studied Martin's hand. His lifeline—the one that curved around his thumb—was hardly there, just a faint scratch. But the line for fate looked as if it had been seared into his skin, a dark crease cutting across his palm from his wrist to the base of his middle finger.

He turned his hand over and laced his fingers through mine.

"Shall we walk?" he asked.

"Okay."

We hadn't gone very far when I gave an involuntary shiver. He stopped. "It's cold," he said, and letting go of my hand, he shrugged out of his hooded sweatshirt and passed it to me. Underneath, he was wearing another short-sleeved polo, baby blue this time instead of that vivid blue of his eyes.

"But now *you'll* be cold," I said.

He looked down for few seconds at his bare forearms, as if he were concentrating on his own skin.

He shrugged. "I don't get cold, I guess. At least not yet."

"Oh," I said. What the heck was that supposed to mean? I took his sweatshirt and pulled it on. It felt wonderfully warm and it smelled nice, like the pecan cookies my grandma baked that time I stayed at her house when Nick was born. "Thanks."

I started walking in the direction of the river, which was always my favorite place to go when I needed to clear my head or when I wanted to draw, which pretty much amounted to the same thing. Martin walked beside me, and as we passed the little houses on my street, it occurred to me that if he was here, if he was real, he'd have to live somewhere. Or…*my God*, if he really was from my dream, maybe he thought he was supposed to live with me! Maybe that was why he kept riding around the block.

"My house isn't far from here," he said.

"Did you—" I started, but my voice sounded too sharp, even in my own ears. I softened my tone and tried again, "It almost seems like you know what I'm thinking."

He tilted his head, considering. "Yeah," he said. "I do. Cool."

"You're kidding, right? You couldn't…I mean, can you tell what I'm thinking now?" I tried to call up something unlikely. A mermaid? A picture frame without any picture in it? Will across the lunch table with burrito on his face?

He frowned. "That's too many," he said.

"How about now?" I concentrated on the most random thing I could imagine: a box turtle I'd found near Pandapas Pond last fall and kept for a few weeks in a crate in my room. I envisioned the turtle's mottled shell and bright red eyes. Then I remembered Will had told me red eyes indicated it was a boy-turtle and had teased me about naming him Miss Elizabeth Bennet.

"A turtle named Elizabeth," Martin said, but he still wasn't smiling.

My skin prickled. "That's quite a trick." The idea of someone going into my brain and picking up stray thoughts *was* kind of cool. But creepy. What if I didn't want him in there? "How do you do it?"

"It's not a trick. It's like part of me is still up there." He tapped my forehead with his pinky. "I can hear stuff."

"Could you…could you maybe *not* hear it?"

"Sure," he said. "Sorry." He took my hand again and held it as we walked.

After a few seconds, I asked, "Does that mean 'sure' you won't do it, or 'sure' you won't *let on* that you're doing it?"

"I'll try not to do it."

I'm thinking of a number between one and ten, I thought, and then looked at him out of the corner of my eye to see if he picked up on it. He seemed not to notice, so I went on, out loud, "So, where *do* you live?"

"Oak Drive," he said. "There was an old house for sale and I—we—got it."

"Who's we?"

"My parents," he said. "And me."

"You live with your parents?" I asked, but what I meant was: *you have parents?*

"It appears so."

As we walked on, I flipped the idea back and forth in my head: it *appears* he has parents, it *appears* he's real. He sounded as surprised at all this as I was.

"It's not—you're not living in the old Lucas house?" It was the only house on Oak Drive that had been up for sale, but the last time

55

I'd seen it, it was basically uninhabitable. The paint was peeling, the front steps had fallen in, and there was a hole below the porch where groundhogs had chewed through. I'd always thought it was kind of romantic, though, in that shabby Victorian way.

He nodded.

"You're in that old house with parents?" It was as if everything had shifted overnight. "And you're really...?" I just let the question sit there, hoping he'd finish the thought for me, but he just nodded again.

"Really...?" I repeated.

"It appears so."

"You say that a lot."

"You say 'really' a lot." His grin looked kind of like the one from the dream, but different, too. A little confused.

"But what I mean is: you're really...*new* here?" I found the idea vaguely freakish and I was half-hoping he was going to tell me no, that this was all just a joke, a segment in one of those prank reality shows.

"You could say that," he said.

"This is so weird." I shook my head. "I don't know what to believe, what's real and what's—"

"What's not? I thought we'd gotten that part straight." His smile faded into a straight line.

"I didn't mean you," I said. "Sorry."

"Nothing to be sorry for," he said.

We turned down the winding side street that ran perpendicular to the river. The front yard of the ranch on the corner was over-loaded in that obsessive-compulsive way with concrete birdbaths, fountains, and three-foot-tall statues of mostly half-naked Romans. Beside the cluttered front stoop, a concrete pig received the blessing of the Virgin Mary.

I took a breath, looked up at Martin, and decided to get it over with. "So, how did you get here?" I asked.

He rubbed his bare elbow and looked at me through the corner of his eyes. "I was hoping you could tell me."

"All I know is…" I lowered my voice, worried that maybe I had this all wrong and he was just some eccentric guy who happened to look like the guy in my dream, and who happened to be biking in my neighborhood, and who happened to be able to read minds, and who happened to examine his own skin like it was a new Sunday suit. I mean, he hadn't outright said it, had he? *I was the one in your dreams.* And maybe all that other stuff was just coincidence and I was going to sound crazy. "All I know is that you were in my dreams, and then you were in my driveway."

"But you brought me here, right?"

"Me!? With what? Fairy dust?" I tried to sand down the edges in my voice. "I mean, I didn't *do* anything. I just dreamed."

We'd reached the river, which ran low but which still had that comforting rushing sound. The leaves were turning, and a few had already fallen into the water and been trapped by the rocks. On the other side of the bank, the branch from a willow tree had fallen onto the roof of the pump house; it looked like an ugly green wig.

"Well, however I got here, I'm here now," he said. To prove it, he took my hand and raised it to his cheek. He gave me one of those soulful, smoldering looks that only happen on TV. I could feel a slight stubble beneath my fingertips. And I started not to care so much where he came from; I only cared that he was here, that he was, at that very moment, lowering his lips toward mine for what I could only assume would be the most surreal kiss of all time.

Our lips touched. It was good. More than "good," which doesn't have nearly enough syllables. It was poet-good. Rock-star-good. Biker-revolutionary-underwear-model-good.

"Thanks," he whispered. He drew back and looked deep into my eyes. Then he kissed me again.

"But I didn't, I didn't..."

And then I closed my eyes and stopped thinking about all of the things I didn't. I started thinking about the things that I did.

Chapter 9

I wasn't cold anymore. Martin's lips lit something inside me and I felt only heat. When we kissed, it was as if I'd known him forever. But there was an itch I couldn't quite reach, somewhere on my spine, maybe, reminding me that I hadn't. I'd known him for thirty minutes, not counting dream time, and I wasn't sure how to count that anyway.

I could hear a rational voice whispering: *Be careful, Annabelle.*

But I'd been careful forever and where had it gotten me? A life sentence in my hometown. Plus six months with Daniel Kowalski for bad behavior.

Martin's hands ran up and down my back. I could feel his fingers making little swirls on my skin that matched the swirling in my brain. Somewhere through that swirl, I felt my insides tilt and I thought about how he'd been on the boat—so intense and sexy and sweet. It was like he was programmed for this. A prepackaged romantic dream.

He lifted his lips from mine. "I'm not programmed…"

I looked up, dazed.

"...and I'm not packaged," he finished.

"But you are a—you're a dream, right?"

He didn't seem sure how to answer.

"Was," he said finally.

"That's the same thing."

"Not even close."

"But you *were* a dream." *A superhot dream,* I thought, remembering the way the muscles in his back flexed when he dove into the water.

He grinned and gave a slow, sexy nod, and I knew he knew what I was thinking. My cheeks grew warm. "I thought you weren't going to get into my head," I said.

"It's hard not to when we're close." He dropped his hands to his sides and took a small step back.

I looked up. The morning light had an uncertainty to it, as if even the sky hadn't made up its mind about what kind of day it was going to be.

"My mom's probably wondering where I am," I said finally. "We should go back."

"Okay."

We turned together and walked away from the rushing water, without skipping even one rock. At the edge of our driveway, he took my hand again. "So, should I meet your mom?"

"You've had a lot of experience meeting parents, then?"

"Nope. None."

I started laughing, that nervous laugh that comes out when your body can't think of anything else to do. "Sorry," I said. "It's just… *this* feels like a dream."

"I've been in your dreams, Annabelle," he said. "And this isn't like one at all."

"What do you mean?"

"Well, for one thing, you weren't so worried in your dream. For another," he leaned over and whispered, "if this had been a dream, we would have gone swimming."

He was right on both points. "What would you even say to my mother, if you met her?"

"That I'm new here?" he considered. "It's true. As far as it goes."

I was going to say "not a good idea." I was going to tell him to go home. But I was afraid that if I did, he'd disappear back into the ether or wherever he came from. Anyway, my mother stepped out on the porch and made the decision for me.

She folded her arms over her bathrobe, which she must've forgotten she was wearing. "That was a long minute," she said.

I dropped Martin's hand and started to walk toward the house. He touched me, lightly on the back, like a blind person, following along.

Nick came out on the porch, too. "Hey," he said. "The bike dude."

Martin reached out his hand toward my mother. "Hello," he said. "I'm Martin Zirkle."

"Hello, Martin," my mother said. "Nice to meet you." She gave me a funny why-didn't-you-tell-me-about-this-guy look. I didn't know what kind of look to give back.

"Nick," Nick said.

"Martin," Martin said.

"I heard," said Nick. "Do you live around here?"

"We just moved into the old Lucas place," he said.

"Oh, I'd always hoped someone would see the potential in that house," my mother said. "I'll bet you have a lot of fixing up to do. Tell your mother I know the name of a good contractor, if she needs one."

"Thanks," Martin said. "But we're good. My mom has a couple of crews working on it already."

"Already?" my mother said. "I went by there last—"

"Hey!" yelled Nick. "It's Will! Hey, Will!"

At first I thought Nick was saying it just to mess with me. Correction: I *hoped* Nick was saying it just to mess with me. I wasn't ready for Will, the King of Logical Thought, at this particular, deeply illogical moment. But the distinct putt-putt of his Jeep got louder and then stopped.

I turned and waved and pretended I was glad he'd stopped by.

Martin watched me, concentrating.

"He's a friend," I blurted out.

Will slammed the car door and walked toward us. "Hey, Annabelle," he said. But he was looking at Martin. He was the usual Will, wearing his old jeans. Today's T-shirt was emblazoned with $C_8H_{10}N_4O_2$, which I happen to know is the chemical formula for caffeine. The reason I happen to know is because Will told me, but that hardly mattered. What did matter was that Will and his shirt and his rational, piercing mind were all standing on my porch with my bathrobe-ensconced mother, my annoying brother, and the boy of my dreams.

"Hey," I said.

"I tried texting," he said.

"I didn't have my phone," I said. "Oh. This is Martin. Martin, this is Will."

"I saw you at school yesterday," Will said.

"Really?" Martin said. "I didn't see you."

"Hey, Mrs. M," Will said. "Nickel breath." Will's adopted and doesn't have any brothers, so sometimes he borrows mine. Nick likes it, because it gives him practice hurling insults. Not that he needs it.

"Geek fart," Nick said, grinning.

"Is that all you've got?" Will said, at the same time my mother said, "Nick!"

"He started it."

"There is a difference between breath and…that other," she said. "Apologize."

"Sorry," Nick said.

"No worries," Will said.

Martin looked cold, but not because of the weather.

Will looked at me, finally. He seemed to be waiting for something.

"Nice sweatshirt," he said.

I glanced down at the blue sweatshirt I was wearing. The shoulder seams hung down to just above my elbows and the sleeves were bunched where I'd pushed them up so they wouldn't hang over my hands. Obviously not mine. Obviously Martin's.

"I still have some French toast left," my mother said. "If anyone's interested."

"I'm always interested," Will said.

"I've never tried it," Martin said.

"Well, come on in, then," my mother said, like it wasn't odd that someone had never tried French toast. "You'll love it."

"They must not have had that in Egypt," I mumbled to Martin, when the others had gone ahead of us.

"They didn't," Martin said. "They had figs."

Chapter 10

Will sat in the empty chair at the end of the kitchen table, where my dad would have sat if he'd stuck around. Martin sat in my seat. My mother set out clean plates. "So, Martin, what brings your family to Chilton?" she asked as she lifted the skillet off the warming element at the rear of the stove and forked out slices of French toast.

"Well." Martin stared at the exposed eye of the stove with apparent fascination. "We've always wanted to live in a place like this. You know, good people..." He gave me a meaningful look. "The mountains. The river. It's a great place to live."

"That's what Dad always said," Nick piped up. "'A great place to live, but I wouldn't want to visit.'"

Some of the "greatness" must have worn off for my dad, I thought.

My mother ignored Nick and poured glasses of milk for Martin and Will. "Let me know if there's anything we can do to help you settle in. I'm sure we'll see you around." She picked up her purse off the counter. "Come on, Nickie. Get your shin guards on," she said as she ushered my brother out of the kitchen. "I need to get ready, too," she added, fingering the belt of her bathrobe. "I can't cheer you on in this. Annabelle, you can see to your guests?"

Martin was eyeing his plate with a perplexed expression, head tilted, hands by his side. *Oh hell,* I thought, *he can run around on a football field, no problem—but he doesn't know how to eat with a fork.*

Okay, Martin, I thought LOUDLY—trying to transmit brain-waves in his direction. *If you are still listening in, pick up the bottle of syrup and pour a little on the toast. Then take the fork...*

I wasn't sure if he heard me or started watching Will and mimicking his gestures. I suppose it was possible he knew all along. At any rate, Martin finally started eating—and enjoying—the French toast. If he was in fact copying Will, I was just relieved that Will didn't decide to do his belch-as-a-compliment-to-the-chef routine. Will says it's acceptable in China.

It might have been easier if Will *had been* in China, instead of watching Martin saw away at his food like someone who had never used utensils. A big chunk of syrupy toast shot off his plate and stuck to the pantry door.

"So, Martin, you play football?" Will said. "That must take a lot of coordination."

I gave Will a *smart-ass* nudge on my way to the sink for a sponge. As if sensing my irritation, Martin threw Will a hard look. "That's right."

Will returned the look. "So how is it you know Annabelle?"

The air in the room sparked. It was like one of those westerns where Gary Cooper is out in the middle of a town's deserted main street, staring down an outlaw at ten paces.

"We're close," Martin clipped. "And you?"

"What do you mean *me?*" Will looked genuinely pissed—which was almost as strange as everything else that was happening. I could count on two fingers the times I'd seen him really angry: When Mr. Wilkenson accused him of plagiarizing a science fair project, because he thought no fifth grader could truly discover which type of fuel burned the cleanest in a combustible engine; and when he got into a shouting match with Daniel Kowalski after a history class debate. He said it was about politics. I didn't believe him.

"I mean," Martin said, "how do *you* know Annabelle?"

"If you were close you wouldn't have to ask that question."

Martin grabbed my hand and pulled me onto his lap. "Close enough?"

Okay, forget the western. It was more like that thing where dogs pee on their property as a message to other dogs.

I pushed Martin's hands away and stood up. "I think breakfast is over," I said. I waited for them to leave, but neither of them moved, so I gave them both disgusted looks and went out on the back deck.

The sky looked worn out now, like a secondhand dress. Across the fence, Miss Kallan's flowerbed, which had bloomed profusely all summer, had gone to seed, except for a few last airy purple blossoms. I exhaled and knocked a few leaves off a plastic lawn chair. I waited another minute, giving Will and Martin time to leave. But when I returned, they were sitting where I'd left them, as if a witch had cast a spell, freezing them in ice.

"Annabelle," my mother called from the door. "I'm taking Nick to his game."

"Wait up." I ran into the hall. "I'm coming, too."

I used to go to all of my brother's soccer games, but once I hit high school, my mom gave me the option of staying home. Since most of the games were at eight o'clock on Saturday morning, I skipped them more often than a respectable big sister should. But this wasn't an early game and suddenly nothing was more appealing than watching a bunch of eighth graders chasing a ball around.

"You're *coming*?" Nick asked.

"Love those Tornadoes!" I said.

"We're the *Hurricanes*."

"Go 'Canes!" I said. "Just give me one minute."

I returned to the kitchen. "I have to go to my little brother's soccer game," I said. "So you'll have to leave. But I'll see you later." I said that more to Martin than to Will, but I meant it for both of them.

"How about lunch tomorrow?" Martin asked. He grabbed my hand, like tomorrow was an eternity away.

"Okay," I said. "Pick me up at noon?" I wriggled my hand loose and shrugged out of his sweatshirt. "Here."

"You keep it." Martin tried to hand the sweatshirt to me, and I would have taken it just to hold onto that pecan cookie smell, except I felt a little weird with Will around.

"That's all right." I pushed it back and slipped on a sweater that was draped over the back of my chair from a few days before. "Come on." Both Martin and Will followed me out of the house.

Nick and my mom were already in the car. I got into the backseat and rolled down the window.

"See you soon, Annabelle," Martin called.

Will didn't say anything. He didn't even wave.

Chapter 11

My mom hummed along to the radio and Nick sat in the front, tossing his soccer ball up, then head-butting it into the windshield.

"Stop it," my mother said. "Do you want me to have an accident?"

Nick put the ball on the floor, but he jerked around every so often, heading an imaginary ball. He looked like he was at a hard-core show instead of sitting in the car, listening to classic rock.

We arrived at the field. "Manning!" the coach yelled, before we'd even opened the doors. "Get over here! Take a knee."

I followed my mother to the sidelines and helped her stretch out a beach towel.

"So," she said when we sat down. "Martin seems nice."

"He does, doesn't he?"

"What can you tell me about him?"

"He's *nice,*" I said.

"I got that part."

"He lives in the old Lucas house."

"Have you met his parents? What do they do?"

"How should I know?" I said.

My mother made a dramatic flourish with her wrist, like a Shakespearean actor. "And that, my friends, is a conversation with a teenager."

The coach had finished talking to the team and Nick was on the field, ready to play.

"Darn," my mother said. "I like it when he plays offense better."

"Maybe next half," I said.

"Will didn't look very happy."

"Mom, come on!"

"I'm sorry. I'm just relating what I saw."

"Will's fine," I said.

She raised an eyebrow and turned back to the field as Nick booted a ball away from the goal.

"Way to go, Nickie!" my mother yelled, and I could see Nick cringe. He hated to be called Nickie in front of his friends.

I started clapping. As long as I was there, right?

"He's a good-looking boy, I'll say that for him," my mother said.

I didn't know for a minute if she was talking about Nick or Will or Martin, but the way she was smiling at me, it had to be Martin. I couldn't help it. I smiled back, then looked away, down the sidelines.

Some of the moms were gathered together, drinking coffee and not even pretending to watch the game. But most of them—and all of the dads—had their eyes glued to the field. Well, except for Mr. Muncy, who was stuffing an entire Happy Meal cheeseburger into his mouth and watching Mrs. Muncy. They were separated, and he wanted to reconcile, but she was having a secret thing with a married fireman. Except in Chilton, nothing's a secret, so even my mom stayed on top of gossip. She didn't repeat it to anyone but me, though, because when my dad left, she was gossip herself.

Mrs. Muncy came over and stood behind us. "Did you see someone is fixing up the Lucas house?" she said.

My mother got to her feet. "I just heard something about that."

"Gorgeous," said Mrs. Muncy, who was in real estate. "Bob and Lynn Zirkle. They got it for a steal, but I'll bet they'll spend seventy thousand fixing up the outside alone."

"It'll help the neighborhood," my mother said. "I always hated seeing that house empty. What do you know about the Zirkles?"

I put my head on my knees just in case my face turned red.

"He's a writer. She's an architect. They have a boy about Annabelle's age."

"Really?"

"Go Nick!" I shouted, because I had to shout something.

"Business is good?" My mother tried to continue the conversation, even though it felt over.

"Steady," said Mrs. Muncy. "These past few years we've seen a real upturn in the market. Chilton is *thriving*. Everywhere else around here, even Roanoke, is Deadsville. I can't explain it. Must be something in the water."

My phone buzzed and I pulled it out of my pocket.

"It's Serena," I told my mom, standing up. "I'll be right back." I walked up the hill where I wouldn't be overheard and sat down in the cold grass. The day had grown brighter, but it still wasn't warm.

"So, did anything happen?" she asked. "I've been dying to know!"

"Everything happened," I said.

"Details!"

I paused a second, for dramatic effect. "He came over," I said.

"He did?!" She squealed.

"He was riding his bike in front of my house when I got up—you know, like circling the block."

"That is *so* romantic. And then you came out and fell into his arms and the music swelled and you looked deep into his eyes—"

"Not exactly," I said. "But we went for a walk."

"Was he just like you'd imagined?"

"He was great," I said. "*Is* great."

She squealed again, as my phone beeped. Talon was checking in. "I'll call you back," I said.

"You can't leave me hanging!"

"I'll call you back. I promise."

I switched lines.

"Well?" Talon said.

"He came over."

"Dream Boy?"

"Yup."

"Get out!" she practically screamed through the phone. "What happened?"

"Well, I shouldn't kiss and tell…" I said.

"You *kissed* him?" Talon said. Emphasis on *kissed*.

"I—"

"You kissed an alien!"

"Shut up," I said. It was just like Talon to turn this into a tabloid headline. "Martin is—"

But I didn't have a good idea of what Martin was. I was working on an answer, when a shadow blocked my sunlight.

Will.

He had a strained look, like the time he swallowed an entire pack of Bubblicious, even though everyone says that gum takes seven years to digest. I don't remember why he did it—maybe to prove that it *didn't* take seven years—but I do recall that afterward I put my ear up to his belly and it made a strange gurgling sound, like a mating whale.

"I gotta go," I said into the phone. "Will's here."

Talon started to protest, but I cut her off.

"Really," I said, "I'll call you later." I turned my phone off and slipped it in my back pocket.

"Hi," I said, in a softer tone than he deserved. "What's up?"

He sat down. "I don't really know."

"Oh." I looked out at the game. Nick was on the sidelines, but some kid on his team was dribbling the ball furiously down the field and the parents were screaming like it was the World Cup. He was almost to the other team's goal before some tank of an eighth grader got a foot in there and kicked the ball out of bounds.

"So, how were the Pacers?" I finally asked.

"Great," Will said, "but I guess you were…" He trailed off.

"I was out with Talon and Serena."

"Yeah. Right," he said.

He drummed his fingers against his leg. "So." He paused. "What's the deal with that guy?"

"Well, I guess he's…He's new in town."

"Yeah. *Very new.* I meant, what's the deal with you and him?"

I twirled my hair around my finger, tight enough to stop the blood flow. I tried to think of something to say that would be simpler than the truth. "I guess he likes me."

Will didn't say anything, waiting. Patient, right?

"And I like him." I looked in his eyes. They were what you would call hazel, a sort of mixture of green and brown, but today they seemed flecked with gold. "I want you to like him, too."

Will was still quiet; he just sat there like a tree someone had carved initials into.

"What was that crap this morning, anyway?" I asked.

"I don't know," Will finally spoke. "I thought he was kind of a prick."

"No," I said. "I mean all that crap from *you*. All that 'How is it you know Annabelle?' stuff. You're not my dad."

"Clearly."

"Then why were you acting like it?"

"Is that how your dad acts?"

I could tell he regretted saying those words the moment they were out. He, of all people, knew how I felt about my father. When my dad took off, it was like he couldn't get far enough away from us. "Nick, Bellie, I have to follow my bliss," he'd said. What he didn't say was that his bliss would lead him to *Alaska*. So we get a postcard with a picture of glacier and a polar bear and a note that says it's too expensive for him to fly back and see us at Christmas.

"I'm sorry. I don't want to fight with you. It's just, you didn't even know him yesterday and now you're..." He trailed off, like he wasn't sure how to finish that particular sentence. "It's like he appeared out of thin air or something."

"I know Martin better than you think," I said. It seemed I kept walking that line between something true and something not true, real and not real. "Give him a chance, okay?"

Will looked at me as if he was about to say something important. Then it passed. "Okay, sure."

"You have to like him," I said. "You're my best friend, right?"

"Right. Of course. What else?" He looked past me, toward the soccer field. "Halftime," he said. "You want me to go or should I stay and watch the rest of the game?"

"Nick would be psyched if you stayed."

"Go, Nick," Will said, but his voice was kind of off. I looked at him. "What? This is my cheering voice. You just don't recognize it because I never cheer."

"That must be it," I said.

He tried a smile.

I thought about telling him what was really going on. That Martin wasn't...But I couldn't even be sure *what* Martin wasn't.

Real? Human? My boyfriend? I mean, we'd kissed, but that would only qualify as a marriage proposal in a Jane Austen novel, and I wasn't sure those people even kissed; they just wrote letters. And as for the human part...well, I wasn't sure what I thought about that, either.

I lay back on the hill. The few clouds were just clouds—not rabbits or fire trucks or seashells. And one was a tiny, perfect button. Will lay beside me.

"Cold?" he asked.

"A bit."

He reached over and rubbed my arm for warmth.

After a minute, I said, "Look, none of this really means anything." I was talking about Martin, but Will's hands stopped moving.

I looked up at his face. Not movie-star perfect like Martin. Ms. Sage had talked about the Greek ideal of male beauty in art class. It was all symmetry, proportion, harmony. Not to mention some serious beef. Like there was a cookbook recipe for the ideal man. Will's face, with its uneven cheekbones and crooked smile, could be considered good looking in an unconventional way, but it was far from ideal. Still, there was something in that face I liked. The way it told me things. My favorite was that bright look he'd give me when he'd just said something really funny and was waiting for me to laugh. Right now, he had a look I didn't see much—a tightness around his jaw, like he was holding something back.

"Hey." I rolled to my side and chucked his chin. "What're you thinking?"

After a second he said, "You know, when we were kids, anything seemed possible. That's what everyone told us: we could be whatever we wanted. If we could dream it, we could be it, right? But we had to grow up first. We had to do what they told us to, read what they told us to, think what they told us to. So we go along, doing, and reading, and thinking, just like they said. And every year that we get bigger, the world gets smaller. Until all those things we've been telling ourselves were possible—all the things we've been thinking were maybe already happening—they don't even make a blip on the radar anymore."

I propped myself up on one elbow so I could look into his eyes again. "I don't know," I said. "I think things can still happen. Things we never expected." *Things like Martin.* "You're the one who said I could wake up and everything could be different, right? Well, maybe it is."

"When'd you get so perky?" he said.

"When'd you get so pessimistic?"

"Probably around the same time. Yin and yang and all that. The balance of the world."

We heard cheers then, but not for us, and not for the Hurricanes, either. The tank from the other team had scored.

"Tough break," Will said. He started cheering for Nick for real then.

I yelled, too. It didn't seem likely to make much difference, but we kept at it. Who knew what a little yelling might do?

Chapter 12

The little girl is lost. She has been left here, and I am trying to find her, to lead her back home.

Beside the lake, the ground is soft, but full of bony rocks that tilt under each step.

I hear movement—something shifting in a line of trees beside me.

"Hello?" I don't know her name.

A twig snaps. In a rush, two black birds flap off a branch and disappear into the darkening sky.

It is growing cold. I need to find the girl.

"Hello?" I call again.

"…Hssss…" A moistness gargles in the mud below me.

I look down, confused, as a thick brown snake, newly hatched, ripples from the clay between my feet.

I stumble back, away from the snake, alarms blaring in my head.

Across from me, maybe six feet away, a small figure shuffles out from behind a tree.

The little girl from my dream about Josh. The one abandoned on the shore.

Her face is shadowed, but I know it is her in that white tea-party dress.

"Don't look," I say, hoping the snake won't spook her. "Hold still."

But the girl walks toward me—her hands over her face, as if we're playing hide-and-seek, and she's It.

She counts with each step. "One. Two. Three..."

At "Four," she raises her foot over the snake. "Watch out!" I yell, but as if she hasn't heard me, she sets her foot down. The snake flexes, spiraling itself around the girl's ankle and up her calf. It rubs its head against the girl's leg with the purr of an eager cat.

The girl bends down, curious.

"No! Get back!"

She drops her hands from her face, and the snake stretches up and wraps itself around her head. She stands, the snake masking her eyes like a blindfold.

I want to move toward her, but I have no control of my limbs. The ground between us becomes a river of snakes. Some are brown, some black, some gray with bands around their necks. The girl keeps walking, oblivious.

"Stop!" I shout. But again, she doesn't hear. I flounder backward, sinking into the mucky border between lake and land. A large black snake slithers toward my feet.

Chapter 13

I've never been the type to freak out over nightmares. I figured dreams were just dreams—my mind's way of talking to itself. If the dream was frightening, well then no big deal; I simply had something frightening that I needed to say.

But now I knew how real dreams could become.

So yeah, if you call running into my mom's room at the break of dawn and catapulting myself onto her bed "freaking out," then I guess you might say I freaked out.

Luckily, my mom, who had been up late all week, was groggy enough that she just mumbled, "Okay?" and flopped over, mid-snore.

I had plenty of time to stare at the beige ceiling and contemplate life, the universe, and the relative likelihood of a bunch of snakes slithering up the side of the bed and carting me away to my doom. On one hand, it seemed pretty far-fetched. On the other hand, so did Martin.

In the end, though, it was Martin, not a passel of snakes, who carted me away. And not to my doom, unless an overload of butter and sugar could be considered instruments of the apocalypse. I thought we'd be walking or riding bikes downtown, but Martin showed up in a shiny red sports car, like something Mac Z would drive. It had soft leather seats and smelled like cinnamon, and for once instead of overthinking (*Where'd it come from? Why cinnamon?*), I hopped in and enjoyed the ride.

Our lunch date turned out to be breakfast—not breakfast time, but breakfast food—because that's what he wanted to eat. I guess he liked my mom's cooking.

"You need some pancakes to go with that syrup?" I asked, handing him a napkin.

"That's a joke, right?"

We were sitting in an orange vinyl booth at the MELET SHOPPE, which would have been OMELET SHOPPE, except some drunk hunter had shot out the O.

"It's a joke," I agreed. "What I mean is: that's a LOT of syrup." I looked at the pool of liquid cascading off the edges of his plate.

Martin smacked his lips in a way that wasn't gross, like if an old person did it.

I smiled. "So I take it you didn't eat, you know, before?"

"Not much," he said. "In fact, I'm not sure I even *have* to eat yet. I think my body's still getting used to...being a body."

He raised a wedge of pancakes on his fork and crammed it in his mouth. "It's surprising how infrequently people dream about food. Food causes dreams. Like pizza. But people don't dream about actually eating it. Except grapes. A lot of people dream about eating grapes."

"Oh." I made a mental note to look up grapes in my dream app, but I was starting to think Cynthia Rêve was out of her league.

"Grapes and strawberries," Martin continued. "Or maybe it was just my people."

"Your people?"

"My dreamers. Like you."

I tried to take this in. "So I'm *one* of your 'dreamers'?"

"Well, sure." He looked at me, tilting his head in that high-frequency-dog-whistle way.

"I don't know why, but I thought you were, oh, you know." I was thinking *mine*, but what I said was, "I thought you were new."

Martin put down his fork and extended his hands, flipping them back and forth, back and forth, examining them. "I am," he said.

I took his two outstretched hands and held them across the table. Together we made a little slanted roof for his pancakes. It seemed like a romantic gesture, but really his hand-flipping had started to bug me. "Tell me about the others."

"There's not much to say. They were just people."

"Like girl-people?"

"Some."

"And that means what? Dozens? Hundreds? Thousands?" There must have been an edge to my voice, because Martin eyed the exit and shifted in his chair.

MARY CROCKETT AND MADELYN ROSENBERG

"More than a hundred," he said, "probably not so many as a thousand."

"And in these dreams you…did what?"

"Lived, I guess. I mean, lived the way we live there."

He looked at me to see if I was getting it.

"Most of it wasn't so bad," he said. "Some was, but the dreaming never lasted very long. It was the in between that was the worst. It lasted forever."

"In between?"

"Between dreams. When we don't do anything. We just wait."

"Wait?" I was an echo.

He dropped my hands and leaned back in a stretch, as if talking about it made him tired. "Like there was one woman who dreamed she was in a doctor's office. In a waiting room? She was waiting to find out if she had cancer or not, and I was one of the people in the waiting room."

"Did she have cancer?"

"I don't know," he said. "I didn't go into the examining room; I was just waiting. But when you're a dream, that's what you're doing all of the time. You have no idea how long it can be, waiting for the next dream." It didn't sound so different from the waiting I was doing: waiting for the weekend, for my dad to call, for my turn in the bathroom. Waiting to meet a boy. "Unless you're *in* a dream," Martin went on. "And then you're, you know, doing whatever the dreamer has in mind—swimming in a lake or something."

"I thought swimming was your idea," I said.

84

He picked up his fork and held it like it was the neck of a guitar. "It was your dream, Annabelle. Not mine."

I pondered for a moment. "So dreams have dreams, too?"

"No!" He dropped the fork, making a loud clatter on the tabletop.

"Sorry. I didn't mean—"

"No, no, it's just...where I come from, the ones who try to dream, well, they're not very nice."

"I see," I said, though of course I didn't see. "Like, how?"

"Well, it's not natural, is it? For a dream to take control. The whole thing about being a dream is that it's not up to you. Where you are, what you do. You just have to accept it."

"But that's crazy. It's not like *we* control what we dream." I picked up the syrupy plastic menu from the little stand behind the ketchup. "We don't place an order. *'I'll take Being-president-for-a-day, with a side of Flying Monkeys.'* Dreams just happen. And even if our subconscious *is* what makes things happen, our subconscious is"—I tossed the sticky menu onto the even stickier table—"sticky."

We were quiet for a minute, and in the silence, I kept thinking about all of the dreams I'd had—and the nightmares, too, like last night's snake extravaganza, which Cynthia Rêve says represents temptation, sexual feelings, or hidden fears. Whatever. I certainly didn't choose any of that. I hardly get to choose how I live when I'm awake, much less when I'm sleeping. I thought about those hundreds of dreamers Martin had had—all controlling him. "So in a dream, have you ever kissed—" I stopped, embarrassed, but he laughed.

"Yes," he said. "Haven't you?" I thought about Daniel, and then I tried not to think in case Martin was in my head.

I nodded. There was a pen on the table, and I picked it up and doodled a blue jay on the flat part of my palm just under my thumb. "But did it ever—"

Maybe he was in my head because he seemed to understand what I was asking without me finishing. "This is all new to me, Annabelle. I didn't realize it could happen. There were rumors," he stumbled over his words, "but I didn't really believe—I've never been here."

"But why?" I asked. "Why now? Why me?"

He reached across the table and touched the back of my hands. His fingers were sticky, too. "I think it's *because* of you somehow," he said. "You're special, Annabelle. You're...perfect."

That word again. My heart shot straight into my throat and I started to cough. I took a sip of water to settle myself, but ended up coughing it up, too. Out my nose. Smooth. I grabbed a wad of napkins from the little metal box and covered my face.

"Did I say something wrong?"

"It wasn't wrong," I said. "It was just that no one's ever said anything like that to me before."

"I have," he said.

"Yeah, but..." That was then. In dreamland or whatever. It was different hearing it in real life, with the glare of the everyday all around me. The orange plastic booth with a little tear on the seat, the stained ceramic mug, the jittery light from the ceiling fans.

"Right," I said, pointedly changing the subject. "How does it all work then? How did you get here?"

"Who knows?" he said. "In old stories, there was *our* world, the world of dreams—the place *you* go when you dream. And on the other side, there was Earth, which was empty except for shadows. They say a dream crossed into the shadow Earth through a tunnel of mist. And she became the first dreamer."

"That'd be like...what? Our first human? Are you saying she came from your world, that she was like Eve?"

"What's eve?"

"*Who*," I corrected. "It's a name. Our first woman. *Eve*." Which made me think about last night's serpents again.

"The dreamer didn't have a name," he said. "But her dreams were so powerful, they spun a cord between the worlds—yours and mine." Martin's eyes grew distant, like he was looking out a plane window. "The legend says she would walk along that cord between the worlds. And sometimes she'd lead others from our world back with her to earth. They lived with her there. So, I guess if she was your first woman, they'd be your first people, right?"

"Weird." I was getting tangled in all this talk of different worlds.

"Of course, it wasn't like that for me," he went on. "I didn't see any rope or a tunnel of mist or anything."

"What did you see?"

"It happened so fast. Everything flexed at once, and then contracted." He paused, looking for the right words. "I felt like I'd been squeezed inside the nozzle of a vacuum. And I was here."

"Vacuum," I repeated, but so softly he couldn't hear me.

"I've heard stuff about that, too. And these stories aren't so old. They say one dream escaped to your world by running through fire. One crawled through pipes. Compared to them, I got off easy. Not that I ever took it seriously, the stuff I heard."

I think this was the first time in my life that my jaw literally dropped. "So there are others like you? And they come through pipes?"

"Yeah, I guess it sounds strange."

"You think? Pipes!"

"I'm not saying it happened that way," he said. "They're just stories. It's not like I know they're all here exactly."

He rubbed his jaw with the flat of his hand.

I waited for more but it didn't come.

"Anyway, I'm here now, right?" He nodded his head a little too emphatically. Maybe he was avoiding saying something, or maybe the sugar from the syrup just kicked in. "And I bet the longer I'm here, the more human I'll be."

"Oh." I could actually feel my mind whir. "You're not human now?"

"No, I totally am."

"But you could be *more* human?"

"Right."

Apparently dream people aren't real big on logic. There are degrees of human-ness? This is the kind of thing that would have made Will zap into debate-mode. Well, this and the pipes.

"Oh my God." It just hit me. "Do you have a belly button?"

88

On the boat, what I'd seen of his body looked totally normal, but suddenly I wasn't sure if I'd noticed his belly button.

He rolled his eyes and lifted his shirt just enough for me to see a standard-issue belly button and a few dark hairs trailing down his stomach. If it were Will, I would have poked him. With Martin, I just tried to breathe.

He pulled his shirt down. "What if I didn't have a belly button?" he said. "Would you still…"

I waited to see what word he'd use, but he just left it hanging, which was not a bad thing, given that we'd known each other a grand total of twenty-seven hours.

"It would just be hard to explain," I said. "You have to admit, it'd be a little weird for you in the locker room after a football game."

"It's already weird in the locker room after a game," he said. "How is slapping someone with a wet towel a sign of friendship?"

"It's a guy thing," I told him. "Anyway, you're the one who decided to play football."

"I thought you decided that."

"I don't think so," I said. "We hate football."

"You mean there are others like *you*?" he teased.

"Look, as much as I'd like to take credit, I don't think I had anything to do with the fact that you're…here. And I certainly had nothing to do with the fact that you're on the football team."

"You had everything to do with the fact that I'm here," he said. It was the surest he'd sounded about anything. "You remember that kiss, in the water? It was electric, like the edge of everything blurred. Nothing like that had ever happened to me before."

I looked down, suddenly shy.

"What happened to you, after that kiss?" he said.

"I...I woke up," I said.

"That's what happened to me," he said. "I woke up. Here. And as for football," he went on, "maybe you didn't plan all of that consciously, but did you ever consider that maybe you had a subconscious desire to have a boyfriend who's a member of the football team? Like you said, the subconscious is sticky."

I'm not the sort of person who constantly turns into a tomato, but I felt my cheeks flush.

I was torn. Part of me homed in on the word "boyfriend." The other part of me was pissed. I most certainly did *not* have a desire to date a football player, subconscious or otherwise. Just like I most certainly had *not* chosen a name like "Martin Zirkle."

This time it was Martin who flushed. "In case you wondered, Annabelle," he said softly, "there are some things that are just mine."

I fully expected to pay for lunch, but apparently lots of people dream about money because Martin had some and knew what to do with it.

We walked down Main Street, where every shop that hadn't closed was cute and struggling and mostly useless. Martin stopped in a flower shop (useless until now) and came out with a bird of paradise. It looked spiky, but was soft. "These must be the wings," I said, touching it.

"They had other flowers. But you're different, so I wanted you to have something different."

I pulled the flower to my face. It smelled sweet and ripe, like peaches topped with vanilla ice cream. "It's exquisite."

"So are you."

"Do you have to say stuff like that?" I asked.

"You don't like it?"

"No, I mean do you *have* to? Do you have any choice or are you, you know, compelled?"

"No, of course not," he said, though he didn't sound quite so confident this time. "There's a certain *track*, I guess you'd say. Like my house, my parents, football. There's a place I'm supposed to fit in. But once I got here, my mind was my own. Finally."

I tried not to wonder if I was just another part of his track. "And you're here," I said.

"Yes." He grinned at me, and honestly, his smile could power a third world village.

When he reached out his hand, I took it.

"Can you hear what I'm thinking now?" I asked.

He nodded. "Though it's farther away. I can feel things shifting."

"Shifting," I repeated. "But you weren't going to listen anyway, right?"

"I didn't think I'd have to, but you don't say what you're thinking."

"I don't always want to say it." I turned and looked at him. *Kiss me.* I thought. *Kiss me now.*

He leaned forward, took my chin in his hand, and did.

He smelled of syrup, tasted of it. When he pulled away, a passing car honked and someone let out a rebel yell. I touched my finger to my lips, feeling off-balance, and dazzlingly awake.

Chapter 14

"Ve have vays of making you talk."

Talon's accent was straight out of a B-grade movie. *The Gypsy Bride of Düsseldorf.*

"I thought we were supposed to be concentrating," I said. We sat across from each other on Serena's four-poster bed, our fingers lightly touching the arrow-indicator-thingy from Talon's Ouija board. "Anyway, I've already told you guys everything."

Which wasn't precisely true. In all my phone conversations and texts the day before, I'd been as elusive as possible. Plus after lunch, Martin had asked me not to tell anyone about how he'd gotten here. Even though I'd already told Talon and Serena that I'd seen him in my dream, I was now supposed to say he was from Philadelphia and it was all just a big coincidence.

"Let's see." Talon was all American now as she addressed the Ouija board. "Has Annabelle told us everything?" Slowly, as if a magnet were drawing it there, the indicator moved to "no."

"See?" Talon quirked one eyebrow up in a No-More-BS gesture, and I felt a wave of sympathy for her future children.

"We just took a walk," I said. "And went to lunch…and talked and stuff."

"What stuff?" Serena asked.

"Well"—I had to give them something—"he's an *amazing* kisser!"

Serena literally clapped her hands.

"Tongue?" Talon asked.

"Some," I said. "He's really sweet. Kind of clueless, but *hot* clueless."

"That wouldn't have anything to do with him being from another planet, right?" Talon had a propensity for one-track sarcasm. As usual she was right on target, but I couldn't let her know that.

"Shut up," I said. "Okay, he looks like my Dream Boy, but not totally-totally. He also kind of looks like Sean Farrell." Sean Farrell is the lead singer for Sideways, my favorite band of all time. Besides the Pacers, they were the only band who ever came through Chilton because they were actually *from* Chilton. "I mean, who wouldn't dream about him?"

I picked up a wedge of zucchini from the tray Mrs. Mendez had set out for us. You couldn't come over to Serena's without digesting vegetable matter. The last time I visited, her mother fed us eggplant, pine nuts ("pignolia," her mother called them) and a pile of unidentifiable leaves that took forever to chew. I think that's why Serena drinks so much Diet Coke and stuff whenever she's away from home.

I pointed at Talon with the zucchini in a way that I hoped made me look convincing. "You dreamed about Spice. Does that mean

Spice is an alien? Anyway, Martin's from Philly, which, last time I checked, is in this galaxy."

"I thought he was from Egypt," said Serena.

"He was only there for a year or something."

"Yeah." Talon squinted and tucked her hair behind her ears—which is the same thing she does when she watches cop shows on TV. Not a good sign. "And Chilton, Virginia, is the next logical stop on his world tour."

"Why not Chilton?" Serena interjected. "Mr. Stauffer says with the Internet, you can live pretty much anywhere and work out of your home." Serena has a huge crush on Mr. Stauffer, our guidance counselor. She says she doesn't, but then she quotes him on everything from organizational strategies to paradigm shifts.

"There you go!" I said with more enthusiasm than was warranted. "And anyway, I think I must have remembered the dream wrong."

"Hold on," Talon said. "You dream about this guy and then *poof*, he appears. And he not only appears, but he shows up at your house and sticks his tongue down your throat. And now you're all 'tra-la-la my Dream Boy didn't have a freckle on his arm so it wasn't him.' Come *on*, Annabelle. This is *cosmic*. You've got to admit, something's up." She addressed the Ouija board again. "Is something up?" she asked.

We put our hands back on the board and slowly, the indicator moved to the letter U, then P, then U, then P, again and again until I took my hands off to make it stop.

"You made it do that," I said.

"Did not," Talon said. Serena put her hands out for me to inspect, to show that she, at least, was innocent.

I've never known quite how Ouija boards worked. I mean, it's not like I believe there are a bunch of spirits just waiting for us to call on them and ask them dumb questions like "Who will I marry?" But at the same time it doesn't seem like Parker Brothers could manufacture a game where you rely on someone to cheat and make the little thingie move. That's not exactly a business plan, is it?

I rested my fingers back on the indicator. Talon was being a total contrarian. Had I been all freaked out (*I kissed a dream who came to earth through pipes!*) she likely would have acted nonchalant (*Just as I suspected all along.*). But since I was understating things, not to mention *omitting* them, she was determined to stir up drama.

"It's surreal! Who's with me?" Talon raised her arms like she was talking to a huge crowd instead of just Serena and me.

"Of course, it's surreal," I said. "With my love life, *any* guy showing up at my house and sticking his tongue down my throat is surreal. And just for the record, he didn't 'stick his tongue down my throat.' Our tongues just sort of touched. Like they were bumping into each other. It was nice."

"But he is"—Talon said this slowly, as if I'd just had an emergency lobotomy—"the same...guy...from...your...dream. You said so Friday."

"It's just a coincidence. End of story."

"You are one sucky liar, Annabelle Manning." She went back to the Ouija board. "Is Annabelle lying?"

And this time, I couldn't help myself, I did cheat, to keep the indicator from going to yes. I couldn't tell if Talon and Serena were pushing back or not, but the spirit didn't tell us anything in the end, just kind of shuffled around a little in the middle.

"Okay, next question," Talon announced. "Is Martin Zirkle an alien?"

"GUH!" I took my hand off the indicator. "Can we move on?" I wanted to change the subject and besides, Talon was right about the lying thing. I could never quite wrap my face around a lie, ever since my very first fib, when my dad asked if I had eaten all twenty-two of the lollipops I was supposed to tape onto my kindergarten valentines. "It wasn't me," I'd said. But my lips were coated with red sugar and I couldn't look him in the eye.

When I faced my dad I was alone. This time, I had Serena.

"You're missing the point," she told Talon, folding her arms, too. "First of all he is so *not* an alien. And second of all it doesn't matter where he came from. What matters is he's hot and sweet and... what else did you say he was?"

"Clueless?" offered Talon.

"Romantic," finished Serena. "He got her *flowers*."

"Technically he got me *flower*, singular," I said. "But it *was* romantic. Now ask a question." We put our fingers back around the edges of the indicator.

"What is—" Talon began.

"Not a me-and-Martin question," I interrupted.

"What is your name?" Serena asked. The indicator swirled over the board, stopping on the letters A, S, C, O, and T.

"Your name is Ascot?" I asked.

"Just 'Scot,' maybe," Serena said.

"You're *wearing* an ascot?" Talon asked. The indicator moved straight to "yes" and the three of us cracked up.

We moved on to debating whether or not Serena should get her belly button pierced. (I was *Why?* Talon, who had already pierced her tragus, was *Why not?* The Ouija board was *Goodbye.*) Then Serena's mom poked her head in the door.

"You girls staying for dinner?"

"Thanks for the offer, Mrs. Mendez, but I have a thing with my dad," Talon said.

"Annabelle?"

"Oh, thanks"—I thought of the pine nuts—"but I have to get going, too."

"Next time then. Serena, I still want you to try on these hiking boots to make sure we have the right fit." She tossed a box on the rug. "You know I don't like you girls using that thing, especially on Sunday." She sighed. "But as long as you're using it, ask about my necklace. I still can't figure out where I put it." She shut the door behind her.

"Where is my mother's necklace?" Serena asked.

"S, L, E, L, F."

"Slelf?" Serena said.

"Maybe he means shelf," I said. "Like bookshelf or something."

"We have a lot of shelves." Serena moved away from the Ouija board and started to unpack her boots. "So what's the 'thing' with your dad?"

"Dinner at Sushi Palace," Talon said. "He's never been; I've never been. We're 'opening ourselves up to experiences.'"

"Sushi in Chilton is an experience all right," I said. "It's like roast beef in…I don't know. India. Is that something The Doctor suggested?"

"What else?" Talon grimaced.

I looked down at Serena's feet, now clad in industrial-strength pink boots. "Nice."

"I needed some new ones before our trip to Black Beak." Serena clicked the toes of her boots together.

"So you're still going AWOL over homecoming?" Talon asked.

"It's not like I have any better options," Serena said. "It's too bad really. I would have liked to see Annabelle all dolled up with her new boy."

"Oh crap! Crap crap crap!" I bit my lip. "I sort of made plans for homecoming with Will."

"Will. Really?" Talon had that cop-show look again.

"We were just going as friends."

"Well, then, tell him *as friends* that you're making other plans," she said, still squinting.

I didn't want to think about that conversation—especially not after all his weirdness yesterday. "Anyway," I said, "Martin hasn't asked me."

"Hasn't asked you *yet*," Serena amended. "I don't even *have* to ask the Ouija board that question."

"All right, then. How about this?" Talon rubbed her hands together and then put her fingertips on the indicator. Serena and I followed suit. "Oh great and powerful Ouija, what does homecoming have in store for our sweet little Annabelle Manning? Will it be everything she could hope for—the night of her dreams?"

"B, E, W, R, E, G, R, L."

"Be We Are Grill?" asked Serena, taking her hands from the indicator and shaking them out. "Be Regal?"

"Beware G.R.L?" Talon asked. "Who's G.R.L.? Do you know anyone with the initials G.R.L.?"

"Beware GRILL," Serena said. "No barbecuing on homecoming."

To me the interpretation seemed obvious but I didn't share it: BEWARE GIRL.

The girl in the dream. A warning.

But whether the warning was for her or for me, I couldn't say.

Chapter 15

I didn't have any nightmares on Sunday night, which made it a lot easier to face Monday morning. Instead I focused on my good dreams, and on the one that had come true and had followed me to my locker and kissed me on the cheek in front of God and Mr. Stauffer.

I avoided mentioning homecoming—to Will or Martin, though I'd been thinking it at the top of my lungs.

It probably seemed weird that I even *wanted* to go to homecoming since it was such a disaster last year, and since technically it fell under the category of "school spirit." But I did want to go. For one, it was a chance to show Daniel that I'd gotten over him. And for two, it was a chance to spend the night leaning against Martin and listening to music, both of which are good things in themselves, but which, when combined, are amazing. At least, I thought they would be amazing. I guess I'd never know unless Martin asked me to homecoming. It wasn't that I thought he didn't like me. Even given my usual insecurities I was pretty sure he did. I mean, he kind of had to, right? But I didn't know if Martin *knew* he could ask me. Or should. Or if he even danced.

When I got to the lunchroom, Will, Paolo, Talon, and Serena were already in our spot. I didn't see Martin anywhere. I moved to the end of the table next to Will and opened my bag lunch. I'd packed PB&J, an apple, and some carrot sticks wrapped in aluminum foil, which is SO middle school, but is at least edible. Then I had a panic attack. What if Martin came to lunch but didn't sit with me? What if he did sit with me and he and Will went all Testosterone again?

I felt him looking at me before I saw him, but when I did, everything seemed all right. He was coming out of the cafeteria line, and he was smiling. He wouldn't be for long. I should have warned him about cafeteria food when he called Sunday night. "I just wanted to hear your voice," he'd said, and my heart beat like I'd just run a six-minute mile. We'd talked for two hours, and I'd kept my head under the covers so my mom wouldn't hear me. And even though he wasn't there, I'd felt like we were alone together in a cave.

Now my heart was beating fast again. We were in a wide-open space and Martin was walking toward me.

I gave him a half-wave.

"Who are you—oh," Will said. He had a camera on the table in front of him and he was trying not to drip mustard from his sandwich on it.

"You'll be nice, right?" I said.

"I'm always nice," Will said.

"Not always."

"I'll be nice." He raised his hand like a Boy Scout, though he'd never been one.

I squeezed over and made room for Martin, completely ignoring Talon and Serena, who were elbowing each other and mouthing words like "finally." Martin sat down. He was wearing another blue shirt that matched his eyes—did he own anything but blue?—and jeans.

"Miss me?" he asked. Then he made eye contact with Will. "Hello, Will," he said and, after a pause that went on for a beat too long, he added, "Math...fascinating subject, isn't it?"

I looked at Will. Today his T-shirt read "I eat π for breakfast." I hoped Martin was responding to the T-shirt, not thinking that "math is fascinating" was a normal topic of conversation.

"Indeed," Will said, all politeness, though his jaw was tight. "How are you adapting to life in Chilton? It must be quite a change from Philly."

"I love it here," Martin said.

"So, I guess you're a big Eagles fan?" Will asked.

"Sure, I like eagles," Martin said. I nudged him under the table with my foot. Even I knew that was a team of some sort.

Will raised an eyebrow in a "something's fishy in Denmark" way, but he went on to comment on some guy who, from the drift of the conversation, must have been the team's new assistant coach. Martin nodded, clearly lost.

"Um, Martin, these are my friends. Serena." She waved,

watching us like she was watching one of my mom's old romance movies. "Paolo." He nodded his head once, a weird, knowing smile on his face that made me want to slug him. Martin nodded back. "Talon." Talon reached a hand across the table to shake his. I think she wanted to make sure he wasn't made of alien goo.

Martin smiled at everyone and picked up his fork.

"Steak!" he announced.

"Ew." Serena said.

"Ew?" Martin said.

"They *call* it Salisbury steak," I explained. "No one knows what it is really."

"Ground beef," Serena said. "Only schools don't use the best beef. They use the worst beef. And gravy."

"They call it gravy," I said. "It's really—"

"Plasma," Will finished.

"You mean plasma like the kind in your blood?" Martin looked a little paler.

"No, no," I said quickly. "It's edible. It's okay." I gave Will a dirty look, but of course he was all "What?" especially since I started it.

Talon started humming the theme from an alien movie.

"So he likes Salisbury steak!" I muttered at Talon. "So what?"

Then Martin tasted it and it turned out I was wrong. Martin didn't like Salisbury steak. Maybe he was human after all.

He looked like he wanted to spit, so I pointed to his napkin, but right at that moment Stephanie Gonzales started walking toward our table and he swallowed instead. His eyes flashed the way most guys' eyes flash when they first see Stephanie Gonzales. Like they've never seen a girl so perfect before. Only Martin's expression was slightly different. It was like he *had* seen her before and was happy to see her again.

"Marty!" She stopped at our table—stopped, instead of walking past us.

"Steph."

She called him Marty! He called her Steph! I knew I shouldn't have left that stupid football game!

"You were on fire Friday night!" She sounded like one of her cheesy cheers.

"Um, thanks," he said. "So were you."

She laughed and flipped her hair. "Are you sure you want to sit here?" She looked at me. "No offense." As if that could somehow *not* be offensive?

"I'm comfortable," Martin said, but he didn't look comfortable. His smile was a little too determined, and he sort of gripped the edge of the table, like he was trying to keep himself from jumping up. "This is crazy, isn't it?"

"Crazy," I said, but they both ignored me.

"So, how's it going?" Martin said.

Stephanie put one hand on our table and leaned down, putting her cleavage on prominent display. "How's it look like it's going?" Only Stephanie could make *how's it going* an invitation to show off her boobs.

"Good," he said. "Great."

"We're sitting over there." She pointed to her table. I wanted to see Talon's face but I was afraid if I looked away, Martin would stand up and follow Stephanie right into the sunset. Actually, I was afraid he'd do that even if I didn't look away.

"I'm fine right here," he said. "But we should get together and… finish our talk."

"I'd really like that," she said.

When she was gone, Talon kicked me under the table.

I gave her a weak-tea smile.

"She's a friend," Martin said, soft enough so that maybe I was the only one who could hear. "From before."

"Before?" I muttered. "Before Friday or—Oh my God." She was one of his dreamers! Just the thought of it gave me itchy skin. Stephanie Gonzales had dreamed about Martin. She'd probably kissed him and her tongue had probably—

"That's not it," Martin said. He looked at me meaningfully, like he wanted me to read his mind for a change.

I knew Will and Talon were trying to listen to every word we said. I searched my head for a code word, and for once I was grateful that Martin *did* know what I was thinking.

"So she's…she's from Philly?" I whispered.

His eyes said yes.

She's one of the others, I thought. *She's somebody's Dream Girl!* And this time he nodded.

"Was," he whispered.

"I have to throw this away," I said, wadding up my napkin. "Keep me company?"

We walked to the trash can.

"Whose?" I asked. "Billy's?"

"I couldn't say," Martin said. "I don't think I should be discussing this with you anyway. It's too much."

"You bet it's too much."

"Annabelle—"

I looked back at our table where everyone was watching us like we were a reality TV show.

"Let's go back," I said. "Before everyone gets suspicious."

"They're already suspicious," he said. "Look. You go back. I need to tell Stephanie something."

But I didn't want to face my friends. What did he want to tell Stephanie that he couldn't tell me? When he went to her lunch table, I followed, and stopped near one of the big blue columns that, I suppose, was meant to keep the cafeteria from collapsing. I crouched down and pretended to tie my shoe.

From my vantage point, I could see Martin bend over Stephanie as her full, red lips whispered something surely poisonous in his ear.

"All right," Martin said, and then added in a deeper voice, "Hey, Billy."

"Hey."

"I have cheerleading this afternoon." Stephanie made it sound like shaking pompoms was on par with curing cancer. Then Martin said something I couldn't hear and she answered, "It's a date!"

A date! I was thinking. *She just wants to—*

Whap. Martin drummed the side of his head with his hand, as if he were trying to get water out of his ear.

"You know what else we should do," she said.

"What?" At least he couldn't read her like he could read me.

"Homecoming." She said it casually, the way only a girl like Stephanie could say it. "For old time's sake. I'm certain Billy wouldn't mind."

"Uhh…" This from Billy, who didn't sound as certain.

"What's homecoming, exactly?" asked Martin.

Like he hadn't gleaned anything from all of the brain scanning he'd been doing the past two days! I reached down and tied my other shoe.

"A dance, silly," she said. "Everybody goes. It's the only thing to do this weekend. It's the only thing to do all fall, really. You know, *Chilton.*" She said the word like it was a joke between the two of them.

"It's beautiful here," Martin said. "It smells good."

"You have so much to learn," she said.

"I can't believe it's really you, Steph."

"Uhh, hey—" said Billy.

"So, how about it: homecoming?" She talked over Billy as if he hadn't spoken.

"You said—" Billy started.

"Yeah, I know, we're going, Billy." She sighed. I could almost hear her lips turn down in a pout. "But Martin can come, too, can't he?"

"I really think I should go with Annabelle," Martin said.

"Well, I guess if you like that sort of thing," Stephanie said, as Billy muttered, "Damn straight."

I was having more uncharitable feelings about Stephanie and I was having them at the top of my lungs. Brain.

Martin dug his fingers through his hair and glanced toward my column.

"So, later?" he asked Stephanie.

"Be there with bells on," she said.

"People wear bells?"

"You're so silly!" She laughed, but it was fake.

A second later, Martin peeked around the pole and helped me up. "You know," he whispered like he was letting me in on a secret, "I can't hear a thing when you yell like that."

"I wasn't yelling. I was thinking."

"Don't think so loud," he said. "It's like a siren going off in my head."

"Sorry," I said. *Better?* I thought in a softer voice.

"Better."

"So, you know Stephanie pretty well, I guess?" I asked out loud.

"I told you. We're just friends."

"Just friends," I said, but I was thinking, *Not if she has anything to do with it.*

"Maybe it's like your Will situation," he said.

"What Will situation?"

He looked at me like I was the clueless one. "Never mind," he said.

We started to walk toward our table again, but he stopped.

"There's a dance next weekend," he said. "Homecoming?"

I shrugged, but I stopped breathing. "What about it?" I said.

He got down on one knee—I swear to God, one knee—right there in the cafeteria. "Will you go with me?"

The whole cafeteria was watching us, but I didn't care. I looked at Martin's face and those warm, honest eyes that liked me and maybe even more than liked. I knew he could read my mind but I wanted to say the answer out loud anyway.

"Yes," I said.

Chapter 16

When we got back to the table, I was too amped up to eat my sandwich, so I just nibbled on carrots while I watched Martin poke at his Salisbury steak. He was like some sort of Greek god.

I thought of the guys in the romance novels that my mom sometimes read: "broad-chested" and "chiseled" with "dark waves of hair," "piercing eyes," and "smoldering lips."

Okay, maybe the lip part was a little over the top, and Martin's waves were more golden than dark, but the rest was pretty much him. And, he was mine. Sort of.

He looked over at me and his lips (maybe smoldering a little) curled up at the edges in this delicious, sexy way.

Talon and Serena stared at us like they'd scored front-row seats and Martin was the headliner. Meanwhile, Will kept turning around and snapping pictures.

"What are you doing?" I asked him.

Snap.

"A panoramic," he said. Snap.

"Oh."

Snap. Snap.

"That wasn't panoramic," I said.

"You've got jelly on your face," he said. "Just capturing the moment."

Snap. That one was of Martin. I had a sudden fear that he wouldn't show up on film, like a vampire, but Martin didn't seem worried so I tried not to be, either.

"Would you stop?" Talon said. "You're so annoying."

Snap.

"Yearbook," Will said. "I'm getting candids."

Martin stood up.

"I have to go talk to Coach," he said. He touched my cheek. "See you soon." To everyone else he said, "Nice meeting you."

"A pleasure as always," Will said.

After he left, Talon gave Will a look. "What is *up* with you?"

"I'm being polite," Will said. "Chivalrous."

"I'll bet Martin wears a gambeson," Paolo muttered.

Will gave Paolo a nudge and then picked up his camera, focusing this time on me.

"So," he said. "Homecoming."

"Yeah." I looked down. "About that." I wasn't sure where to start, so Will did.

"I guess all bets are off," he said.

"You're okay with that?"

He shrugged and took the camera away from his eye. "I believe you're the one who said if we hadn't found someone by home-coming we would go together. And if I'm not mistaken, you found someone."

"Yeah," I said again. "I guess I did."

"So," he said. "Live long and prosper and all of that." He gave me that little Star Trek finger sign with his free hand.

"Are you still going to go?"

"I'm shooting it for yearbook," he said. "I guess I have to."

"Alone?"

"There's always Bessie." He held up his camera.

"There must be someone you can ask."

"I wasn't even going to go at all until you brought it up," he said. "Now I've got this assignment so, you know, whatever. I'll just go and snap a few pictures and leave. It's no big deal."

"I don't think Talon's going yet."

"Talon hates homecoming," he said. He looked across the table at Talon. "Right?"

"Thank you for not acting like I'm invisible," she said to Will. To me she said, "I don't hate it. I loathe it."

"See?"

"There has to be someone—"

"Look, Annabelle," he interrupted. "I don't need you playing matchmaker for me."

"Yeah, but—" I started.

"Can we drop it?"

"Sure," I said. But I didn't want to drop it. I wanted Will to be happy. As happy as me. "So, you're in the photo lab this afternoon?" I asked, intentionally changing the subject.

"Yep."

"Maybe I could help out?" I was searching for some reason to hang around until after football practice anyway.

He looked at me like I'd just sprouted a second head, but then he smiled. A little tense around the eyes, but still a smile. "Yeah, okay," he said.

Chapter 17

The photo lab was a big low-ceilinged room in the annex at the back of the school. No windows—and from the looks of it, the janitors had pretty much written it off circa 1995. It was bright enough, but it had a strange sawdusty smell, and the boxes in the corner had easily been stacked there since the Clinton administration. To the back was Chilton High's version of a "media center" with video cameras, a few TVs, huge umbrellas, lights on metal stands, and for some reason that I couldn't quite fathom, a big old-fashioned microwave. On the other side were long shelves packed with junk, and a tall black tube that served as a door of some sort. "DARKROOM," it said. Beneath was a bumper sticker with a camera that read, "Help! I've been shot!" and another that read, "Photographers do it in the dark."

Will was sitting at one of the computers, uploading his pictures, and across the room a few random guys huddled around a Goth chick who was drawing something with a fat, black marker.

"Hey." I took a seat next to Will.

"Hey." He nudged my knee with his knee.

"This the stuff from earlier?" I asked, pointing to the computer screen.

"Yep. A day in the life."

Each picture flashed on the screen for a moment in a sort of slideshow. A group of sophomore girls with too much makeup voguing in front of the trophy case. Mr. Stauffer sitting on the edge of his desk, his eyes squinting in that "I'm listening" face he makes. A kind of artsy shot of test tubes filled with different colored powders. The Lobmans' Japanese exchange student, Akiko, smiling over her shoulder as she walked down the hall. Two guys running off the soccer field, a haze of blue mountains in the distance.

"These are solid," I said. "You have a great eye."

"Just one?" He looked at me, deadpan. "I always thought both my eyes were equally great."

I gave him a kick. "You are soooo smooth," I said.

"Smooth like ex-lax."

"Smooth and gross," I added.

"Like ex-lax."

The pictures from lunch flashed by next. I'd been there, right beside him the whole time, and it had seemed like he was kind of goofing off, so I was surprised by what he'd managed to capture. In his photos, all the confusion of the cafeteria seemed much more interesting than it had in real life. It was as if by freezing its motion and drawing a frame around its edges, everyday stuff had taken on some deeper meaning...truth, even. Each frame had a little story: Billy Stubbs tossing a crumpled milk carton toward the trash can in a high perfect arc while Trina Myers checked out his butt; Melanie Butler, whose hair color changed with the weather (orange today), puckering her lips as if she was just about to curse at Clive Porterfield, who was half-sitting, half-standing, trying to explain something.

Will stood. "I need to work on some prints while these upload. Wanna come?"

"In a minute," I said. I was waiting to see the photo he'd taken of Martin, wondering if it'd be, I don't know, *there*. But what I saw first was not Martin; it was me. I had a little jelly on my chin, as promised, and a huge grin on my face. I looked prettier than I thought of myself as looking. And happier than I was used to feeling. Then there was Martin in profile, beautiful as always, slightly out of focus, but even so, good-looking enough to be a high-end underwear model. There was another picture of Martin, too, this one from behind. He had a small tattoo on the back of his neck, two small, squiggly lines, like waves. I wondered why I'd never noticed it. But maybe I had; it looked somehow familiar. Before I was ready to stop looking at him, Serena appeared, a mahogany curl coiling over one eye as she offered Paolo a rutabaga chip.

"Can you get me a copy of those?" I asked him. "I might want to use some for sketches."

"That's quite a compliment, coming from Chilton's resident artist."

"You're an artist, too."

"I just like to take pictures," Will said. "Anyway, the camera only

117

sees what's going on outside. Your drawings show what's inside. It's like you make this invisible connection between what you're thinking and feeling and what the person who sees your work could be thinking and feeling."

I blushed. "Nick would love it if my head swelled up so much I couldn't fit through my doorway. He's always wanted my room."

Will nudged my knee again. "Come on," he said.

I followed him to the darkroom door, which was really this cylinder, with a piece cut out. Once inside, you stand on a circle and slide the door so that the entrance into the cylinder becomes your exit into the darkroom. That way you don't allow in any light from the outside. Pretty much, it works the same way some of my mother's spices work: saltshaker technology.

"Voilà," said Will, even though he was taking Latin instead of French.

The darkroom was, as expected, *dark*. It took a minute for my eyes to adjust to the eerie red light—the same kind they used in the mad-scientist display for the haunted house at Dixie Caverns each Halloween. They actually set up the haunted house *inside* the cave, which went on for about a mile underground. That way you got that wet-spooky feel of being trapped underground with the campy-spooky feel of a vampire popping out of a rustic wooden coffin. Will's favorite was the guy in a bloody flannel shirt who chased people with a revving chainsaw (as he said, "How can we know he's not a sociopathic townie who *really* wants to cut us all to bits?"), but the one that always got me was the crazy woman with matted hair, singing off-key to a dirty, headless baby doll. In the past, I'd always liked being scared, running from somebody else's nightmares. Now that I had had my own, I wasn't sure I could face Dixie Caverns. I wasn't sure I could even face the darkroom.

The red light blared. And the whole place smelled like the inside of a can of ant spray. But my eyes adjusted, and I didn't see any snakes.

Will showed me how to focus and expose the negatives, and then slip the photo paper in various trays of chemical solutions to develop and fix the prints.

"We shoot digital for the yearbook," he explained, "but Heller makes us do it old-school for class."

We were working on the roll he'd taken two weekends before at Olde Salem Days, a street festival in a town nearby. Little kids with balloons, people looking at baskets, a woman whittling a primitive fertility-goddess figurine, that sort of stuff. One of me, Talon, and Serena talking to this old guy who had a 1906 Model-T Ford that he promised to give us a ride in if we ever came back to Salem when the streets weren't so crowded.

I put in another negative strip and focused on a close-up of Talon licking this huge double scoop of pineapple frozen custard that a cute dairy farmer from Franklin County had given her—free of charge. Everywhere we went, older guys drooled over Talon; she had a quirky beauty that high school boys didn't even seem to notice, but college-age guys found irresistible. Not that it did them any good. She took the free ice cream or the waived cover charge or, once, a huge stuffed rainbow-striped frog—and went on her way, untouched.

I zeroed in on Talon's nose. "So, about homecoming…"

I could hear Will, who was looking over my shoulder, suppress a groan.

"I have an idea," I went on. "Macy White."

"What?"

I turned. I was pressed uncomfortably close to his chest and for a minute I felt this kind of flicker in my stomach, and Will was looking down at my mouth and I couldn't swallow. He seemed tall, suddenly. My mind flashed blank and I felt myself straining upward, rising on the balls of my feet.

Then Will moved back, like we'd been caught kissing.

"What?" he asked again.

"Macy, for homecoming," I said, though I was having trouble concentrating on my words. "You could ask her."

He closed his eyes, then opened them again. "It's all right. I have it covered."

"What do you mean you have it covered?"

"I'm going with Talon."

"Talon?" My head was swirling. "But she hates homecoming—"

"Yeah, well. I guess she changed her mind."

"When?"

"During P.E.," he said.

"Oh. Well. That's great then," I said, trying to make it sound like I sincerely meant it. Which I should have, right? I'd suggested Talon.

Will had a date, one who hadn't stolen away Daniel Kowalski. And Talon was "opening herself up to new experiences" that did not involve her parents, The Doctor, or another piercing.

Will took out his contact sheet and held it up to the light. He circled a picture of Talon's ear with a black Sharpie. The picture was close. Not close enough so you could see earwax or anything, but close enough that it went beyond looking like an ear and started looking like something else. Tunnels. Or a seashell maybe. Her gold studs just looked like part of the landscape.

He circled another, and I viewed it through the loupe. It was a little boy looking lost among a bunch of kneecaps.

"I hope you helped him find his mother after you took that picture," I said.

"She wasn't far away," he said. "The assignment was to show emotion."

"I thought all photos showed emotion," I said.

"Nope," he said. "Many photos feature fake smiles, which offer the appearance of an emotion—like happiness—but not the actual emotion itself."

"But isn't fake happiness an emotion?" Sometimes it seemed like I was in a perpetual state of fake happiness. *I'm so happy you found your bliss in Alaska, Dad." "We're doing great, Aunt Caroline. Four-course dinners every night." "Daniel who?"*

"Hmm." Will frowned into the loupe. "I'll have to take that one under advisement."

I savored my almost-victory as Will circled a picture of an old man bent in front of a shelf of carved wooden bowls, his face etched like an ancient tree. Then he circled a picture of me and Serena and Talon. "This one's not for Heller," he said. "But there's nothing fake-happy about it, is there?"

I looked at the photo under the loupe. It was taken before Martin, when I was busy hating Chilton, worrying that I was going to get stuck here all alone, like my mom. But I wasn't alone; I was with my friends. And I had to admit, the smiles were real.

Will moved forward to some photos he'd taken over the weekend—wildlife shots from the river, Chilton's watery border. The mountains stood tall in the background, turning the town into a postcard. A dead tree. A squirrel, which stared right into the camera so his eyes followed you, like the Mona Lisa. Three deer and one deer butt, which made me laugh. A close-up of a snake, which turned my stomach to ice.

"When did you take these?" I asked him.

"Yesterday. Why?"

My breath came quick, as I forced out a "no reason."

"It's a northern water snake," he said.

"It looks evil."

"Nah," Will said. "It's harmless."

I closed my eyes for a minute, and prayed that Will Connor really did know everything.

Chapter 18

At four thirty, right around the time football practice would be letting out, I left the darkroom and headed over to the field with the idea that I might get a ride home with Martin. Coach Masterson had the guys running plays, so I hung back behind the bleachers. There was some loose change on the ground. I picked up a nickel and a dime before I thought about how pathetic it would be to become known as the Girl Who Picked Up Coins Under the Bleachers. I decided to stoop only for actual bills, but I didn't see any.

The sun caught the silver of a crushed soda can and I kicked it toward the back fence. Just beyond the chain links, something long and black glinted in the grass. I flinched. A snake?! A big fat...oh, a big fat *hose*.

I probably just had snake on the brain since seeing Will's photo. But it got me thinking. If Martin could walk out of my dream, what's to stop anyone showing up in Chilton? Or any*thing*. Like those snakes. Or that lost girl. Or whatever else we can dream up.

Maybe, I thought, I should try to dream something amazing. World peace or endless cupcakes or Gandhi. As if I had that sort of control. As if anyone did.

My dream dictionary app has a calculator feature that shows how many dreams someone has had in their lifetime, based on the average person over the age of ten hosting around five dreams each night. According to the app, I've had approximately 12,485 dreams since my tenth birthday. *None* of which have come true. Except this one.

With that kind of record, it was clear: Martin was a fluke. Or maybe I should say *miracle*. When I looked out to where he was dashing across the field, his body almost musical as he flexed and ran and dove, the word *miracle* definitely fit. He was beyond perfect. Way too gorgeous for our shabby little world. I tried to think quietly, and it must have worked because he didn't look at me, the way he had in the locker room, the way he had at lunch when I hid behind the pole. Masterson had them run a lap— Martin, graceful, in the lead—and then they all started heading toward the locker room.

Just as I was about to step out and call to him, Stephanie— Chilton's other "miracle"—came out the back door of the gym. She was wearing shorts that cut just below her butt, as if they weren't shorts at all, but some sort of bathing suit. It was crisp out—not shorts weather. I could smell burning leaves. Stephanie stood with one hip stuck out like she was waiting for a bus. As the guys ran toward the locker room entrance, Martin stopped. Billy stopped right behind him, but Stephanie waved him on, saying something high and sharp that I couldn't quite make out. I was too far away to hear his response, but he stomped past them while Martin, hands on his knees, caught his breath. *Was this their date?* I thought, and then cursed myself for thinking it so loud.

Walking together toward a big tree at the edge of the school grounds, Stephanie and Martin looked like they went together, a couple who belonged in a sportswear catalog.

They were on the opposite side of the field now. The only way to get near them without being seen was to go around the school building.

I walked quickly—not a run, but fast enough to lose my breath. I always thought of Chilton as small. Why was the school so big?

When I finally reached the other side, they were sitting under the tree. I still couldn't hear what they were saying. It seemed impossible to get any closer without them noticing me. Maybe I could disguise myself—wrap a shirt around my head or go to the theater department and nab a wig. Suddenly, the image of me with a T-shirt turban coiled over a frizzy gray hair extension flashed into my mind. First I was picking up change under the bleachers like some pitiful troll. Then I was thinking about dressing up like one. Was love supposed to turn people into trolls? Is that how it worked? Was this Crazy Annabelle, the Sequel?

Stephanie flipped her hair over one shoulder and reached up to stroke Martin's arm. *Stop it, stop it!* This time I couldn't quiet my thoughts, but even so, Martin didn't look my way.

Instead, he stood and held out his hand to help Stephanie up. He was shaking his head as they walked back toward the gym.

The wind blew their voices my way, but I could only make out parts of sentences.

"—so far—" Stephanie said. "—safe." (Or maybe "waif.")

"—looking?"

"—living a lie," Stephanie said. "—orary."

"—living—" said Martin. "—choice."

What did he mean? I was his choice? He had no choice? What???

I had stayed after school for two hours so that I could score fifteen cents and hear a grand total of ten words. One of which was really only a half-word. All this drama for "orary"!

Then Stephanie leaned into Martin, the way I leaned into Will sometimes. Okay for friends, but too close for Martin and that she-wolf. My brain shouted at her to back off. But she just clasped his shoulders and whispered something in his ear.

I felt like I needed to take a shower, or at least wash my hands. Okay, I told myself. This was insane. After Daniel, I had promised never to let another guy make me so nuts. And here I was, booking the first flight to Crazy Town just because, well, because the hottest girl in school was stroking some guy's arm. My guy's arm. But regardless. Get over yourself, Annabelle Manning. For one thing, you've known him for, what, the entire span of a weekend? So it's not like he's really *your* guy. Even if he did come from your dream. And for another thing, he either likes you or he doesn't, and no amount of psychosis on your part is going to change things. Unless it changes things for the worse.

I went to the front of the school and sat on the curb. Will's Jeep wasn't in the parking lot, so I called my mom for a ride. When her old Volvo finally came rolling up in the circular drive and I jumped in, I was, I firmly told myself, leaving Crazy Annabelle behind.

"How was your day?" Mom asked when we stopped at a light.

What could I possibly say to a question like that?

It was great: Martin asked me to homecoming.

It sucked: Stephanie Gonzales was boobinating my new boyfriend.

It was great: I got proof positive that, as suspected, Stephanie is not human.

It sucked: No one cares if she's human or not when she wears those shorts.

"Swell! And how was your day, Mom?" my mother said to make up for my silence. "Why, Annabelle, thanks ever so much for asking!"

"Sorry," I grumbled. "How was your day?"

"Busy, and I'm dead on my feet," she said. "Macaroni and cheese for dinner tonight, if you don't mind. I'm too whipped to come up with something else."

That much, at least, was normal. I wonder sometimes what exactly she does at work—do they strap her to a treadmill and make her run?—because she's *always* dead on her feet. It doesn't seem like you'd get such a workout as the activities coordinator for a retirement home. I mean, her clients don't move very fast. The place is called the Preserve, which makes it sound like it should be some kind of wilderness camp for bears, but as far as I can tell, it's just a normal retirement home with the normal boring wall art and embarrassing smells.

When we got home, Nick was sitting in the kitchen at the computer.

"Annie," he said. He'd called me that when he was little.

My mother tossed her keys on the counter. "Nick, you know you're not supposed to get on there without an adult present."

"I need to show Annabelle something," he said. "It's important."

He clicked the mouse and I peeked over his shoulder. It was an email from "LaskaDawg." My dad.

My father rarely called us, and he wrote emails even less frequently. When he first left, we heard from him once a week. Then it became once a month. Then every month or two. Now we pretty much only heard from him on birthdays, when he sent twenty dollars cash—which my mom said did *not* count as child support—without even writing a note. And when we did talk, our conversations were of the I'm-Fine-Salmon-Are-Pink-Hope-Everything's-Peachy variety. "You know how it is on a fishing boat," he said. But actually, we didn't know at all.

The email was copied to both of us, so I knew it would be in my inbox, too.

It was written all in lowercase letters.

annabelle lee and saint nick sorry so long no talk. good haul in august. salmon spawning now so season is over. still swamped but had to drop you a line to tell you the news. i'm getting married! can you believe it? her name is elana and she's great.

wedding in dec. over xmas, maybe. elana insists you two be there so guess what? i'm flying you out! told you she was great! pic enclosed. hope all is good with school and that your mom is healthy. xoxo dad

"Whoa." There didn't seem to be anything else to say.

Nick clicked on the attachment and brought forward a picture of my dad, barely recognizable behind a full beard, with a blond woman, her face red with wind. She had a nice smile, I thought, disgusted.

"Did you see this coming?" I asked Nick.

He shook his head. "I can't believe we're finally going to get up there!"

"What?" my mother said. "What are you talking about?"

"We're going to Alaska over Christmas," Nick said. He didn't mention the marriage part.

"I hope he's paying for it," my mom said.

"He says he's flying us out."

"Isn't that the coldest season?" said Mom. "And the darkest? He couldn't ask you during the summer like he's supposed to?" She poured some salt in the macaroni water—way too much salt. "Damn." She tried to fish it out with a big metal spoon, then dumped the whole pot in the sink and started over.

I knew it had been four years since my dad had left and these things happened and blah blah blah. But it still didn't seem right that he was marrying someone else. My mom hadn't even gone out on a date.

Plus, it's been pretty ugly around here since he left, money-wise. Not like we're going to live at the Rescue Mission or anything. But we're not bathing in champagne every night, either. What gets me is that my mom could have had a real career if she'd lived somewhere like New York or L.A., but she stayed in Chilton for my dad. And then he jumped ship and she's stuck here, like great-aunt Caroline says, with the kids and the bills and the old people.

Now he was getting married. And he wanted us there.

Or, wait. Elana wanted us there. My dad didn't actually say *he* wanted us.

My mother got the water on to boil with the right amount of salt this time and dried her hands with a dish towel.

"Now," she said. "What's this about Alaska?"

Nick looked at me, a look that said, *she's going to find out sometime.* I gave him a look back that said, *and she's already pissed off.*

"Dad's getting married again," I blurted out.

My mom turned a little pale, but she stood up straighter and poked out her chin. "Well," she said. "Good for him. And good luck to her, whoever she is." She put her hand on her head, like maybe she was getting a migraine. "Who is she?"

"Elana?" Nick said, but it was a question more than an answer. It was really the only thing we knew about her—her name, that she had blond hair and a red face, and that she was "great." I started to list in my mind all the things I didn't know: if there was any actual reason my dad *thought* she was so great...if she had a last name or if she was just "Elana" like Adele or Rihanna...if the blond was from genes or Clairol...if she was really as young as she looked (twenty-nine? maybe twenty-six!)...if she was from Alaska or had just ended up there too on account of her bliss...if she had kids of her own that were going to start calling my dad "Dad"...

My mom came up behind us and looked over Nick's shoulder at the computer.

"The beard suits him," she said. "Keep an eye on the water, Annabelle, I'll only be a minute." And she disappeared into the bedroom.

"Do you think she's crying?" Nick asked. I was impressed. Sensitivity wasn't usually his strongest virtue.

"No," I said. "Maybe. I don't know." I paused a minute. "How do you feel about it?"

"I'm happy about Alaska," he said. "I've always wanted to go."

"Me, too," I said.

"Everyone thinks it's awesome that my dad lives in Alaska."

"I know exactly what you mean," I said, and I did. Everyone thinks it's cool to have a dad who lives there, but it's only cool if you get to go to Alaska and see real glaciers and moose—not just pictures of them on a postcard.

The water boiled and I added the macaroni. I thought about adding peas, which my mother sometimes puts in the macaroni and cheese to give it extra health. But then I figured if she was leaving it to me, we could skip the pea part. By the time everything was ready, my mother had done whatever it was she needed to do and she kept the conversation nice and perky. She said she was glad my father-the-fish-mogul was doing well enough to bring us out to the Last Frontier, even if was going to be too dark for us to see it.

After dinner, I called Martin to hear his voice, but when I told him my father was getting married, he just said, "Hey! That's great!"

"Is it great?" I asked.

"Of course marriage is a great thing. You want him to be happy, right?"

"Sure," I said.

Then I told him about my dad living in Alaska, but I don't think I said it right because Martin thought that was great, too. "The Land of the Midnight Sun!" he said. "Cool!"

"Yeah, it's cool," I said glumly. "Guess this is my big chance to get there."

"Wait," he said. Digesting. "You *don't* want him to be happy?"

"No," I said. "I do."

"But you're upset about him getting married?"

"Well, yeah. Can you…can't you tell?"

"Let me see," he said and there was a short pause. "No."

My room felt colder. "I stayed after school today—I saw you and Stephanie talking," I blurted out. "Did you know I was there? Could you hear me?"

"No," he said. He sounded surprised. "Wait, no, there was something, like static, but it didn't make sense. That was you?"

"Maybe." If he couldn't hear me, what did that mean? I was surprised at how empty I felt at the thought that he was no longer in my head. But maybe it was a distance thing.

"You were watching?" he asked.

"I guess that's kind of—" *What? Creepy, insecure, nuts?* I didn't fill in the blank. "What were you doing with her anyway?"

"She's a friend," he said. "We were talking."

"Oh." I was torn between wanting to wind myself into a knot of shame and wanting to ask him what the hell they'd been talking about.

"So come on," he said.

"What?"

"Tell me."

Tell me? That was like my mom's *How was your day?* question.

"About what?" I asked.

"You. Your dad. Whatever's on your mind," he said.

It came out in burble. "I don't know this woman. I've never even *heard* about her. And all of a sudden she wants us there for the wedding and my dad is booking our flights and she's going to be my stepmother, not that I'll ever think of her that way."

I paused, waiting for the part where he says "That sucks." Only he didn't say, "That sucks"; what he said was, "When are you going?"

"Christmas break." I tried again: "My dad's lived in Alaska for years and, you know, he's never brought us out to visit him before. Doesn't that sound weird to you?"

"He sounds like a man in love." Martin went right on painting silver linings around every cloud I conjured. It was like trying to argue with Little Orphan Annie.

Finally, I told him that I had to get some reading done and he wished me good night. He said he could see the moon outside his window and it was the same moon that cast its glow (he actually used those words "cast its glow") down on me at my house, so he could sleep, knowing we really weren't far apart. I didn't bother mentioning that we really *weren't* so far apart, since his house was only about five blocks away. Not to mention that it was eight fifteen, way too early for sleep. But his voice was low and husky when he said it, and it gave me the chills—the good kind—just the same.

I opened *Frankenstein*, skimmed a few pages, closed it again, then glanced at my cell. No messages.

What are you doing? I texted Will.

Creating world peace. You?

Blah, I texted back.

Blah what?

Blah my dad is getting married.

????

Over Xmas. Bridezilla! It was probably unfair, but I wasn't really worried about being fair.

!

Sucks, I texted.

Sucks. I'm coming over.

Don't bother, I wrote.

See you in 5, he said.

Chapter 19

I was standing outside when Will's Jeep pulled up to the curb. Instead of waiting for him to get out, I hopped in.

I'd cleared it with my mom, who still wanted to know the who, when, and where of any outings, but generally didn't give me a hard time. Plus, I was with Will. My mom trusted him, maybe more than she did me. I knew I had to be back before ten o'clock since it was a school night, but otherwise the world was my oyster. Not that I like oysters—but I didn't like the world at the moment, either.

"Where to?" Will was wearing a worn flannel shirt, untucked, and his hair hung down over the collar.

"Anywhere that's not here."

He put the car in drive and pressed down on the accelerator. "That bad?"

I shrugged in the dark.

"I bet we could get as far as Texas before the Jeep conked out," he said.

I wasn't sure if he was serious or not—but my mind was cast with an image of the two of us stumbling down a deserted road, Will's Jeep hazed with smoke in the background, the eerie neon light of some slasher-movie motel ahead, and the faint rumbling of a chainsaw in the distance.

"I don't think so," I said.

"Well, if Texas is out, how about the next best thing?"

"Which is?"

Will grinned. "The Texas Grill."

BEWARE GRL flashed like a neon sign in my brain. Maybe Serena was right. Maybe it was the *Grill*, not the *girl*, I was supposed to avoid.

But the idea that I was supposed to watch out for a *grill* seemed beyond ridiculous. True, the Texas Grill was in one of Chilton's rougher neighborhoods—all repair shops, warehouses, junk cars, and weeds. It was as far as you could get from Chilton without passing the city limits. I'd never been inside, but Will and Paolo had braved it a couple of times and spoke with reverence about something called a cheesy western. Plus, I'd told my mom, who hates me "just driving around" that we were getting something to eat. This way I wouldn't be lying.

"Drive on, James!" I commanded in my best (but still lame) British accent.

Will steered us down toward River Road and I scanned through the lists on his iPod. Nefarious Rodents, Meltdown, Lamb of the Apocalypse.

"Geez," I said. "Do you get this for the music or the band names? Burning Fur? Really?"

"They're good," he said. "A sort of glam rock-opera thing. If you're in the mood."

I highlighted the first track and pressed play. After a minute of bone-rattling drums and dramatic wails, I turned it off. "I'm not sure what would have to happen for me to be in the mood for *that*, but it wouldn't be pretty."

The dark hills rose and fell behind the river.

After a while, Will said, "So, your dad…"

It was a statement, not a question. Meaning I could talk about it if I wanted to but didn't have to if I didn't—which made me realize that I did want to talk.

"He's starting over," I said. "And he didn't even tell us about her. I'm pissed, but it's not like I have a right to be pissed. I mean, I should probably be happy for him."

"Of course you have a right to be pissed. He's your *dad*—not your great-aunt Caroline or whoever."

"Good old Aunt Caroline," I said, and sighed. "At first I thought they were getting a normal divorce. Like Talon's parents. You know, he might get an apartment in Blacksburg and we'd see him Tuesdays and Thursdays and every other weekend. But when he left, he just…left. He'd never really wanted much to do with the whole idea of family, even when he was with us. You know what he called us? 'You people.' 'I can't think straight with you people around.' He said we made him crazy. My mom would tell me,

137

'That's just the way he is.' But now he's starting a new family with Elana. So maybe he's not down on family. Maybe he's just down on our family."

"*He's* messed up, Annabelle, not you." Will ran his fingers through his hair and looked over at me.

He reached over and tapped out H-I-S-L-O-S-S in Morse code an inch above my left knee. When he finished, he left his hand there. It was supposed to be comforting, but a jolt of something hot shot up my thigh. I put my hand on top of Will's, thinking it would make that burning feeling go away, turn it into something friendly and safe, but instead the heat just kept rising until my stomach turned waffly. I pulled my hand away. Will moved his hand away, too, more slowly than mine.

He kept his eyes forward on the road and he *looked* normal. See Will sit. See Will drive. Drive Will, drive.

I guess it was my problem, not his.

Correction: no problem at all. I was just hyped up emotionally, right? The hot feeling was probably related to something *emotional*, not genuinely hot. Plus, Martin had gotten all my hormones surging and now they had just started leaking out in non-Martin settings.

Anyway, I hadn't grown up in the heartland of Virginia without learning that handy southern skill of ignoring what I didn't want to see.

We arrived at a small rectangular building that looked as if it had been built out of Legos. It had a big neon arrow on the roof that simply read "EAT" and a hand-painted window that read "The Texas Grill: Good Food Since 1959." Outside and in, it was all white and red like a cloth picnic napkin. A burly guy with a white hat and apron was bustling behind the counter, chatting up the clientele, which consisted of a pair of middle-aged guys in wifebeater T-shirts, a few drunk college kids, an old guy, and a cop. Only two seats remained at the counter—one was between a college girl and the old man in a moth-eaten gray cardigan, the other was on the end beside the cop. A framed sign on the wall announced, "We seat 1,000 people. 10 at a time."

"I guess we're nine and ten," I said to Will.

"Or nine hundred ninety-nine and one thousand," he said. "Hungry?"

"Starving," I said.

"Sit," he said, nodding to the space between the cardigan guy and the college girl. Will stood behind me until the college girl zigzagged out, and then he took her stool.

The cheesy western was basically a burger with a fried egg on top. And the chili, which they spelled "chile" like the country, was a thick, whitish broth with beans. Mustard was the only acceptable condiment. Will said that if I asked for ketchup, the counter guy would heckle me for wanting "sissy sauce," so I ate what was put in front of me. And it wasn't that bad, though I'm sure Serena's mom would have said just breathing the air in there could have clogged our youthful arteries for good.

So maybe the Ouija board really was warning me. It just didn't know how to spell "cholesterol."

Then again, it didn't know how to spell "grill," either.

We finished and Will paid. "Workman's comp," he said.

"That's for people injured in the workplace," I said. "I wasn't working."

"Being his daughter is work," he said.

"I think I got laid off," I told him.

"Nah, it's like the Supreme Court," he said. "Lifetime appointment."

Will got me home in plenty of time for curfew. I didn't want to leave, but I opened the car door and stepped out. My mom had a full-blown Crap-a-palooza going on in her private life; I didn't want to add anything more to the lineup. "So, thanks," I said. "This is just what I needed."

The air outside smelled like someone had lit a fire in a fireplace, but I knew it wasn't ours. I started to walk toward the house.

"Annabelle." Will got out of the car and followed me.

"I forgot," he said, and he put a thick envelope in my hands. "The photos you wanted."

"You could have just emailed them," I said.

"I know. But as long as I had the equipment…"

"They were really good. Thanks."

"No problem," he said. "Plus, they're evidence."

"Of what?"

"That you can smile."

"I smile," I said. "I've been smiling more than ever lately."

"I know. I just hope—"

"What?" I waited for him to say something prophetic and comforting about my dad.

"That you're being careful." Careful? Oh my God! This wasn't about my dad. This was about Martin. Was he having a *sex talk* with me? He must have known what I was thinking because he quickly added, "I mean in general. You have to be careful with—everything."

Whew.

"Yeah, okay," I said. I hugged him. "I'm glad we're friends."

He squeezed me a little tighter for a second. "You're my first memory, did you know that?"

"What?"

"The first thing I remember, from when I was a kid," he said. "You were on that swing, going so high I was thinking you might just keep going, that you'd flip all the way over, make a full circle. But then you jumped off." He brushed his thumb across my forehead. "You had a scrape right there. Like from a bug bite you'd scratched."

"You never told me that."

He was looking at me so closely I felt my face grow warm and the skin on my neck started to prickle. I took two steps back and sat down on the stoop outside the kitchen door. Will sat, too. It was dark but not dark enough to see stars.

"I think about it sometimes," he said.

"But Will, we were *four* when we met. That can't be your first memory. I mean, there must have been something before that."

"Maybe I blocked it out. I guess it wasn't a very happy time... you know, before I was adopted. That's what struck me about you on that swing. You were *so* happy. It seemed like you were from another world."

"I'm sorry." I reached out and gave Will's hand a squeeze. "You don't remember anything at all?" He'd never really talked about his life before he'd been adopted. I always thought he just felt embarrassed about it or something, not that there was anything to be embarrassed about. It never occurred to me that it was a black hole.

"I get flickers sometimes, but it's fuzzy. Grayish."

We stayed on the step and talked until the courthouse clock four blocks away struck ten. We could just make out the dim chime from our house if everything else was very quiet, and tonight was almost too quiet, as if the air was holding its breath. "I should go in before my mom starts to worry." I stood and shook out my legs.

"See you tomorrow?" Will said.

"Of course." I squeezed his hand once more, and then the door banged shut behind me.

Chapter 20

It is beautiful on the water. The fading light seems dark and myste-rious, in the way velvet and tarnished lockets seem dark and myste-rious. I drift in a small rowboat, the water carrying me nowhere I intend to go. In the dim light, I cannot see far enough to make out the shore, but I believe I am on the same lake where Josh and I sailed and swam, where we kissed and he became real.

I lie back, dragging my hands through the cold water on either side of the boat. Tendrils of seaweed skim through my fingers, and I close my eyes. My mind starts to wander, as aimless as the boat, when I feel something thick and muscular wrap around my wrists. It is not the seaweed. An animal, maybe? It tightens and pulls. My eyes fly open and I see snakes wrapped around each of my wrists like handcuffs. There are other snakes, too, rippling through the water.

They begin to slither up the sides of the boat—shimmering as they pool in the boat's hull. One of them slinks over my toes. I jerk my feet up, but the others keep sliding toward me.

Maybe I can charm them, with my brain, with a song. But

controlling the snakes is as unlikely as controlling a wisp of fog. I try without success to wrestle my wrists loose. Snakes are coiled all the way up my arms now, holding me tight. Panic rises in my throat. I crane my neck to look behind for some way out, but the blackness outside the little circle of the boat is now absolute.

It is when I turn my head back that I see her again. She sits in the boat facing the opposite direction. The abandoned girl from the dreams. Her white dress gleaming as if it were its own source of light. Hair limp around her shoulders like a yellow fog.

"Help me!" I cry, even though I don't think she can hear me.

She doesn't turn, but she must hear me after all, because her small voice echoes my words in a singsong tone: "Help me!"

A large brown snake starts to edge toward her waist. I struggle to free myself as I call, "Watch out!"

The girl doesn't move, except to raise her arms above her head in a V and let out a long, low hiss.

In a unified motion, as if they were part of the same muscle, the snakes snap their heads toward the girl. At once, they slither to her from every direction, up her legs and back, spiraling around her waist. They rise and rise, climbing one over the other, braiding themselves together into a writhing mass.

The serpent—for the combined parts now move like a single organism—is huge. Thicker than the girl's waist. Far longer, if stretched out, than the entire length of the boat. It drapes itself across the girl's shoulder, its head nestled against her neck. The girl still does not turn around, but when she lowers her arms, the enormous viper trains its red eyes on me. It rears up, opening its wide jaws. It is going to strike.

Something hisses in my mind. It wants to swallow me whole.

I struggle again, but my arms are still wrapped in snake flesh, immobile.

"Help me, help me," the snake hisses, but it is the little girl's mocking voice I hear.

——————

I searched for Martin before my French class, ignoring Ms. Gilchrest, who stood in the halls clapping and yelling "*Vite! Vite!*" I didn't have to search very hard; he was leaning against my locker, drawing sighs and stares from idol-worshiping freshmen. Seniors, too.

"I had a dream—" I said, but he put his hand on my arm and drowned my words with a kiss.

"About your dad," he began, then paused, like he was hoping he was saying the right thing. "I'm sorry."

"Thanks." Thoughts about my dad and Elana still swirled around in my head, but some of them had been swallowed by the mottled black snakes from last night. They encircled my brain, the way they'd encircled my wrists, and squeezed.

"And I'm sorry I didn't know I was supposed to be sorry. I'm still figuring some stuff out."

"Me, too," I said.

"So does this make it a bad time to invite you to meet *my* dad? My parents, I mean. They want to have you over for dinner."

"I'd love to meet them," I said. I'd been curious about his parents;

I wanted to make sure they were real. Whenever I pictured them in my head, they were wispy and translucent. Projections. Ghosts.

"The thing is…" he started, but then stopped and pulled me to the side of the hall, out of the flow of people. "The thing is, they're not really like me."

I waited, thinking he'd go on. When he didn't, I said, "Oh. I see." *Not.* I was clearly as clueless about his family baggage as he had been about mine.

"Good," he said. "Tonight, okay? After practice. You want me to pick you up?"

"I'll walk." I smiled at him. "I know where you live."

I didn't see Martin again until lunch. We'd been sitting for about two seconds—just long enough for me to take too big a sip and dribble water all over my chin—when Stephanie came up and whispered in his ear. It sounded like a hiss.

Clearly the snake in Will's photograph was a cosmic coincidence. This was the *real* snake. A perfect match for every one of Cynthia Rêve's interpretations: temptation (his), sex (hers), and hidden fears (mine). Ms. Rêve bats three for three!

Talon shook her head. "Can't you put a stop to that?"

"He's his own person," I said, committed at least on the surface to being the new non-crazy Annabelle—the Annabelle who had enough confidence not to sweat it when her boyfriend was being pursued by a serpentine cheerleader. The Annabelle who could wait, patiently, for his attention.

Talon hadn't said what she thought of Martin, other than

agreeing about his general hotness. She was "reserving judgment," which was not a bad thing. Serena, who had already judged, was ready to sing at our wedding. Will had also judged—but not in the good way. I had hoped, since he was off finishing a photo project during lunch, it would give Martin a chance to shine.

"Excuse me," Talon said to Martin, when Stephanie left. "Would you care to share with the rest of the class?"

He looked up, confused.

"It's rude to whisper in front of other people." Talon cupped one hand beside her mouth and whispered, loudly, "In case you didn't know."

Sometimes it was hard to figure out what Martin didn't know. He knew everything about throwing and catching a football, and enough about math and English and chemistry. But sometimes he didn't understand painfully obvious stuff. And a few of his social graces needed refinement, I guess.

"And you're disrespecting Annabelle," Talon said, taking a bite of celery, which she'd snagged from Serena's lunch bag.

"I know where my loyalties lie," Martin said. He smiled at Talon and touched my arm again. "But Steph and I are old friends. I don't want to be one of those guys who abandons his old friends when he meets a girl."

How did he learn about THAT in dreamworld?

"Very insightful," Talon said. "I don't like the friend, but I approve of the sentiment." She dropped her voice. "Just don't whisper."

"Thank you," Martin said. "Your approval means a lot to me."

He grinned. I was so relieved. He was making a joke. Sort of. And Talon was laughing. Sort of. At any rate, she threw a Cheeto at him, and everyone knows that throwing a Cheeto is a sign of friendship.

Finally, school ended. I still had a couple of hours to kill before going to Martin's, so Talon and Serena and I took off for Goodwill to find some dresses for homecoming. I could have asked my mom for some money, but I hated to bug her; every month when she sat down to pay the bills, she got a semi-glazed look and started tugging on her hair. And anyway, some amazing stuff comes into Goodwill. If Chilton weren't so small, no one would know where it came from.

Of course Talon, who has plenty of money, is the one who found a dress.

It was filmy, sleeveless and black, like something Aria Timpane would wear in one of her music videos. She spun and put her hands in the air, then back to her side.

"You are so getting that," Serena said. She found a white scarf and swooshed it around Talon's neck. "The picture of elegance, *n'est-ce pas?*"

"It's really beautiful," I said. In my mind's eye I saw Will pinning a white rose on the black gauze just above Talon's breast.

"You didn't find anything worth trying on?" Talon asked me.

"Guess not. But there's one more place I want to check." We headed to the antique store. In the back, they had vintage dresses that didn't cost so much because most of them had small imperfections—a moth hole, for instance, or an underarm stain. But they still looked mostly beautiful, like you'd come from another time.

Serena, who still liked playing dress up, was too busty for most of the dresses. I was too flat chested. But I found one dress, periwinkle blue, my favorite color. It was sleeveless with a square neckline and a smooth, shiny bodice that went to a V at the waist. I couldn't find any imperfections, unless you count the fact that it was about fifty years out of date.

I touched the skirt, thinking about all that dress must have lived through: first kisses, romantic sunsets. And it was still here, still treasured enough that someone had saved it for years, maybe taking it out of the closet every so often just to stir up memories. A true-love dress. Not right for someone like Daniel Kowalski. But maybe just the thing for Martin Zirkle.

"You look like a princess," Serena said when I tried it on.

"It's the epitome of awesomeness," Talon agreed.

Mrs. Finch, the pinched-face saleslady who smelled like lemon drops, didn't seem to mind that I paid her in mostly one-dollar bills. "I can always use the change," she said, as she wrapped my dress in tissue and tucked it in a paper bag. "You got yourself a lovely, didn't you, dear? This old dress, she's got life in her yet." With a quick wink, she added, "Just like me, dear. Just like me."

Chapter 21

Before Martin, the old Lucas house had been a faded gray. The green roof was flaking, the shutters dangling off their hinges. Each summer, the neighbors reported the lawn as a rat hazard and the town came with a John Deere to mow it down.

Now the lawn was short. The green roof was newly shingled, and the rest of the house was painted a sunny daffodil that still looked wet. I rang the bell and waited for the house to dissolve in a puff of fairy dust.

"You look perfect!" Martin grinned when he opened the door. He probably would have said the same thing if I'd shown up in a clown suit, but I'd worn a green T-shirt and a black skirt—the flouncy kind, like hippies wear. "What do you think of the house? It's great, right?"

"It's great," I said. And it was, like something from a magazine. I stood on the porch, suddenly afraid to go inside. What if the house really *did* disappear, and we all disappeared with it?

"You're probably the whole reason I'm even in this house," Martin said.

I gave him a blank look.

"You know," he said, leaning against the door. A real door. Oak.

"Uh…" I said, not sure why it was so hard to be straight with him. I took a breath. "No, actually, I don't."

"That dream," he lowered his voice, "with my house."

I racked my brain. I remembered a week or so ago waking up with the feeling that something was about to happen in a dream, something about Josh…Josh, who was of course Martin. But Nick had burst in and started talking to me before I was even fully conscious, and the dream, like so many others, had drifted away—a snowflake, one of thousands.

"You don't remember," Martin said. "You had the dream. It was *yours*. But it's *my* memory?"

"Lots of people can't remember their dreams," I said. I could still hear the hissing from the last dream I *did* remember.

"But it's funny, isn't it? You make everything happen, but it isn't real to you. I'm the one who remembers."

"I don't make everything happen," I said. If I did, I'd have done some home improvements of my own. "I don't make *anything* happen. What was it about? The dream?"

"We were on the street, walking toward each other. You were wearing an old-fashioned dress and I was in a sailor uniform. Everything looked like the color had been drained out of it. Just white or gray. Except the house. It was lit up, golden. When we got close enough that we could almost touch, you turned and started up the walkway. I went after you, but the dream washed out."

I could see every detail. In my mind, I translated it to a sketch, the house colored in like my childish drawings that my grandma kept on her refrigerator even after the colors faded and the edges curled. I wondered, briefly, about the way dreams faded and curled under the light of morning—what I remembered, what I didn't. It was like I had a whole other life I didn't know about, a life someone had erased.

"Martin, is she here? I thought the idea was for her to meet *us*."

"Coming!"

Martin led me down a hallway and into a large, airy kitchen where his mother stood over a cutting board piled with fresh herbs. She wore her hair red and spiky and she had these thin, rectangular glasses that made her look like a German architect. Which, of course, she was. (An architect, anyway, not German.)

"Welcome!" She came over and shook my hand. Warm. And real. "Martin's told us everything about you."

"A lot of things," Martin said. "Not everything." He smiled at her almost the way a kid would smile at a mother, but not quite.

"Pretty," his mother said. "And not overdone. I like that. You know, Annabelle, I feel like I know you from somewhere…Like I've known you forever."

I smiled, but my smile wasn't exactly normal, either.

"I'm Lynn," she said. "Bob will be down in a minute. He's just finishing something in his office."

"What's he finishing?" I didn't mean to be too nosy, but I was curious. I'd asked Martin about his parents, but his answers had been incomplete and he kept changing them, like when you're filling in a multiple-choice question on a test and you can't decide between A or D.

"He's writing a magazine essay about home renovation," she said. She snorted in a way that made me feel somehow better. "'Write what you know,' they say."

"The house is lovely," I said.

"Thanks to my lovely wife," said Martin's dad, who appeared at the door in a black T-shirt and jeans. He was tall and had the same blue eyes as Martin, the same wavy hair that looked like he'd just combed his fingers through it. "She always has just the right touch. You should see what she did to our place in Philly."

"Was that a big house, too?" I asked.

Lynn froze, her eyebrows together. She craned her neck around to look at Bob. "An apartment, wasn't it?"

He nodded. "Right. An apartment in Philly. You know, the rat race." He dropped his hands and took a seat at the counter. "That's why we came here, a fresh start. Out with the old, in with the new. Or, in this case, I suppose, in with the remodeled. All it really needed was some fresh paint, some Mexican tiles, and new toilets."

"Don't talk about toilets in front of Annabelle," Lynn said. "We just met her."

"It's okay. You said you felt like you'd known me forever," I said. They both laughed, like I was on late-night TV.

"Well," Lynn said, "the gazpacho is ready and I just need to finish up the spinach tartlet. Martin, why don't you show Annabelle around? But don't take her away for too long."

"Your parents," I said, when we were out of earshot. "They're really—nice." Which was, I guess, what I'd have said about anybody's parents. But they genuinely *were*. They seemed to really like—love?—each other. Yeah, they were a little hazy on where they'd lived last week. But so what? "They're so happy."

"They're my parents," he said, with a shrug.

"But they haven't *always* been your parents."

"As far as they know, they have," he said.

"Don't they remember anything from before?" I asked.

"I don't think so. They have memories," he added, watching my face. "I'm just not sure the memories are real."

"But *you* remember where you really came from. Why do you remember when they don't?" I finished.

"I have a theory," he said. "Come on. We can talk in my room." I had a million questions, but my old questions kept getting replaced with new ones. *Do all dream-people know when they're in someone's dream? Do they wear clothes when they arrive or do they show up in their birthday suits? What was the deal with that freaky girl and all those snakes?*

I followed Martin upstairs to his bedroom—a generic, catalog bedroom. Inside was a single bed, neatly made, a rolltop desk, where his schoolbooks were stacked, a wooden wardrobe, and heavy navy curtains that blocked the light.

"So what's your theory?" I asked.

"I think they came with me," Martin said, "like it's part of what happens. I know for a fact that Bob was a dream. I remember him. But it's like both he and Lynn got blanked out. They know nothing about where we really came from, but they have these odd recollections of our 'real' life as a family. A vacation we took to the Grand Canyon, stuff like that. Only I've never been to the Grand Canyon, at least not that *I* can remember. Lynn says I rode a mule named Juliet, but then, well, you saw it—both she and Bob have no idea where we supposedly lived in Philadelphia. There are things they just avoid talking about. I think their memories are…what was it you called me that first day? Prepackaged?"

I walked to the window and looked out. Someone's sheepdog was on the loose and peeing on the boxwood hedge across the street. "So how—"

"You know what a wake is?" he cut in.

"Yeah." I turned back to face him. "We had one when my grandma died."

"I don't think so," he answered, confused. "Wake: you know, from a boat?" Which got me thinking about the snakes again.

"That's what Stephanie calls it—the wake. She thinks her mom was swept along in the wake of her arrival. Just kind of plucked from the slipstream."

I had seen Stephanie's mom at a Back-to-School night. Serena said she'd been a beauty queen. She was all done up and glossy. But also somehow flat—no laugh lines. I'd heard Stephanie complain about her a thousand times, which is a lot given that we didn't really speak.

"They have a…I guess you'd call it a 'backstory,'" Martin went on. "But they get confused if you ask too many questions."

"Weird," I said. And it was. "Speaking of questions. I had a dream last night. A really vivid one. I was on a boat with these snakes and—"

"It wasn't our boat, was it?" he asked.

"I think it was. And then the snakes all got together and formed this ginormous snake, only I think it was really her. It's like they were all laughing at me." Even though they sounded absurd when I heard the words spilling from my mouth, it was a relief to finally get them out. Like once I did, they didn't have the power to hurt me.

"It's stupid," I said. "I've had nightmares before. Just not like this one. At least not since you."

His smile melted me. "Was I a nightmare, then?"

I shoved him, playfully, the way I shove Will. "You know you weren't."

He stepped closer then, taking my hand and drawing it slowly back to his shoulder. He placed it where I had pushed him a moment before—but so gently that it was like a small bird landing on a stalk of wheat.

"Can you make them stop? The nightmares?" I asked.

"I wish. But how can I? I'm here now."

We sat down on his perfectly made bed and he held my hand in his, rubbing my palm with his thumb. How many times had my mother eased me back to bed after a nightmare with those very words? *It was just a dream. I'm here now.*

I thought about Martin's theory and what else might be here

in the wake of his arrival. Like a single stone tossed in a lake—the ripples just keep spreading out.

Martin leaned in for a long, hard, movie kiss.

"I've been waiting all day to do that," he said.

I tried to get my breath back but it didn't come. He pressed his face to mine again and I was back in a dream, a good one. But something about it didn't feel right. It was too perfect, if that's possible. Like I wasn't me sitting there, but some ideal version of me—and his kiss could make me forget the other me, the one who's not ideal.

"Here. Let me show you something."

Standing, he went to his wardrobe and pulled out a dress. "For homecoming," he said, holding the dress out to me. "It's perfect, right? I thought it was perfect. I picked it out myself."

So now Prince Charming was my fairy godmother, too? I thought about him on one knee in the cafeteria. Maybe all of his dreamers had wanted a fairy tale. Maybe I had, too. But not this part.

The dress was a puffy chiffon explosion in Pepto-Bismol pink. "Oh!" I exclaimed, standing up. I took the dress in front of me and studied myself on the full-length mirror attached to the inside of the wardrobe door. It looked like I should be starring in a douche commercial.

"It was my mom's idea," Martin said. "Because I told her things were…tight at your house."

I hadn't mentioned that to him—at least I don't think I had. But maybe I'd been thinking about it more than I realized. "How did you know my size?" I said. "Most guys wouldn't."

"I'm very observant."

"Well, thanks. This is great." I lay the pink ruffled monster down on the bed and hugged Martin.

"So you like it?"

I answered with a kiss, so I wouldn't have to lie. A part of me wondered if Martin had been doing the same thing.

Chapter 22

Martin was waiting on my porch when Serena pulled into my driveway the next afternoon. She and Talon were dropping me off after our standard Wednesday post-school hangout at the coffee shop. The Doctor had recommended a weekly "gal friends decompression session," so Talon's father paid for our lattes and pastries. Serena got her sugar fix, I got more $C_8H_{10}N_4O_2$ than was good for me, and Talon got "enhanced mental health," aka, the pleasure of using her dad's credit card with abandon.

Leaning back against the porch post, Martin looked like he belonged in the Men of Chilton superstud calendar that the Junior League puts out each year. "Ladies!" he said as Talon stepped out of the passenger seat.

He bounded up to Serena's Beetle and helped me out of the backseat like he was escorting Cinderella from her carriage. Then, with a flourish, he presented me with a large paper shopping bag.

"Your dress!" he pronounced.

When I looked clueless, he added, "The one I got you for homecoming."

"Right!" I tried to sound enthusiastic. I don't know if it was my subconscious talking to me or not, but I'd ended up forgetting the dress at Martin's house when he'd driven me home. And I'd spent a good bit of the morning purposefully continuing to forget it.

But here it was, like a homing pigeon, back in my hands.

"I thought you picked the perfect dress." Talon turned to Martin. "She's already picked the perfect dress."

Martin looked at me. "You didn't tell me that last night."

"I had other things on my mind," I said. "Anyway, it was a beautiful gesture and I didn't want to hurt your feelings by telling you I already had a dress."

"But now it's like I've hurt yours." His shoulders visibly slumped.

"Aw," said Serena. I could tell it was taking all her self-control to keep from springing out of the driver's seat and giving him a hug.

"Well, listen, Martin." Talon was speaking for me again. "What you did was nice. I mean, nobody does it, but it was lovely. And, Annabelle, not saying anything about it was also lovely, but I think you two need to stop being lovely and talk to each other."

"Thanks for the insights, Doctor," I said. "We talk."

"All of the time," Martin agreed.

"You know what?" I said. "I'm wearing Martin's dress."

"Only if you want to," Martin said. He looked at Talon as if for guidance.

She nodded. Beside her, Serena nodded, too. Of course, they might not have if they'd seen what was inside the bag.

"So, we gotta get," Serena said, as Talon climbed back in the passenger seat. "But I want to see you in your dress, Annabelle. Send me pics!"

Serena's Beetle backed out of the driveway. I waved. Martin waved. I watched him from the corner of my eye, amazed at how perfectly he fit onto the canvas of this world. The soft rise of the mountains behind him, the sun lowering toward the horizon, the sky a lacy blue—and there, below, Martin. Perfect, beautiful Martin, waving like a politician on a parade float.

We went inside; Nick was doing his homework at the kitchen table. I was half hoping he would call Martin "fart breath," but he just said "hey" and went back to his math.

"Martin and I are going to my room," I told my mother.

"You can't stay down here?" my mother said.

"I want to show him something."

"Leave the door open." She smiled, but not with her eyes.

"Why does she want us to leave the door open?" he asked when we were upstairs. He sat down on the edge of the bed, but I pulled him down so we were both sitting on the floor—which seemed safer, considering my mom's exceptional radar when it came to me and boys. I hoped he couldn't see under the bed. It had been too long since I vacuumed under there, and the dust balls swirled like small galaxies.

"Because she doesn't want us fooling around," I said.

"Oh." He smiled a little.

"What?"

"There's a lot of that in dreams, you know. Things are different here."

"In a good way or a bad way?" I asked.

"I like it here. But there are some things I miss."

"Tell me more about *there*," I said. "The place you come from."

He let out a puff of air. "I don't even know where to start."

"The beginning's usually good," I suggested.

"That's just it," he said. "For most dreams there are no real beginnings. Only middles. Then we just sort of…drift."

"It sounds…" I searched for the right word. "Peaceful?"

"No," said Martin. "It's like being empty, but there's an awfulness to it, too. Limbo. But worse than limbo. You're not your own." His eyes turned dark, and his right hand clenched and unclenched like a pulse. "Even when you're in a dream, living, sometimes you might as well be invisible. A girl might dream she's on a train. She sits there with an empty notebook on her lap and a Miss Piggy toothbrush sticking out of the backpack and she hardly even notices all the people around her. But they're there."

Wait. I'd had that toothbrush when I was eight. I was pretty sure I had also had a dream about a train, though I couldn't quite recall it. It hovered carefully on the edge of my memory like one of those tiny plastic toy birds that balances on its beak.

"And those people stay there," he went on, "riding train after train. They don't just show up in her kitchen the next morning."

"So you're saying I was lucky."

"I'm saying *I* was lucky. It was…listen, you know how you feel about Chilton?"

I thought about my map-dot of a town. Beautiful enough, but nothing happening. No energy. No pulse.

"But how would you feel about it if you couldn't," he reached out for my lucky river rock from my bedside table and held it between his finger and thumb, "if you couldn't even decide whether or not to pick up a rock? Maybe you'd want to pick it up, just hold it for a second, but that wasn't your role. Or maybe you'd be compelled to pick it up, and then in another second, it might turn into a feather or a bullet or a chunk of ice. You couldn't decide about anything. And that's the *good* time. Most of the time, you're…nowhere," he said. "You wait and drift. It's like you're not alive."

I thought about my recent dreams, when I'd tried to yell, but with no sound, when I'd tried to move, but my wrists remained trapped. I thought about the people at my mother's nursing home, the people who just sat on chairs, their walkers in front of them but nobody going anywhere. They were like statues that breathed. Alive, but not.

"And you couldn't go anywhere," I said.

His eyes got a lighter, mischievous look. "We did find a few ways to pass the time," he said. "Diving. We weren't supposed to."

"Diving. Like diving in water?"

"Sort of," he said. "It's more like…Have you ever had a dream and all of a sudden someone shows up who doesn't fit in? Maybe you're in your elementary school and a fireman drops from the ceiling and does the hula and then disappears."

I knew exactly what he was talking about. I thought about the first time I'd seen Martin in a dream. He was Josh, then. I was dreaming about my dad in Alaska, and all of a sudden Josh showed up, just for a few seconds, like an eagle on top of a glacier. Then he'd disappeared. I always thought that was just the nature of dreams.

"That's dream diving," Martin said. "It's kind of like bungee jumping or something, but without the cord. We push ourselves into someone's dream, just to see what's happening, just to live—or almost live. It's a rush, like football. We can't sustain it, though."

"You dove into my dream?"

He nodded.

"Just popped in out of the blue?"

Martin smiled self-consciously. "I'd seen you before, on that train. But you didn't notice me."

"No way," I said, taking a long look at him. His perfectly sculpted face, his muscular body. "How could I have *not* noticed you?"

He shrugged. "Guess you were looking at something else."

"So that time in Alaska, you were in my dream *on purpose*. It wasn't just chance. I didn't invent you."

"You did and you didn't," he said. "I was already there, or someone like the person I am now. But your dreaming gave me... *more*, if that makes sense. And those other times—on the street outside my house, at the lake—you called me back. I didn't mind," he added quickly. "I was glad to go. More than glad. I wanted to see you. And I wanted to...I wanted to get out."

"Yeah, I know that feeling," I murmured, thinking of all the hours

I'd fantasized about leaving the grit of Chilton, Virginia, behind me. Like my dad. Why couldn't I follow my bliss for a change?

"It's a rush, you know?" he said. "A release. Once you do it, it's kind of addictive—it's hard to stop. There are some dreams—the bad ones—that don't stop with diving. They want it to be *their* dream. To own it. Control it."

Like the girl, I wondered. Was that what she wanted?

"Why did you keep coming back?" I said. It was a leading question, but I wanted to hear him say it.

"You were special," he said. "I guess maybe I got addicted. To you."

He leaned forward to hug his knees, and I studied the tattoo of little waves at the back of his neck, the one I'd seen in Will's photograph.

"Those waves. Do they stand for anything?" I asked. Again I had the feeling that I'd seen them somewhere before.

"What?" He sat up, slapping his hand over the tattoo, as if it were a mosquito.

"Well, like Talon's tattoo. She's got a Celtic friendship wheel. It represents the complex lives of friends."

"Oh. Do you have one?"

"My mom won't let me," I said, though to be honest I was kind of glad. I hated needles. "What does yours mean?"

"It doesn't mean anything," he said.

"Maybe it has something to do with the water," I said. "That's where we first kissed."

"That could be it," he said. His voice sounded funny, but I didn't

165

push it. "You told your mom you wanted to show me something," he added, clearly changing the subject.

"My drawings," I stood and walked over to the bulging cardboard portfolio on top of the table in the corner of my room. He couldn't read my mind anymore, but maybe looking at these would let him back in.

Martin joined me at the table and hefted the portfolio into his arms.

"You did all of these? That's amazing." He put the portfolio down and started to unwind the cord that held it shut.

"Thanks," I said, stilling his hand, second-guessing myself. Half the time I didn't let Will see my drawings, even after they were done. "Let's look at them later. I don't know why I brought it up."

"But I'd like to—"

"No, really," I said. "Later. Please." I took him by the wrist and led him back with me to the window seat. "Hey, I have a question: what about stuff?"

"Stuff?" he asked.

"You know, like all the stuff in your house. Where'd it come from? Did it just show up as part of the whole 'wake' thing?"

He shook his head. "I guess you'd say Lynn is…efficient. The woman can shop."

"But it must have cost a fortune. The house, the repairs, everything." I knew it was tacky to mention even the concept of cash, but I couldn't help myself. "Where'd the money come from?"

"I asked my parents the same question when we bought my car, but they just act like it's all taken care of. They got a loan."

"How could they possibly—"

"Lynn can be pretty convincing. It's sort of like the mind-reading thing you and I had going. When we first got here, Lynn was pretty hard—okay, let's say impossible—to resist. You just did what she said. You just did."

"Geez..." I whistled. *Introducing the Amazing Lynn Zirkle, hypnotist extraordinaire.*

Martin scooted me closer and then slipped his hand down to my hip. "Look, I know a bunch of this doesn't make sense. But that's not the most important thing, is it?"

He was right. The most important thing was that he was here. With his hand on my hip. He leaned in, brushing his lips against my ear.

My mother's make-out radar went off like a buzzer.

"Annabelle!" she called from downstairs.

"Yeah?" I called back.

"Will's here."

"Oh," I said quietly. *Oh.* Will and I got together every Wednesday to watch *The Wild Side*. Tonight they were releasing a geriatric game show host, a singer, and a slutty reality show star in the middle of the Grand Canyon with nothing but a loaded backpack, a llama, and a camera crew.

Martin's hand slid from my body. "Will's here," he repeated.

I stood and pulled Martin to his feet. "Come on."

Chapter 23

We found Will at the kitchen table, explaining the Pythagorean theorem to Nick.

I tried not to think about the pissing contest Martin and Will had had the last time we'd been together in this room. "Hey." I aimed for casual. "You're early."

"I brought pizza." Will pointed to two boxes from Giovanni's on the counter. "Triple veggie for you and Mrs. M, Hawaiian for the squirt." When his eyes hit Martin, he said, "I didn't see your car."

"I walked," Martin said.

"Right…Nice night for it." Will was clearly *not* saying something, clearly holding back. It's possible he was just choosing a tactic, but I decided to take it as a sign that he was making an effort to get along.

"So, you guys thirsty? We have milk, probably soda, water?"

Martin shook his head, and Will picked up a glass of water he'd already poured and said, "I'm good."

I went to the counter, cracked open a box, and sniffed the

warm pizza. "Yum, thanks," I said to Will. And then to Martin, I explained, "Will and I usually watch *The Wild Side* on Wednesdays. Have you seen it?"

Since Martin had only been in the Land of Television for the past few days, I was pretty sure he hadn't. I mean, what kind of freak would dream about *The Wild Side*? But then again, it might just be one of those things he mysteriously *knew*. Anyway, I thought asking would make things sound more normal in front of Will.

When Martin shook his head, as I guessed he would, I went on, "They get these super-cheesy B-grade celebrities and abandon them in a cave or something, and they have to find their way back to civilization. You want to watch with us?"

"Hey, I didn't mean to interrupt whatever you and Martin—" Will said.

"You didn't," I said, which was more polite than true. "Martin was dropping something off. Let's just—"

"I was leaving anyway," Martin said.

"Don't be—"

"No, really, Annabelle. I need to get going," Martin said, and before I could argue, he was out the kitchen door.

After a second, I followed him, pushing the door back open just as it clicked shut. I called out, "Hey, I'll..." But the driveway was empty. He'd taken off so fast he might have been swept into space. I shut my eyes, feeling tilted and lost. The way I'd felt when my father left. Crazy Annabelle rippled under my skin.

When I turned to Will, I wasn't thinking with my rational

brain—the brain that could have told me, if I'd bothered to ask, that this was not Will's fault.

"What'd you do that for?" I demanded.

"Uhh." Will glanced around the kitchen, like he was missing something. "What?"

"You wanted him to leave."

"I didn't *do* anything. I've been giving him a chance, like you asked me to. And what I want…what I want is beside the point."

"What's that supposed to mean?"

Will stood up, knocking his chair slightly crooked. "I always mean what I say with you, Annabelle."

"Dude," Nick piped up from his corner of the table, "she's just PMS-ing. You know how girls are."

"I do not have—Arrggg!"

Nick went on in a fake-announcer voice, "Tune in next time to *Drama Teen* and see if Annabelle's head actually explodes."

"Hey," Will said, "cut her some slack." Because it was Will, Nick listened.

"Let's go for a ride," Will said. "Come on."

For a full second I studied the dull rose pattern of the linoleum floor. Then, without raising my head, I looked up. Something about Will's face reminded me of a moth I'd once seen trying to get into a window. I remembered how it just kept battering itself against the glass pane, battering and battering until its wing tore.

I was still mad, but I grabbed my jacket. "Tell Mom," I said to Nick, "and save us some pizza." We headed out.

The night was cool and the air felt fresh against my cheeks. Just getting out of that kitchen and into the Jeep helped me breathe. Will took his own advice, giving me space. At the stop sign at the end of the street, he turned left toward the highway. He coasted for a minute in silence.

"You want to talk about it?" Will finally asked when he drove up the on-ramp.

"'Bout what?"

"I guess that answers my question."

"Guess it does." After a second, I added, "It was sweet of you to bring pizza. Sorry. I'm just feeling crappy. Forgive me?"

I studied Will's not-Greek profile. Unreadable.

"Of course I forgive you for that," he said.

After a second, I repeated, "*For that?* There's something you don't forgive?"

"Look, Annabelle, let's just—"

"No, tell me."

Will didn't answer, but instead checked his blind spot. Then he switched into the passing lane, blowing by two bikers and the van for a carpet store. Finally, he said, "There's nothing to tell. I don't think you could do anything I wouldn't forgive eventually." He didn't sound particularly happy about it.

"Well, that's something, I guess," I said. "Meanwhile, I can't imagine *you* ever doing something that would even *require* forgiveness. Other than being a jerk to my—to Martin."

"Saint Will." He sounded even less happy than before.

"You're a saint for putting up with me," I said. "Speaking of which, where are we going, exactly?"

"Where do you want to go?"

I played with the knob to the glove box. "Is there somewhere we can walk?"

"Sure."

Will took the next exit, then down a back road that cut through the woods.

"Isn't this the way to Pandapas Pond?" I asked. I thought of the lake from my dream. Of the girl and the boat and the snakes. "No. You know what? I don't need to walk. I'm good here."

"You sure? The pond looks cool at twilight."

"I can't," I said. "It's just—I had this weird dream about a lake. It kind of freaked me."

"What happened?"

"I don't want to talk about it. It was scary."

"We should drive, then." He pulled a U-turn and headed back toward the highway.

"It's stupid, I guess."

"Maybe," Will said. "But maybe there's more to it. I mean, dreams aren't *all* in our heads, are they? What if they're just another type of reality? That's what the Iroquois believed. And Australian Aborigines. For them, the real world began as a dream."

Now *Will* was reading my mind. Except for the aborigine part. "Australian Aborigines?"

Will shrugged.

"That's a big can of suck, though—if nightmares are real," I said.

"Maybe not like we think of real," Will said. "But I've always felt dreams are something more than what's *exclusively* inside us. They're part me, and part something else. As if they have a life of their own."

"Tell me about it." That was the scary part. That the snakes, the girl—whatever it was coming after me in my dreams—could somehow take up a life on this side of the dream/reality Mason-Dixon line. The way Martin had. And Stephanie. And the pipe people, whoever they were.

All that was beyond my control—but this girl, it didn't feel random anymore. I was beginning to think she was *stalking* my dreams. Like she wanted something from me. And I'm pretty sure it was something I didn't want to give.

"I keep thinking about it," I said. "The nightmare, I mean. I've put all my conscious effort into figuring it out, but I can't."

"That could be your problem," Will said.

"What do you mean?"

"Maybe what you need is an *un*conscious effort."

"Okay, sensei." I gave him a friendly shove. Not enough to mess with his driving but enough to let him know I thought he was full of it. "I'll be sure to give that a try."

I hadn't done anything when my father left. Or when Daniel broke things off. I just let life roll over me. I sulked and stomped and holed up in my room to cry. Reacted, instead of acted. But that wasn't going to cut it this time. This time I needed to *do* something.

The trick was figuring out exactly what I was supposed to do.

Chapter 24

A flash.

Dark space.

The girl is twirling, her white dress fluttering out around her.

"Kill the dreamer," she sings.

A glimpse of streamers, glitter on a glossy wooden floor.

———————

Thursday started out like that "ideal day" you see in movies—the sky stuffed with fluffy clouds that all looked as though they were just about to turn into teddy bears or hippopotami.

It was Spirit Day, so everyone wore blue and gold T-shirts. The girls wore ribbons. Some of the boys covered their backpacks with blue and gold duct tape and sprayed their hair with blue and gold dye. Wally Ferguson was going around with a two-foot stuffed blue devil perched on his shoulder like a parrot.

It was weird. Martin was the newbie, but I felt like the one seeing everything for the first time. This kind of spirit-wear used to look to me like a prison uniform for the jail that was my hometown, but now it looked…colorful. Almost fun, even. I'm not sure why. Maybe it was just delirium after a week of restless sleep. Or maybe it was the fact that Martin was little-kid excited about the whole thing. Like jump-up-and-down excited. Not that he was *literally* jumping up and down, but still.

He said he'd "never done a homecoming parade." Of course, I hadn't, either, but that was by choice. At least, I'd had the chance. I thought about what it must have been like for him—stuck in someone else's head. He might not have even known parades were possible, just because someone else hadn't bothered to dream about one. It didn't seem fair.

And now here he was, at the center of it all. Happy. And I was happy to see him happy. Neither one of us discussed his Houdini act the night before. I for one was content to stash away that particular scrap of drama.

While I didn't go all out, I did wear a blue shirt with my jeans. And in the bathroom after lunch, Serena wrote "Let's Go" on my cheek with blue eyeliner. Talon dressed all in black and accused us of reckless abandon.

There was a shortened football practice so the players wouldn't sprain something before the game, and Mr. Ernshaw graciously postponed the due date for our essays on "The Atom: Democritus to Bohr." So after school, as planned, I worked with Martin to decorate the team float. It was basically a flatbed truck with lots of streamers and electric lights and signs that said things like "DEVILS ROCK" and "GO FIGHT WIN" in glitter paint. At each end, there were goalposts made of PVC pipe. A six-foot card-board football was attached to each side of the truck on a big metal spring, so it sort of jiggled in midair.

The parade route was only five blocks long and took a grand total of fifteen minutes, but even so, the town went all out. The shops and restaurants along Main Street decorated their windows in blue and gold, and the Chilton Chamber of Commerce tied hundreds of helium balloons to street lamps along the route.

Talon and Serena skipped the whole float-decoration thing, but they showed up a few minutes before the parade started. They were there for moral support since Martin would be on said float, and I dreaded the idea of standing alone on the sidelines like some black-and-white sweetheart in a World War II movie, waving while my hero marched by.

In the long run, it didn't much matter since I was standing on the south side of the street and my hero ended up on the north side of the float. I saw Martin's profile for a second, but by the time I got my hand up for a wave, he'd already passed.

I could tell Serena, like me, secretly got into the spectacle of it all—the cheering and band and the big foam glove-thingies that you put on your hand to make you look like you have a huge blue number-one finger. Talon, on the other hand, was her usual snarky self.

"Go, fight, win? Hello. Haven't you people heard of a noun? And where would the world be if everyone decided to go, fight, and win? It'd be a disaster zone."

"Yeah, but, Talon, this is football." I waved my big blue finger in her face. "Where would we be if we *didn't* go, fight, and win?"

"Well, the team would be in last place," she considered, "and I would be somewhere that wasn't so noxiously color coordinated."

"You don't have to be here, you know."

"I know," she said. Then to show that she was just being difficult because she enjoyed being difficult and not because she actually wanted to be difficult *elsewhere*, she took up the red feather she was wearing as a pendant and used it to tickle my ear. "But if I weren't here," she said, "who would point out the irony of the Fellowship of Christian Athletes screaming 'Let's Go Demons'?"

I put one arm around Talon's shoulder and the other around Serena's and gave them both a squeeze.

"Hey, where's my homecoming date?" Talon asked.

"It wasn't my turn to watch him," I said, although I usually was the one who knew where Will was hiding. I wasn't exactly sad he wasn't there, since mixing Will with Martin was sort of like pouring vinegar over baking soda. But I was used to seeing the world half through my eyes and half through Will's, and I liked the way his half helped me refocus my own.

I got out my cell phone. Hey, I texted Will. Where are you?

I didn't get an answer, so I texted again. I'm at parade with S and T. Whoohoo.

I waited, then tried again. You there?

Still nothing. I put my phone back in my pocket.

The cheerleaders marched by next. It was cold, so they were

wearing panty hose under their skirts, which made their legs look tan and shiny. They were doing this skip-step-shake-their-bootie kind of thing. Lots of pompom action. All culminating with them putting their fingers on their butts and making a sizzle-hiss to rhyme with "class." When she strutted by, Stephanie Gonzales was close enough that I could have reached out and touched her shoulder. Her dark hair was up in a ponytail, and in the sharp slant of late-day sun, I noticed two squiggly lines on the back of her neck. I sucked in a breath. They were faint, a pinkish-gray, not the deep black of Martin's. It was as if they'd faded over time. But they were the same lines. The same mark.

He'd said they hadn't meant anything. He'd said it was just a tattoo.

He'd lied.

It doesn't matter, I told myself. It can't. So what if they have matching tattoos? It wasn't like they'd gone off to the tattoo parlor on a Saturday night and gotten the his-and-her special.

But I was lying, too. I knew there was a bond between the two of them, not made of ink, but of dreams. And maybe that was worse.

After the parade, I asked Serena for a ride home before Martin could track me down. I didn't want to see him, and I didn't want to see the person I would likely become around him. Crazy Annabelle could take the night off. I needed some rest.

If I could only sleep without having to dream.

Chapter 25

I am running down a path in the woods. It is dark, thick with moss. The trees on each side of the path grow dense and gnarled. Behind me, there is a dull scraping, like something being dragged across the forest floor. Scraps of far-off music shuttle along in the wind.

Ahead, a hazy light pulses. I sprint toward it. The path opens, and I burst into a clearing.

In the center, on the large flat stump of a tree, sits the girl in the white dress.

She sews something, the needle pulling taut and then looping back. A wisp of smoke rises in the air and she begins to hum under her breath. A lullaby?

The distant music in the woods—the murmurs caught like torn paper in the wind—had been hers.

She doesn't look up, though I sense she knows I am there.

In her lap, I see what she is working on—a dirty rag doll with brown yarn hair and broken button eyes. She is sewing thick red stitches along the side of the doll's neck.

"Martin!" I shout. He can tell me why this girl is haunting my dreams. He can tell me what I need to do.

And then he is there—without warning, like a jump in a snippet of film. Not exactly himself, but a sort of hologram. I feel like I am watching him through a pane of tinted glass. He stands on the other side of the girl, facing her, facing me. I can tell he wants to come to me, but he doesn't—or can't—move.

I stop, catch my breath. "What is it?"

The girl's voice is in my head, small, like a bird. "That's right. Ask him. He knows."

She stands and for the first time looks at me.

Only, her eyes are wrong. They don't fit that little girl face; they are an old lady's eyes—washed out, so pale that they'd almost turned completely white. Worst of all, they are pricked with a tiny red pupil, like when someone takes a photograph and the flash isn't quite right.

She walks to where I am on the edge of the clearing. I feel a clammy sickness in my gut. Her voice rises and deepens in my mind. "I'm going to get you." She holds up the rag doll and turns it to face Martin. "I'm going to be you."

My own body also turns, like a puppet. "Why—" I start to speak, but my throat closes on itself. Someone is choking me from behind. Strong hands clamp around my neck. I haven't seen the girl move, but she is suddenly closer, both her hands firmly around the doll's thin neck. She squeezes and I feel the fingers around my own neck constrict.

The girl jerks the doll, and its arms flail. At the same moment, my arms flap and spasm.

"I'm going to be you."

Fighting for control, I raise my hands to my neck to pull the girl's invisible fingers away. They feel small and brittle, like peppermint sticks, and the moment I touch them, the girl shivers, excited, like she is made of electricity.

She laughs and her doll disappears in a throb of light. For a second, the girl's grip releases me, and I can breathe. But then, my own hands creep up my neck—closing tight against my will. I look to where the girl stood at the clearing's opening. She isn't there. I try to pull my hands away, but I can't stop. Under my palm I feel a line of thick, sloppy stitches in the same place the girl had sewn on the doll. I want to gag, but my throat won't open.

Surging in and out, my vision goes painfully bright, then almost black. I feel my brain expanding star-like, too big for my skull, the forest, the universe. I squeeze my eyes shut and tumble down into darkness.

The ground is not hard, as I expect it to be, but…muscly and writhing. Alive. I open my eyes to a landscape bloated with snakes. They swarm me, covering every inch of my body with their leathery scales.

"Martin! Help!" I think the words more than call them.

In the last second before I am lost below the swarm, I concentrate and force my head to turn. I look to where he's been standing.

It isn't Martin there at all. It is Will.

"Will!"

He runs to me, but I am sinking beneath the snakes. They are weaving me in, another cord in their gruesome carpet.

His pained face rises above me. "Annabelle, you know. You know what to do…"

Dying is not what you'd expect. I am there in that dark earth, aware but not alive. I hear Will's voice fade above me. "You can't go, Annabelle. I won't let you."

But I am already gone.

Chapter 26

I watched Martin glide through the crowded halls Friday morning—the morning after the girl tried to strangle me in my sleep. People stepped out of his way, and I could see why. He was gorgeous, confident, strong. The air around him literally seemed to shimmer. He smiled when he saw me, but as he walked closer, he must have been able to make out the panic I was trying to bury under a bright smile and a black turtleneck.

"We need to talk," I said.

He hesitated for a second before answering, "Shoot."

What I gave him, though, was not a single bullet, but the scattered explosion of buckshot, metal bits flying everywhere.

"The snakes were back. They were all over me. And this weirdo doll. And then she choked me—"

"The doll?"

"Martin, the girl. The. Girl. She's following me. In every dream. She won't leave me alone." Images flashed through my mind: the girl as a girl, as a parasite, as a snake, as the sound of a footfall behind me, tracking me. "She says she wants to *be* me. We were in the forest but it was my hands and you were—"

"Shhh. Slow down. *What* girl?"

"You know. You were there, right?"

"What? Where?"

"My dream."

"You saw me in your dream?" he asked, his voice dropping to a whisper.

"Yes."

"With a girl?" He looked pale.

"She was the one on the bank, near the lake," I said. "In that first dream when we kissed."

He took a deep breath, reining himself in. I knew from his look that it wasn't just a fluke. It wasn't just dream diving, or addiction. The girl was haunting me. Hunting me.

The morning bell clanged. "Look," he said. "I need to know what happened. All of it. Start at the beginning."

"Now?"

"Yes."

"But we've got class—"

"Class can wait." Maybe in dreamworld you can skip class and not get in trouble. That doesn't happen in my world. But when Martin drew me down the hallway that led to the gym, I went. He waited for the hall to clear, then pulled open the door to the boys' locker room. "In here."

"Are you kidding?" The thought of a crowd of half-naked

freshmen giving each other wedgies wasn't exactly my idea of a good place to talk.

"No one's in here first period. Coach uses Friday mornings to set the playbook strategy for the game."

I stepped tentatively inside. It smelled like dirty socks, ripe urine, and bleach. "I shouldn't be here."

"What, the girl who sneaks into the field house at Pulaski Stadium doesn't feel right at home?" Martin smiled for the first time since I'd mentioned the dream.

It warmed me, like it always did. "There weren't so many urinals in the Pulaski field house," I said.

Being in there, alone, smiling at each other—that was what I wanted. Not nightmares and panic. I leaned toward him so my head was on his shoulder, my lips reaching toward his neck.

"You're making it hard for me to think," he said.

I didn't want to think, either. "Do you have to think when you kiss me?"

He met my lips and gave me a long, ragged kiss.

And it worked. I didn't think about the nightmare once. I raised my lips again, but he stepped back.

"We need to focus, Annabelle. I need to focus." He sat down across the room on a bench beside the lockers. "Your dreams. I should have listened closer. Tell me everything you remember."

"They're just dreams," I said, backtracking. "It's not like...I'm not going to lose you, am I?" My voice echoed in the locker room.

"Nothing like that," he said, but he rubbed his face when he said it, covering his mouth. I'd played enough poker with Will to know a tell when I saw it, and I would have bet money that he was bluffing. "Tell me what happened," he said.

So I did. The girl on the bank, the girl on the boat, the girl in the forest. The whole spiel.

He started pacing. "She had milky eyes?"

"Yes." I hadn't mentioned her eyes, and there was no way he could have seen them that first time, not all the way across the lake.

He kept pacing, thinking. "And I was in the dream?"

I nodded. "But you didn't quite look like you. You weren't exactly solid. You were," I didn't know how else to put it, "bluer."

"But no one else, right? Not Stephanie? Not anybody?"

"Yeah...no." I hadn't mentioned Will. I didn't want to now. "At the end I looked to where you'd been. Only you weren't there anymore. Will was."

Martin looked like I had sucker punched him in the gut. "I see."

"Oh come on," I protested. "You don't *see* anything, Martin. You can't blame me for something in my dream. It's not like I decide what happens. Anyway, it wasn't real."

"Just what *is* real to you? Is this real?" He picked up a towel that had been abandoned on a bench, wadded it up into a ball, and threw it across the room into a laundry basket. "Is this?" He kicked the bench between us, then turned to face me. "Am I?"

"Don't be stupid."

"It's a simple question, Annabelle. Why can't you just answer?"

"Yeah, well, I'd like some answers, too," I shot back. "That little girl. It's like she's trying to get in my skin. You know her, don't you? Is she a friend of yours? Like Stephanie?"

When he looked up, some of the blue washed out of his eyes, melting his rage away. "No." He shifted his gaze to his feet, his face intentionally blank.

"You're a crappy liar," I said.

"I'm not lying."

"Sure." If he had been made of wood, his nose would have grown two inches by now.

"She's not a friend," he said. "That's the truth." He rubbed his face again.

The bell for second period rang.

"We should get out of here," he said.

Martin and I made our way through the crowded hallway, so close my elbow jostled into his rib...but inside, where we breathed, we could have been on opposite ends of a frozen lake.

"You may as well go to class," he said. "I need to—I'll figure this out. I promise."

He abandoned me outside the art room.

I thought about following him, but Ms. Sage had already seen me. "Annabelle, get in here and pull out your sketchbook," she said.

She'd arranged a bunch of random stuff on a drape of light blue fabric: green plastic grapes, a gray mug holding three pencils and a wooden back scratcher, a metal eyelash curler, a dollhouse stove, the jeweled pink collar for a cat. "Five minutes looking, twenty minutes drawing," she said. "Starting now."

At first, I was relieved to have some time to think things through. But it was more of a curse than a blessing because my thoughts took me nowhere good. I zoomed in on the eyelash curler and began to draw, but I had plenty of time to think: *He's lying. He's freaking, so there must be something to freak about.* Time to think: *Does he really know that girl? What does she mean "ask him"? What does she want from me?*

And then in my brain, I could almost hear the girl's answer. "I don't want something from you. I want *you.*"

While Martin might be lying, the girl was not.

———————

Martin missed lunch. When he didn't show up in the cafeteria, I noticed Stephanie was missing, too. But Billy and Trina were there at the golden table, so it wasn't some football-cheerleader thing. It was a dream thing.

Will was in the photo lab, probably with Paolo, who was also AWOL. So that just left me trying to assure Talon and Serena that nothing was up.

Martin wasn't next to me in chemistry, either, because there was no chemistry. As if Spirit Day and the parade weren't enough to get all of Chilton High frothing at the mouth for the big rah-rah homecoming game that night, the last period of Friday classes had been canceled and we were funneled into the gym for a pregame pep rally.

The team filed in. I watched, wondering if Martin would skip that, too, but he didn't. He stood down there looking gorgeous and mysterious. Stephanie was in the alpha position on the gym floor with her pack of cheerleaders. I slumped in the bleachers and gnawed my fingernails. Randy Simpkins sat down on one side of me. Everyone called him Moon because he marched out of his pants two years ago while he was playing the bass drum during the Christmas parade. Not a big believer in belts, that Randy. Or underwear.

Will came in and squeezed in the empty space on my other side.

The cheerleaders had started a sort of cowgirl-meets-kung-fu routine and Brazen, the worst band in the history of pop music, was blasting over the loudspeakers.

"You know, 'gymnasium' comes from the Greek word meaning 'to exercise naked.'" Will spoke in my ear. "Coincidence? Or do you think that's what Stephanie's going for?"

I shrugged.

"A *shrug*?" Will was outraged. "That's all I rate? No guffaw? No titter? Not even a snort?"

"I don't snort."

He looked at me, then leaned back toward my ear. "What's up? You look shot. Bad day?"

"Bad night."

"Oh." He twisted his neck around, like his collar itched, only he wasn't wearing a collar, he was wearing one of his trademark tees with a picture of a guy wearing a leaf crown like Julius Caesar. "Carpe Weekend," it said.

"I texted you."

"What?"

It was impossible talking over the ruckus of *watch me walking now/ watch me talking now/watch me dance.* I raised my voice. "I texted."

"Yeah, I got that this morning."

"Why not before?" The pep band started playing, which was even louder than the speakers.

"I turned my phone off. Went hiking up to the Cascades. I just wanted to get off the map for a while."

"What's it like there?" I asked.

"What, the Cascades?" Will looked surprised at my question— which only made sense, as we'd hiked to the falls a ton of times.

"No, off the map?"

"I'm not sure I got there." Will smiled, but it didn't reach his eyes. "Turns out there are some things that just keep following you."

"Like what?"

The pep band got, if possible, even louder. Will shrugged. I couldn't hear his answer, but I was pretty sure his lips formed the word "you."

Chapter 27

Martin had football stuff all afternoon.

"I know it seems dumb, to want to play a game when all of this is going on," he said, when he caught me coming out of the gym. "But I never...this is my chance to play. To do real things. Please understand."

"I do," I said. "But what about—"

"We're working on it," he said, squeezing my hand. "I promise. Try not to think about it, okay?"

But by the time the players took the field that night, I'd had a chance to WAY overthink everything Martin had said. Like "we're working on it." I was pretty sure the "we" included Stephanie. She had glared at me in the hall after pre calc like everything was my fault. But it's not like I had asked to be stalked by Little Miss Nightmare with the bleached-out eyes.

Martin said the little girl wasn't his friend. Maybe. But clearly there was something he was *not* saying, too. In my mind, I kept seeing her on the stump, sewing that freaky doll. The place looked familiar, and not just the way things always look familiar in dreams, like when you're in a nightclub in Brazil but you know deep down it's your chemistry class. I was pretty sure I'd been there.

Talon, Serena, and Will had all skipped the game, due respectively to the opera, "the call of the wild," and a chronic allergy to all things involving the Chilton High football team. So I sat alone and kept my eyes on Martin. "TALK TO ME," I thought. "I NEED YOU TO TALK TO ME." Even though he seemed totally wrapped up in the whole run-around-with-a-ball thing, my concentration must have worked at least a little because the minute the game was over, he texted. Can I see you?

Yes! Where are you? I typed quickly.

Locker room. Meet at your house?

It was already eleven o'clock. My mom had given me her Volvo for the night, and the green light to stay out a little past curfew, but I knew she wouldn't be happy about me showing up at that hour with my "gentleman caller," as she'd titled Martin after we'd watched *Glass Menagerie* on the classic movie channel. She wasn't likely to give us much privacy if I did bring him home.

Text me when you get there. Don't go to door.

At home, I slipped by my mom who, since the announcement of Dad's wedding, had started crashing on the living room couch, remote control in hand.

"That you?"

"Yeah, Mom. I'm here. Go back to sleep."

"Ummmhumm," she mumbled and shifted on her side to hug a throw pillow.

I went upstairs and checked on Nick, but he wasn't in his bed. Then I remembered him muttering something about spending the night at Jeremy's. Good. That meant I wouldn't have to make him an accomplice.

I snuck downstairs to the basement. I rarely spent time there, unless Mom made me do the laundry. My dad had planned to turn it into a game room with a pool table and big-screen TV, but he'd only gotten as far as framing in one of the concrete walls with wallboard before he ditched that project and moved on to something else.

I checked my watch. Midnight. Mom had seen me home, safe and sound. She was, by all appearances, down for the count. I could either sneak Martin into the basement or sneak myself out the same way. Out, I decided. The idea of staying in this graveyard of cardboard boxes and dryer lint was way too depressing.

You there? I texted Martin.

No answer. Then, Just pulled up.

Park down street.

As silently as possible, I climbed up the basement steps that led to the backyard. Leaving the door unlocked, I slipped out, crossed the path that led to the front, and ran down the street to Martin's car.

"Better drive," I said as I climbed in the passenger seat. "Mr. Purfoy is a total paranoid. If he sees this car parked in front of his driveway, he'll call the cops. And if they called my mom, I'd be grounded for a month."

"Right," he said. He drove a few blocks over and parked near the river, where we'd spent that first morning together across from the pump house. He turned off the engine and drew me in for a kiss. His hair was still wet from his shower, and he smelled of baby powder. When he pulled away, he grabbed my hand. I liked seeing our hands together, entwined.

"So talk," I said.

"We won the game." He looked a little sheepish when he said it, like a kid who had been caught eating cookies in bed.

"Congratulations." I wanted to smile, but I held it in. I'd been waiting all night for some answers. "So I've been thinking. The girl's not your friend, but you knew her. Right?"

When he didn't answer at first, I squeezed his hand. "Just tell me the truth."

"Yeah. I knew her."

"Who is she?"

"You already said it," he said. "She's a nightmare. She had... Well, I knew she was trying to get into your head for some reason. I just—"

"You *knew* she was trying to get me?"

"No, not like that. I swear." Martin looked down at the floorboard, confused, like he'd suddenly grown someone else's feet. "I didn't know she was a nightmare. We were in someone else's dream, bit parts, and she was asking me about you and if she could come along sometime when I went to see you and I didn't see the harm. I just thought she wanted out of the waiting room, too, but that she needed help. I figured she'd die soon—"

"Dreams die?"

"Of course they do."

"But she's so young."

"She might *look* young, but she's older than anyone I've ever met. I thought it'd be a nice thing, you know. To give her some time outside. But I swear at the time I didn't know she was a nightmare."

"The milky eyes weren't a clue?" I said, hating that sarcasm was my only weapon. He'd helped a nightmare break into my mind? How do you list *that* on a police report? "What do you think she wants anyway?"

"She wants what every nightmare wants. She wants control."

Control. That was something I wanted, too. The control to silence Crazy Annabelle. To bring my dad back. To make Martin love me. Is that what a nightmare is, I wondered—just a regular dream that tries to take control? Does that make me a nightmare, too?

Martin ran his free hand through his hair. "We're all trying to think of a way to stop her, I promise."

"All?"

"The Chiltonians Formerly Known as Dreams," he said. "That's what Paolo calls us."

"Paolo?"

"Stephanie, Paolo, Macy—"

"What? That's insane. I've known Paolo like for—"

"Think about it," he said. I did. Most families had been here forever, Chilton born and Chilton bred. But both Macy and Paolo's families had moved here in the last couple of years. I remembered what Mrs. Muncy said about the real estate market. *Chilton is thriving.*

"Ernshaw is one of you, isn't he?" I didn't know when he'd come to Chilton High, but he had always seemed to me like he might have arrived from a galaxy far, far away. In fact, it wasn't impossible to imagine that he still visited there pretty regularly.

"Nope, but you're close," he said. "Masterson."

I remembered someone telling me Coach Masterson had transferred here from a high school in California. "That's one heck of a transfer."

Through the car window, the sky was cloudless, the stars pale and numerous as goose bumps.

"So you knew Paolo and Macy and Masterson…up there?" I jabbed my finger upward in the air.

"It's not heaven, Annabelle," Martin said. "Believe me. It's the opposite."

"Right."

"And I didn't really know them," Martin continued. "Well, Masterson, yeah. And I'd seen Macy around, but I wouldn't say I *knew* her. Stephanie told me about Paolo. I've kind of gotten to know him since."

I'll bet Will didn't know that. "Who else?"

"I've seen some people around town, but you wouldn't know them."

"I don't even know who's real anymore," I said.

"We're *all* real," Martin said. "Even the ones who haven't made it to Chilton."

I thought about that. "But why Chilton anyway? Why did all of you end up here?"

"I don't know," he said, "but it's good that we did. Chilton's perfect."

That word again. He talked about my town the same way he talked about me.

"Yeah, well," I said, "it gets pretty boring once you've been here for a while."

"It's *because* it's boring, no offense, that it's so ideal. For one thing, everyone *in* Chilton dreams—more vividly than in other places. You'd have to or you'd go insane. But no one dreams *of* Chilton, so we can kind of slip in under the radar. It's like your brother said, 'the perfect place to live, but no one wants to visit.' Not even in their sleep."

"So now it's…what? Some kind of underground railroad for lost dreams? 'Next stop, Chilton, Virginia.'"

"It appears so," he said. "Stephanie thinks that if that girl gets here, it might become an underground railroad for nightmares, too."

I pictured my town taken over by creepy little girls, fanged skeletons, zombies, snakes. It seemed impossible. But Martin, dreams—all of it had seemed impossible when I went to bed last week.

"What do you think?" I said.

"That Stephanie's right," he said. "The girl's after you, Annabelle. That's real, too."

"Why me?" I asked.

"I'm not sure," he said. "But there's something about you. No, don't argue, there is. I saw it. Even that time on the train. She wants you because you're special."

"Give me a break," I said.

"Look, even if you don't believe it, the girl does. And that makes it"—he left the pause hanging for a minute, then he finished—"dangerous."

"For me or for you?"

"For all of us," he said. "I don't know. Maybe she's trying to follow in my footsteps. I'm real. You did that. Maybe she wants to be real, too."

"I told you I didn't—"

"The evidence says otherwise. And it's more than that. What did she say in your dream? She wants to be you. She can't do that if you're here." He said it so simply, like "and she doesn't care for the color blue." But I knew how deep it went.

The car seemed suddenly way too small. I flung open my door. "Air." I stumbled toward the river and started through the woods along the bank. A night bird flew from its branch in a sycamore above me toward the opposite bank of the river, letting out a stuttered chirp.

"Annabelle." Martin came after me and took my elbow, turning me to face him. "You can try to run away from this, but it won't help. Like it or not, we're connected."

I pulled away and darted across the rocky edge of the river. I didn't know where I was heading; I only knew I couldn't stand around listening to what was quite possibly an extended figment of my imagination tell me I was going to be dead at sixteen.

"Hold on, Annabelle!" Martin, who was—damn him, damn me for making him that way—stronger and faster, caught up. I heard the thump of his footsteps right behind me. His hand brushed my shoulder. Just then my foot slipped on a wet rock and I hurtled toward the earth.

Chapter 28

I am suspended. Floating in deep water. Not wet, but the waves are choppy and the undercurrent is strong. My body rises and falls with a nauseating quickness. I am pulled one way, then shoved the other. I gasp, but the air is thin and I can't fill my lungs. Am I drowning or dreaming? It feels the same.

I see nothing.

But no, it is more than that. I see the consistency of nothing. The uniformity of it. What surrounds me is a thin, flat gray. In every direction, for miles, gray. There is no horizon, no spot where land meets sky. There is, in fact, no land, no sky. Only this lukewarm air in which my body twists.

"Martin?" My own voice does not reach my ears. It is all just bluster, a wall of wind.

I hang like that, my body warping in the gray. I try running, swimming, jumping, willing myself elsewhere. I think of my mother waking to find my bed empty, the sheets cold. Will she call my dad? Will my dad stop looking for his stupid fish and start looking for me? I ball my hands into fists and beat the air. My body ignores my will, until my will is gone.

And that's how I stay. All day. All week. A month? A year? It is impossible to tell how long I hang and twist, impossible to tell how long forever is.

I make out voices in the wind. Chunks of words, different accents, languages. I try to move. I try to hear.

Am I in a coma? Am I dead? I don't want an afterlife; I never got enough of the real thing.

Panic rises in my throat, thick like gravy. There is no way out. Nothing to do but wait. But wait for what?

You have no idea how long it can be, *Martin had said,* waiting for the next dream.

Is that what I'm waiting for—for someone to dream? To dream me?

I wonder if I can break in, like Martin did. Like the girl has broken into my own dreams? I still my mind and focus on the even rise and fall of breath. The twisting air around my body seems to settle.

I focus and move toward space, and then I am standing at the end of a narrow dirt lane. My arms move like arms again. I want to kneel down and kiss the dirt. The lane leads to a cottage, mushroomy and fanciful, like something from Snow White. *All around are orange flowers, bright as sunbursts, brighter, even, after all of the gray.*

My legs, still jellyish from the waiting, propel me toward the back door. I pass through, into a kitchen with a potbelly stove and a small wooden table where a grandmother pours tea. Across the table, a toddler in a blue knit dress, no older than three, stands on a chair and plays with a wad of dough. She kneads and squeezes. In the far corner, a canary in a white wicker cage warbles twoo-twoo-twhee. And the little girl echoes back, woo-woo-whee.

I stand behind the girl, uncertain what to do, as they sing again and again. I want to sit down in this bright world and sip tea with a teaspoon of milk, the way my mother makes it. What I want doesn't matter. I stand on the fringe, watching. The grandmother doesn't notice me. The girl does. Her look questions, but I don't answer. I drain out of the scene, pulled backward like a movie on rewind.

Again, I breathe the thin, gray air of in-between, but before I panic, I am somewhere else. Somewhere dark.

An alley, I realize, my eyes adjusting to the sudden night. I am at the back of a big, run-down brick building, something like an old grocery store. All around me, the world is tinged with gray—all except the back of the store, and, at the far side, a black metal ladder bolted to the brick. I climb. I will do anything just to move.

As I go up, I notice a slice of sky above me, prickling with stars. They blink like heartbeats. The colors aren't the usual yellow-white of stars, but like fireworks—ruby, magenta, and willow green. I reach the top and climb out onto the roof.

The night sky spreads out before me, an endless banquet of light, all swirling with wisps of life. There is a different color for every one of the million stars. Or no...it isn't every star, but every constellation that has a distinct shade. As a girl, I had learned to find the dippers, Orion, and the one that makes a drunken W...Cassiopeia?

Will said she was a queen who'd been set in the heavens upside down as some sort of punishment. I've never been able really to visualize it, though. At least not until this moment. Now, the entire sky is throbbing with color and life. The figures of astrology hover around their star clusters, shifting in and out of focus. Two bears, a swan, Pegasus.

"Oh my God. It's amazing." I exhale.

"What was that?" A girl's voice, familiar, anxious, speaks from somewhere around the middle of the roof.

"What?" A deeper voice, a guy's, but mellow, serene. Also familiar, a voice like home.

"I thought I heard something." The girl again.

"I didn't hear any—a meteor!"

Silver blazes down from the sky.

The girl mumbles something I can't make out.

Stepping catlike, silent, I slink closer to the roof's center.

In the darkness, I can trace the outline of two pairs of legs stretched out on a blanket. They are wearing, I think, jeans, and their feet are bare. The rest is obscured by a metal air vent. There is the sound of kissing, and an odd, unpleasant smell, like burned plastic. Fumbling. More kissing.

"Are you sure?" The guy's voice.

Suddenly I feel like the pervert in the back row of the movie theater. It is wrong for me to be here in someone's private dream, but I have no clue how I got here or how to leave. Taking care to walk quietly, I head back toward the ladder.

As I start to descend, I look up at the surreal light show above me.

Maybe there's a message in the stars. I feel myself yanked suddenly backward again—like a hand is on my shoulder, tugging me hard.

A faint voice. "You okay…? Annabelle? Annabelle?"

Chapter 29

It took me a second to realize that a hand really *was* on my shoulder. Two hands. I was lying facedown on something wet and hard. I pushed myself upward and shifted into a sitting position. Martin was kneeling beside me on the slick, rocky edge of the river. Where I fell, what, a year ago? I was not standing on a roof, looking at stars. Not back in the gray—but *back*.

"Are you hurt?"

Dazed, yes. Confused, yes. Hurt? I felt my forehead: a bit sore near my left temple, but nothing bad. "No, not hurt."

"You look a little weird."

"Thanks a lot." I might have just had the strangest, most mind-blowing experience of my life, but I was still a girl. I smoothed my hair.

"How did I get here?" I asked him. I didn't know how else to put it.

Martin looked confused. "We were in the car," he said, "and you took off and you slipped, and then I helped you up."

"And that was when?"

"Just now."

"The *whole thing* was just now?" I asked.

"What whole thing?"

"It took how long, from when we left the car to right here?"

"Um, maybe a couple of minutes."

"So it's still tonight?"

"What are you getting at, Annabelle?"

I pressed my palm to my temple. "It just seemed longer. Much longer. Eons." I pushed myself up. "I was stuck in a sea of gray," I said. "Like your waiting room. And then I was in a cabin and on a roof…" My legs wobbled as I stood, and I put my hand on Martin's shoulder to steady myself. The world tilted, but I stayed standing.

"A sea of gray." He put an arm around my waist to steady me, then lowered his voice, like we were talking in class. "You were there?" Now Martin was the one looking weird.

"That's impossible," he went on. "You couldn't have been there. No one can go between worlds like that. No one."

"You did," I said.

"That's different," he said. "I am—*I was*—a dream. I belonged there. You're…"

"I'm what?"

"You're not." He said it softly.

I shook my head to try to clear it.

Finally, Martin spoke. "This is where I woke up, you know, when I first arrived. Here." He pointed to the muddy ground.

"And that little house," he said. "It was by the lake, in that dream. Our dream. Maybe it's the same place."

I gave him my "huh?" face, which lately had pretty much become my expression of default. I could just make out the small, brick pump house in the dim light. Then I looked back into the even dimmer memory of my dream, and I saw it in my mind, there on the edge of that lake—the same little house perched like a fat duck on the bank.

"You see?" Martin went on. "It was *there* in the dream. And it's *here* in real life. Both. So this," he spread out his arms, indicating the river, the bank, everything around us, "this could be the real-world version of that dream lake. Or the lake was the dreamworld version of this. They intersect. So when you slipped, maybe you just—"

"—slipped into dreams," I finished.

He nodded.

"But we've been here before." I could still feel the shimmer of our first mind-blowing real-world kiss. "If there's an intersection, why didn't we both get whisked into la-la-land then?"

Martin tugged his ear. "Maybe because we were too close together? Or maybe because it wasn't the *exact* spot? Or maybe you weren't looking to get away?"

Or maybe I wasn't wearing striped socks and hadn't had tacos for dinner, I thought.

I took a step; my knees buckled and Martin righted me. "I need to go somewhere I can think," I said. But I didn't want to go back to the car. I wanted to be out in the air. "I'm just going to walk home. You want to come with?"

"Are you sure you're up to it?" Martin asked.

I took a few steps in the direction of the road. "Just tired."

"About that." Martin came up beside me, taking my arm in his as we walked—but not in the romantic, strolling-in-the-park way; it was more a helping-the-decrepit-old-lady kind of thing. "I'm not sure sleep is such a good idea."

I half-laughed, half-yawned. "Yeah, well, it's something we humans tend to do."

"There's no way you could make yourself stay awake?"

"I guess with enough caffeine, I could put it off for a while. But no, it's not like I can just stay awake forever. Bodies don't work that way. In some places keeping people awake is used for torture." Will probably could have given us a list of the countries.

Martin knocked a pebble with the side of his foot as he walked. "I doubt it would make a difference anyway. I mean, she's probably already here, right?"

"I thought you were talking *if. If* she somehow gets here," I said. "And now you think she's already here?"

"Well, I can't know for sure. It's just you said you touched the girl in the dream, the way you touched me—"

"I didn't kiss—"

"No, not kiss. But you *touched* her, and you must have been feeling something, right? A really strong emotion."

"Yeah but—"

"Fear. Love. They're both powerful in their own way," Martin went on. "I've been trying to figure it out ever since I got here. Why me? How you did it. I'm pretty sure it has something to do with the way you touched me. I could feel your whole heart in your kiss, Annabelle. And I think that emotion, that touch, is what got me here."

I'd tried too many times to tell him it wasn't me. This time, I was too tired to argue. Slower now, Martin and I started walking again toward my house.

"So now what?" I said. It was late and I felt fatigue press against the back of my eyes.

"Get some sleep if you have to. Just don't dream."

"But you said she probably isn't even in my dream. You said she's probably already *here*."

"We can't know for sure, right? Just to be safe." He rubbed his palm over his mouth, the poker tell again. Even he didn't buy that "safe" was a viable option.

"Listen, why don't you stay with me tonight?" He took my cold hands and rubbed them in his. "I'll keep watch."

"That'd be nice," I said. "But if we made it through the night, I'd be facing another kind of nightmare with my mother in the morning."

"Your mother," he said. "Sleep with her. I'll watch the house."

He pulled me in, but I didn't lose myself in his kiss. "We'll figure it out," he said.

More than anything, I wanted to believe him.

Chapter 30

In the basement, I rifled through our old camping gear, grabbed my sleeping bag, and dragged it up the stairs to the darkness of the living room. My mother was still on the couch, the television casting a glow that moved the shadows around the room.

"Mom?" I said.

She opened her eyes, not all the way, just part.

"Hey, Pumpkin," she said. "You have a bad dream?"

"Yeah. Can I rest down here?"

"Of course, baby," she said.

I made myself a cup of instant coffee, rolled out my sleeping bag next to the couch, and watched movie after movie. Halfway through *To Catch a Thief* my mother's arm dropped so that she was touching my shoulder blade. With her hand on my back, I fell asleep.

There's a point in a bad dream when you have to wake up; your body jerks, and your eyelids fly open, like a door that's been kicked. For me that point came at 4:43 a.m., according to the mantel clock.

I wasn't sure where I was just before that moment, but I knew I was alone. I'd been looking for the little girl all night, dreading, fearing—but I'd been stood up. Even without her, though, there'd been plenty of horrors. Cynthia Rêve would have had a field day: my mother drowning, my father and his bride holding hands as they jumped off the edge of a mountain, Nick walking out in front of a bus. I must have cried out at that last one because my mother stirred as I woke.

"Honey?"

It was still dark, but something about the glow of the darkness made it feel closer to morning.

"Another dream?" she asked.

I found my voice. "Yeah."

Her hand reached down to touch my forehead. My hair was wet with sweat.

"You want to tell me about it?" she asked.

"No thanks," I said.

She smiled through the darkness. "When you were little and I asked you what you dreamed, you'd never tell me, either," she said. "You were always scared that I'd be scared, too."

Tonight you would be, I thought.

"You were a very brave four-year-old," she said. "But you didn't have to be." She rubbed her eyes and left her fingers there. "Do you think you can dream about something good now?"

There were still a couple hours before morning. "I can try."

"Martin?" she suggested, as her fingers moved away. "Homecoming?"

"Yeah," I said softly. Martin and homecoming. Both had been at the top of my list. Now my list pretty much consisted of "staying alive."

"To be a teenager again," my mother said. "That's what I'll dream about."

"It's not all it's cracked up to be," I told her.

"Yes, well," she said. "Neither is getting old."

We lay there, together in the darkness, but I didn't sleep. When the sun rose, I watched the sky turn from black to gray to an impossibly cheerful shade of blue.

"French toast?" my mother asked when she got up.

For some reason, just the thought of it made me want to cry. "Cereal's okay," I said. "I'm not really that hungry."

We went to the kitchen. I ate a few bites of Rice Krispies and let the rest disintegrate into a soggy mess as I called Martin.

"Hi," I said.

"I've been waiting for you to call. I'm outside."

"Where?"

"In front of your house." I looked out the window and there he was, waving from the sidewalk. It could have been a week ago, his bike at his feet. Only, it wasn't.

On my front lawn, Martin caught me in a hug.

"Were you out here all night?" I asked.

"I said I'd be."

I touched his hand, warmer than the air outside. "Thanks."

"I didn't see her," he said. "What about you? I mean, when you slept?"

I shook my head. "Not that I remember."

His voice was flat. "Did you, you know...*do it* at all?"

It sounded like he was asking me if I had sex or picked my nose or something.

"I dreamed. It was bad. My family was basically decimated. But no crazy little girls." I bit my lip. "I'm sorry, Martin. I tried not to."

"You couldn't help it," he said. "I should have snuck in and prodded you with a stick or something."

"That's romantic." I stretched my back, catlike. "So, what do we do next?"

"Well, I'm thinking first thing is to find out if anyone else has *seen* her. It might give us some idea about what we're up against. We'll track down the other dreamers. Ask if they've had any nightmares. I mean, anyone might have seen her, right?" He shrugged, and a curl of his hair slipped down on his forehead like an exaggerated comma. "We should talk to some of the other dreams, too. They might have known her *before*. If so, they could have some ideas. And we need to do it today. Before the dance."

"Should we even go?" I said. "I mean, a dance doesn't seem very important anymore, does it?" It knew it was stupid, but I still wanted to. The nightmare was dominating my sleeping life. I didn't want her to have power over my waking life, too.

In a flash, I saw a freeze-frame image of the girl twirling in her white dress, streamers littering a ballroom floor. It was like something I'd seen in a dream.

No. It *was* something I'd seen in a dream.

"Martin." I clutched his elbow. "She'll be there. At the dance."

His bright eyes darkened. "How can you be so sure?"

"I dreamed it. But just a sliver of a dream. I don't think it was something she wanted me to see. She was twirling, singing something. It was so quick. I don't remember."

"Okay," he said, but his voice said anything but okay. "This is good, right? Is there anything else you remember from your dreams with her? Have you told me everything?"

Snakes? Check.

Nasty doll? Check.

Freaky girl hunting me down for creepy-time games? Check.

But there was one thing. "I keep thinking about the forest where I saw the girl in that last dream. Like it's important."

"What about it?"

"I don't know. It was different in my dream."

"You came to a clearing and saw the girl—"

"On a stump!" The words stumbled over each other, my mind snapping like castanets. "In the dream, in the dream where the stump was…was a tree, in real life. That crazy tree we saw in the woods! Martin!"

"Annabelle!" he echoed, clearly lost.

"I went camping with Serena this summer, and we buried some mice under this huge sprawly tree that had all these colored bottles tied to the branches!"

Martin stared at me as if a second head had just sprouted from my shoulders. "Why were you burying mice?"

"Not important! What's important is the tree. Martin, the tree! My mind has been going back to that spot. And now I know! I just…" I sputtered out like a sparkler, the cheap kind. "I just don't know why."

Martin took out his phone. "A tree with bottles tied to it, right?" he asked.

I nodded. He typed.

"Okay. Bottle tree. It says here that a bottle tree is an old folk tradition. It's supposed to protect against evil spirits. The empty glass bottles would capture spirits at night. Then you'd cork the bottles and toss them into the river."

"Evil spirits," I said. "Do you think that includes evil dreams?"

When Will told me to make an "unconscious effort" to figure out what I needed to do, maybe he wasn't just blowing smoke. Maybe this is what he meant. My unconscious had tried to show me the tree by taking me back to that place. But in the dream, the tree wasn't a tree; it was a stump. A stump where the little girl sat. Like she had tried to hide it, to cut it down.

But she hadn't cut it down. I had found it.

"Okay," I said. "The tree is up on Black Beak, where Serena is camping this weekend. We have to get the nightmare to those woods."

Martin nodded. "She'll be at the dance, like you said. It's a perfect place for a nightmare. They feed off angst, drama. All that high emotion in one spot, it's like a dream come true for her."

"Ironic." I snorted. *So maybe I did snort.*

"So we find her at the dance and we lure her to the tree."

"With what?" I asked.

"With you."

Oh. *Oh.* Right. It was *me* the girl wanted. For whatever reason.

No more hiding in my room. Like she couldn't find me there anyway. Time to put my big-girl pants on—or my big pink dress on, whichever came first—and do what needed to be done.

Chapter 31

"I'll handle the townies," Martin said. We were divvying up tasks, dreams and dreamers, to find out if the girl had been stalking anyone else. "Jared Wales, Esther Finch, Mitch Grogan, Charlene Muncy. But I'd like you to cover—"

"Jared Wales, the lawyer? He's a dream?" He represented my mom in the divorce, and I'd always suspected he had a mini-crush on her, which was weird since he was much younger than she was.

"No," Martin said. "He's a dreamer. He dreamed Esther Finch."

"The lemon-drop lady in the antiques store? You're kidding."

"To each his own," Martin philosophized.

"What about Mitch Grogan; isn't that Trina Myers's stepdad?"

"Steph says she's pretty sure Trina brought him here. I'll get her to take care of that."

"Okay," I said. "And Mrs. Muncy?"

"She dreamed Coach."

Geez. Mrs. Muncy had been busy. A football coach. A fireman. I wondered when she'd get around to the stable boy. Poor Mr. Muncy with his fast-food gut didn't stand a chance.

MARY CROCKETT AND MADELYN ROSENBERG

"I'll leave you Chilton High," Martin went on. "I talked to Coach and Paolo already. And Stephanie, of course. Paolo said he'd track down Macy. But you've got the dreamers. The thing is, I think some of these people know what they did: dreamed. They get it. Other people think it was just a coincidence. So you'll have to be careful how you talk with them."

"Of course," I said. "Who's being difficult?"

"You know Daniel Kowalski, right?"

Eight months of hurt came hurtling through the space between us.

"Yes," I whispered.

"Sorry."

"It doesn't matter," I said. "Not anymore."

"It might," he began. "He dreamed Macy."

I sucked in a breath of cold air, remembering his arms around her in the hall and that apologetic look he gave me over the back of her shoulder. I remembered how red my face looked in the girls' bathroom mirror, tears that wouldn't stop, the feeling that my world was about to end.

My world hadn't ended, of course. But now, with the nightmare, it looked like my own private apocalypse was getting a second chance.

I raised my head and looked Martin in the eye. "I know how to talk to him," I said. "It's not a problem."

"Good," he said. "Serena is at the campground already, right? So maybe you can call her."

"Serena!" I said. "Who did she dream?"

"Paolo," he said. "Though he says she doesn't know it. She won't admit it, anyway."

It was funny, really, that Serena wouldn't claim her title. She was the biggest dreamer I knew. *Your brain just processed everything superfast and you thought you'd seen her before when you really hadn't.* She'd used that logic to explain Spice; she must have used it to explain Paolo, too.

"Oh, and there's Spice," I said.

"Spice?" Martin asked.

"Talon's dog. She dreamed him and then he showed up."

"Kind of like me?"

"Um, yeah, but smaller." *And stinkier*, I thought.

"Talon, Serena, Daniel, and one more."

"Billy Stubbs," I remembered.

"What about Billy Stubbs?"

"He dreamed Stephanie, right? But why can't she talk to him? Otherwise I'll just be like, 'Oh, hi, Billy, I know we never talk except to exchange mad insults, but I just wondered: Have you had any bad dreams lately?'"

"You don't have to talk to him," he said, and I could hear a tense smile creep into his voice.

"Oh, come on, Martin, if I can handle Daniel I can handle Billy."

"Billy Stubbs may love Stephanie Gonzales," Martin said. "But he didn't dream her."

"Then who did?"

"Will."

For a second, I didn't understand. Then it hit me. "*My* Will?"

"*Your* Will," he said, and it was as if his next words traveled to his lips through a throat full of broken glass. "Or Stephanie's Will, if you'd prefer."

"Says who?"

"Stephanie."

"Well, she lied," I said.

"Oh right," he said. "Sweet, pure Will isn't capable of—"

"You sure you want *me* to talk to him?" I interrupted.

"I can talk to him, if you'd prefer," Martin said. "I'd be glad to. I just thought you might have better luck. Pierce through that veil of sarcasm he substitutes for a sense of humor."

Will has an amazing sense of humor, I wanted to say, but I stopped myself. I knew how much Martin disliked me hanging around Will. If he wanted me to talk to Will, to be alone with him, he had to believe Stephanie was telling the truth. And if she was— oh, but that was impossible. This was Will we were talking about. If he dreamed about anyone it would have been someone like that Japanese exchange student, not Stephanie.

"Fine," I said. "I'll talk to him, if it makes you happy. Talon, Daniel, and Will."

Chapter 32

I'd already planned to go to Talon's house that morning so we could paint our toenails. Talon said as long as we were both going to homecoming we might as well go through the motions. Teenage rites of passage and all that.

Before I went in, I tried calling Serena. No answer, so I left a voice message and then a text: You ok? Call me. Really important!

"Did you decide for sure which dress you're wearing?" Talon asked when she met me at the door. She pulled me to her room and plopped down on her bed, where a half a dozen bottles of nail polish nested on her pillow. "I got pink and blue just in case."

I looked at her.

"What?" she said. "I borrowed them from my mom. Except the black," she added. "I bought the black at CVS. And this white nail marker, so I could do a skull and crossbones on my big toe. Pretty, right? And check out the shoes." She held up a pair of black stilettos with spiked silver heels. "These could be considered concealed weapons in most states."

She unscrewed the cap on the blue polish and handed it to me, but I just stood there so she put it on her bedside table.

"Hey. Did someone die? What?"

"I'm wearing the pink dress," I said.

"I knew it must be awful."

"No," I said. "Well it is, but there's something else." I took a deep breath and started. "This is going to sound crazy…" It tumbled out faster than I'd intended: Martin, the dreamworld, the others, her dog, the whole thing. And it *did* sound crazy, but Talon, true to character, hardly blinked.

"Martin," she said. "I knew it. And Spice, that makes sense. Of course. She would have figured out how to get away. I always knew she was smart."

She shook her head when I got to the part about Paolo and Serena. I skipped the part about Will. I hadn't confirmed it yet, had I?

When I finished talking her eyes were wide, her cheeks flushed.

"Vapor," she said. "Stephanie Gonzales. Spice. Martin. Paolo. Even *Mrs. Finch*. They were vapor until we dreamed them. Gives one a certain feeling of power, no?"

"Vapor," I echoed. I wasn't interested in the science of it. And I didn't feel powerful, though I was trying to.

Talon shook the bottle of black, uncapped it, and started painting her toes. She was getting paint all around the nails, and even when she tried to scrape the extra away with her fingernail, the toes looked splotchy and bruised.

"You know what this is like?" she said, looking up. "It's like *Frankenstein!*"

I eyed her feet sympathetically.

"Not my toes, you idiot. The Vapors! We created them," she said. "Put together a few stitched-up body parts and a spark plug or two, and bam! You're somebody's daddy."

"They're not monsters," I said. I still hadn't gotten very far in *Frankenstein*, but I didn't think a half-dead brute with bolts in his neck quite captured the essence of Martin or Paolo or Spice. Stephanie Gonzales maybe. The nightmare, definitely.

"And we're not their daddy," I added. "It's not like we're responsible for them."

Talon finished her pinky. The black blobs on her feet were like some kind of Rorschach test: Bat? Butterfly? Oil spill?

"But we are!" Talon dipped her brush in the polish and started on her left foot. "We brought them here. Of course we're responsible for what happens to them."

What was it Martin had said? *Like it or not, we're connected.* I guess that means all of us. The dreamers. The dreams. And the nightmare.

"The thing is…" I said softly. "The thing is, there's a girl, a nightmare. She tried to kill me."

"But just in your dream, right?"

"Martin was just in my dream, too."

Talon looked calm, but I saw the brush tremble in her hands.

"Listen," I said. "Have you had any dreams lately? You know, bad dreams? It's important."

"I don't remember any," she said. "And if they're bad, I usually remember."

"Yeah," I said. "You would. Believe me. How about any dreams with a little girl?"

"We could check my dream journal." With two toes still bare, she recapped the polish, reached under her bed, and pulled out a tattered five-subject notebook. The cover, which had once been red, was scrawled with band names and doodles in every direction.

"Dude, how long have you kept that thing?"

She pointed to the middle of the cover, where a black Sharpie heart encircled the words *Vic Vomit & the Esophagi*.

"Guh! That was like, what, seventh grade?"

"Eighth," Talon corrected. "Here's last night," she said. "We can go back from there."

In purple ink, a line had been drawn down the middle of the sheet. "What's that for?" I asked.

"The Doctor told me to do it that way. I write the left side before I go to sleep. It's supposed to be real life, just a regular journal, whatever I'm thinking, what's bugging me, or even a list of the stuff I did. Then I write the other side in the morning. That's the dream."

Talon's left was blank except for a few scrawled lines:

> *There's a place I don't go anymore,*
> *that place with the yellow door,*
> *and behind are all the questions in my mind*

and beneath is a blue wooden floor.
And you're there—
hair on fire, eyes calling me liar
—you're waiting for me there…

"You write poetry, Tal?"

She tapped the lines. "No, it's lyrics. Wendy Kletter. From that song 'Addiction.' The yellow door is supposed to be a pill."

"Oh." It sounded to me like it was supposed to be a door that was yellow, but I guess I never really got poetry. I shrugged and looked at the right half of the page.

going down steps think i'm supposed to be changing the lightbulb
  but don't have any lightbulbs
spice cuts under my legs and i'm going to trip
she's blue-brown like always
i end up on the sand there's sunlight
a pale blue blanket
these crabs that are supposed to talk
everyone's talking about how they talk

I scanned the rest of the page: more crabs, a tiki torch, a guy with a guppy tattoo, two flippers in the sand.

"This wasn't scary, right?" I asked. I didn't see anything even vaguely threatening. Maybe the guy with the tattoo? But come on, a guppy?

She shook her head and flipped back a page.

Friday had a really big bra and a picnic with weasels. Thursday, a man who lived in the sewer. We kept flipping back, but I didn't find anything scary, except for maybe Talon's lack of punctuation. On Tuesday, she dreamed about teacups on the courthouse lawn. Just above it, on Monday, the dream-side was blank, but on the left were two words: *Will* and *homecoming*.

"That's probably enough," I said. "No offense, Talon, but you're seriously weird."

"Thanks." She smiled smugly and started to tuck the book back under her bed.

"Hey." I reached out to stop her hand. "I just remembered: You said that dream about your dog was in here, right? Can I see it?"

"Sometimes I think all my dreams are about Spice," she said, pulling the notebook back onto her lap. "The Doctor says I have stunted energy. She says my subconscious obsession with Spice has something to do with my green chakra, soul/heart consciousness or something." She plucked the waistline of her emerald T-shirt and grinned. "Which is clearly why I look so great in green."

She was right—both about green, which she did look good in, and about Spice. On every page of the last week, Spice had been somewhere, digging up teacups, eating a chunk of cheese—not the main player, but there.

Talon flipped through the notebook again, this time from the front; after a minute of scanning, she handed the open book to me. "This is it."

at the mall food court will—me—annabelle
there's this prissy chick who's all ladidadida lookatme
& some old dude & this crazy little dog &
that library guy with the chin music
…i'm pretty sure annabelle has been checking out
more than books lately (like his butt!)
—in real life, I mean
in the dream we're all just hanging…
i'm like, <u>where's the glue?</u> has anybody seen the <u>glue?</u>
the old dude gives the dog a french fry or something
the dog is choking
the old guy yells
spice spice
that's the dog's name
annabelle runs over & grabs the dog from him
she opens the dog's mouth
and pulls out a bone

"It's official: I now know way too much about you," I said.

Talon shrugged. "I'm an open book." She took the journal from me and pushed the blue polish into my hands.

"In memory of the perfect dress," she said.

Chapter 33

I decided to talk to Daniel next. Talon. Daniel. Will. Sandwich the worst of it in the middle, like burying pimento cheese between two giant slices of bread.

He was no longer programmed into my cell phone. I had deleted him at the end of a small ceremony in which I had burned the notes he'd written me and given away the necklace he'd gotten me for my birthday. It was a gold necklace (though not real gold) and a sand dollar dangled at the end of it, though it wasn't like the beach or sand dollars had ever figured prominently in our relationship. I found out his sister had picked it out, at Belk, which at the time I thought was kind of sweet. Really, it was kind of lazy. Or kind of Daniel.

Deleting his number didn't mean I'd forgotten it, though. I didn't know many phone numbers by heart, what with cell phones making it unnecessary. But I knew his.

"Annabelle," he said when his picked up. Which meant he hadn't bothered to delete me. "What's up?"

"Hi, Daniel," I said. His name felt strange on my tongue. Cold, like licking an ice cube. "I wondered if we could talk."

"We're talking now, right?" No anger. But then, he was the one who had dumped *me*.

"In person," I said. "It'll only take a few minutes."

"I don't know. I'm kind of busy."

"Ten minutes," I said. "Can you give me just ten minutes?" I tried to keep my voice controlled. In my head I was thinking: *You can't give me ten minutes after everything I gave you?*

When he responded his voice was breezy and arrogant, but there was something soft there, too. Or maybe I just imagined it. "You know where I live," he said.

Daniel's house was about two miles from mine. It was a long walk, a not-so-bad bike ride, and a really easy drive. I borrowed my mom's car and drove.

When I got there, Daniel's red pickup, which rivaled my car for time in the shop, was in the driveway.

I thought maybe he'd wait for me outside, but he was nowhere to be seen. I knocked on the front door. His mother answered.

"Annabelle," she said. Her smile was like warm bread. "How are you? Daniel didn't tell me you were stopping by."

I wanted to explain to her that it was business, that she didn't need to smile like that, that I wasn't really friends with her son. Instead I just smiled back.

"He's in his room. You can go on up if you'd like."

Part of me wanted to. I was curious to see how it had changed in our months apart. I wondered if the things I had given him—a rock from the Roanoke River that looked like a little bird, a bottle of cologne, because I was playing at being a grown-up—were still on his dresser. I wondered if he had the same sports sheets on his bed.

"That's okay," I said. "I'm good down here. Could you ask him to come out, please?"

"Of course," she said. This time when she smiled, it was the kind of smile a receptionist gives you at the doctor's office, when she tells you the doctor will be with you in a moment and really means half an hour.

But a minute later, Daniel's feet came thundering down the stairs. He came out on the porch, letting the front door slam behind him.

"Hey," he said.

I could have been anybody.

"I—"

He smiled, and I looked away. I suppose I didn't hate Daniel so much as I hated myself, the way I'd acted when I'd been with him. And even more, the way I'd acted when he dumped me. But somehow, it all amounted to the same thing. I steadied myself by thinking positive thoughts—a trick I'd read about in a magazine and tried out after the breakup to keep from crying in public places.

I am a cool person. I have friends. My mother loves me.

It didn't work then and it wasn't working now. I walked over to his truck and leaned against it.

Daniel followed me. "So what's up?"

All I had to do was find out this one piece of information and I could be out of there.

"Let me rephrase that," Daniel said, studying my face. "What's wrong?"

I wasn't going to tell him everything. There were things I didn't want him to know—like the fact that the first boyfriend I'd had since he dumped me was, to use Talon's word, "vapor." And true, Macy White had been vapor. But as far as I knew, the other girls he'd dated hadn't been.

I thought about lying. I thought about telling Daniel I needed to do a psychological survey for an independent project about dreams. But Will said my eyes always gave me away, and I'd forgotten my sunglasses.

"I'm collecting some information on dreams," I began, which was true. "Bad dreams. I need to know if you've had any."

He gave me a strange look. "You came here to talk to me about my dreams?"

"Yes."

"We haven't spoken in months and you want to talk about dreams," he said. "Why?"

"I'm collecting information," I repeated.

"For who?"

It wasn't the question I expected. I didn't answer.

"If you're looking for closure—" he began.

"This isn't about that," I said.

"I know it was rough for you. I'm sorry." Where had *that* come from? It was like I'd dropped a few coins in the slot and out came this tidy little apology.

"It's been *months*, Daniel. I'm over it. Could you please just answer the question?" My voice was tight, stretched. "Have you had any bad dreams these last few nights?"

I looked directly at him, and his eyes searched mine.

"One," he said, and looked away. "A few nights ago."

"Could you—could you tell me about it?"

"You don't want to know."

"I *need* to know," I said.

"What's going on?"

"Nothing," I said.

"It's not nothing," he said. "It's too much of a coincidence to be nothing."

"What did you dream?"

"I dreamed someone died," he said.

"Who?"

He looked guilty, the way he'd looked when I told him that Talon had seen him with Macy White behind the band room.

"You," he said.

"*I died?*" I forced my voice into a little box—and I put that box into yet another little box somewhere in the back of my throat. But even as I tried to sound calm, the rapid thrum of my pulse pounded against my neck, like something trying to get out.

"I told you it was too much of a coincidence," he said. "I mean

I hadn't dreamed about—It's been awhile and suddenly I was dreaming about you dying."

"Was there a girl in the dream?"

"Seriously? What's going on, Annabelle? A *girl*?"

"Not like *that*. A little girl. Did you see a little girl?"

"I didn't see anything really. I just knew," he said, and it was the first time I remembered him looking afraid.

"I was running. It got dark. I tripped over something. When I tried to get up, I couldn't. But I saw something in the distance. Like the beam of a flashlight. And I knew you were...gone. Then I woke up. That's it."

"Nothing else?"

"Nothing," he said.

"Okay." I nodded, but instead of leaving I took a breath. "So," I asked casually, "you going to be at homecoming?"

"Yeah, sure," he said. "Are you?"

"Yeah," I said. "Yeah. I guess I should probably go get ready."

"It's only eleven thirty," he said.

"I'm a girl."

"You don't have to remind me." He gave me a smile, the kind that was just for me, and I remembered why I liked him once. And also why I didn't anymore.

"I'll see you," I said.

"You're not going to tell me what this is all about?" He put his arms on either side of me, caging me in. "Something's up, Annabelle, I know you."

"You used to."

"Are you going to tell me? Or not?"

"Not," I said, slipping under his arm. "Not yet, anyway. I'll tell you later. If I have to. And hopefully I won't have to."

"Thanks for stringing me along," he said.

"Yeah, well. It's your turn," I told him. I got back in my mom's car. "I'll see you later. Be…" I wasn't sure what to say? Be good? Be careful?

"Be what?"

"Just be," I said, sounding both cryptic and like a flower child from the 1960s. I slammed the door, put the car into gear, and drove.

Chapter 34

When I tracked him down, Will was driving a bucket of balls at All Starz, Chilton's finest (and only) mini-golf/driving range/batting cage/bowling alley/arcade establishment.

"Hey you," I talked to his back. "I didn't think you played golf."

He dropped another ball on the tee. "This isn't golf," he said without turning around. "It's anger management." He swung back and whacked the ball, hard. It flew high and long, just passing the 220-yard mark.

"Why do you need anger management?" Most of the time Will was the mellowest guy I knew. Of course today the back of his T-shirt read "WAR IS NOT THE ANSWER. Unless the question is 'What is raw spelled backward?'"

His T-shirts were kind of like mood rings. And even though his moods were generally in the meh range, there were slight fluctuations: giddy meh ("Free Shrugs!"); grumpy meh ("Three Things I Hate: T-shirts, Irony, Lists"); annoyed meh ("Dear Math, I'm not your therapist. Solve your own problems."); annoying meh ("It's

Tuesday!" which he only wore on Wednesdays). And the War T-shirt? Well, maybe I should have expected a little more edge from the offset.

He whacked another ball—230 yards. "I didn't think I'd see you today," he said.

"You haven't seen me yet," I said. "Check out the toes."

He turned and I wriggled the blue toenails in my flip-flopped feet—a little cold given the weather, but still.

"You came here to show me your toes?"

"No, I came here," I started. I came here to what? To tell you that my new boyfriend is a dream? And so is your best friend (besides me, of course). Oh, and I'm pretty sure *you* dreamed my worst enemy, and there's a possibility that all of us are doomed. How does one say that exactly?

"I came here to beat your ass in mini-golf," I said.

He grinned this time. "Get a club and help me finish off this bucket, and then we'll see."

I didn't say anything on the first hole. I gave myself a little time just to enjoy the sunlight, the vibrant green turf and the elaborately tacky statuary of the various Greco-Roman gods that adorned the golf course.

But as we approached the fifth hole (Aphrodite, one arm outstretched in a graceful arc, the other cupping an almost bare breast), I bit the bullet.

"You know she kind of looks like Stephanie," I began, poking my club at the statue.

"Stephanie?" As if he'd never heard of the girl.

"*Gonzales.*" I watched his face carefully, looking for, I don't know, a flicker of guilt or something.

Will putted and shrugged. "Yeah, maybe. Around the pits."

"So…" I trailed off.

"So?" he echoed.

"So, what do you think of her?"

"She must get pretty cold come February," he said.

"Not *her*. Stephanie. What do you think of Stephanie?"

"I don't."

"Aren't you…Don't you sometimes?"

His eyes narrowed. "What are you talking about?"

"You know, I'd forgotten this, but when she transferred at the start of our sophomore year, you hung out with her some, right?"

"She was new. I helped her find her classrooms."

"But didn't we see you guys at the mall?" I'd just started dating Daniel then, and was so hyped up on my own hormones that I'd hardly thought twice about Will and "the new girl." But now I was thinking about it three times. Four.

"Maybe. What are you getting at?"

"Nothing."

He looked doubtfully at me over his shoulder and knocked the ball. It banked off the far rim of the green and ricocheted toward the hole, where it rolled to a stop just two inches short.

"Good shot," I said as he tapped the ball in.

We walked to the next hole, a loop-the-loop guarded by a statue of Hermes on one winged foot. The messenger god. Or maybe the god of florists.

"Listen, will you tell me something?" I asked Will.

"Something."

"No, I'm serious. Will you not ask any questions, but just answer mine? It's important." I knew that asking him not to ask questions was sort of like asking him not to breathe.

"I could try," he said. "Especially if it means I finally get to find out what is going on with you today."

"Good." I sat down on a little concrete bench beside a bush and he sat beside me, close enough that I could feel the heat of his body, a soft steam.

I started. "I want to know—and I know this sounds weird, but no questions—I want to know if you've had any dreams lately."

Will was silent for a moment; then he said, his voice reluctant, tense, "Everybody dreams."

"Dreams that you remember?"

He nodded.

"And have any of them been, you know, scary?" My voice dropped to a whisper. "Have you had any nightmares?"

He closed his eyes for a half-second, and when he opened them, he looked relieved. "No."

"You're sure?"

"I don't remember any nightmares," he said.

Living with my dad had taught me that sometimes you could tell more from what a person *wasn't* saying than from what he *was* saying. I got the feeling Will wasn't saying some-thing now.

"So what *did* you dream?"

I could tell he wanted to ask me what was going on—deflect my question with another question. But he didn't. "I don't think it's a good idea for me to answer that."

"Why not?"

"Tell me why you're asking," he said.

"I said no questions."

"That's not a question. It's a request." He kept his eyes on the patch of scrubby ground at our feet.

I put my fingers on his jaw and turned his face toward me. "It's important, Will. That's why."

"Okay." He took a deep breath. "I guess maybe I had a..." he looked down at the ground again, "just regular, you know, guy dream."

"Guy dream?" I asked, clueless. "You dreamed about guys?"

He shook his head, "God, Annabelle, *no*. I mean...I can't believe we're talking about this. I mean the kind of dreams guys have."

It took a second before it hit me. "Oh!" I said, too loudly. "You mean THOSE dreams."

"Yeah, well."

"Who about?" I shouldn't have asked, but I wanted to know.

"Why the hell are you asking all this?"

"Were they about Stephanie?"

"Stop it, Annabelle."

"Talon?"

"Will you stop?"

"Maybe some dream girl who doesn't even exist?" Doesn't exist *yet*, I thought.

Will stood and picked up his club. "Look, do you want to finish this game or what?"

"You're such a freaking *guy*!" I said, standing up, too, and shoving him a little.

He caught my wrists and held them where they were, pressed against his chest. "You noticed."

My throat went dry. I could feel the steady throb of his heart under my right palm.

"Well, yeah." And then it hit me, that voice on the roof under the amazing starlit sky...the voice like home...it had been Will's. He was the one on that blanket, his legs entwined with some girl's. The dream I'd slipped into had been Will's.

I pulled my hands away from his chest, but not before I had felt something else—something inside my own rib cage—clench and then clench again and then, finally, release.

"Okay," I said. "I'll play, but first, one more question—and this one you have to answer." I looked up into his eyes. "Last year, did you or did you not dream up Stephanie Gonzales?"

He didn't answer at first. He just looked back at me. I could see the cogs in his mind fit it all into place. "I knew it," he said finally. "He's one of them, too."

Chapter 35

Part of me was glad that Will knew about Martin—knew and believed, so I didn't have to suffer through one of those *Yes-I-sound-crazy-but-before-you-call-for-a-straitjacket-just-hear-me-out* moments. The other part of me was pissed as hell that he'd had the same secret, only he hadn't shared it. What was he afraid of? That I wouldn't believe him?

Okay, granted, I hadn't believed Martin when he'd told me that Will had dreamed up Stephanie, and that was after I'd already knew such things were possible. Still.

"How come you never told me?" I asked.

"Putt."

I hit the ball without looking at it.

"How come?"

A birthday party of six-year-olds had come onto the course and suddenly a dozen kids were running from hole to hole. "Look! It loops!" "You can't be purple! I'm purple!" And (pointing at the statue of Poseidon), "Why isn't that dude wearing clothes?"

I scanned the crowd. No blond-haired, white-eyed girl in a dress. There were no nightmares in mini-golf. At least not today.

Will went over to the hole, pulled his ball out of the cup, and pocketed it. He put his club over his shoulder and walked off the course to a little gazebo with a picnic table. I grabbed my ball and followed.

"There wasn't much to tell," he said. "I didn't know what was going on at first and when I tried to talk to Stephanie about it, she denied everything. There wasn't anything scientific about it. I must have done a million Internet searches. Psychic dreams and brain waves and hypnosis and mind control. Nothing made sense except maybe déjà vu. And Stephanie acted like I was nuts whenever I tried to bring it up. I thought maybe I *was* nuts. Besides, there are some things you just don't want to talk about. To think I unleashed Stephanie Gonzales on the world? It's nothing to be proud of."

"I thought you could tell me anything."

"You were busy with Daniel." He turned and watched one of the six-year-olds turn his putter into a bazooka. Pow-pow-pow-pow-pow. "I think he got us," Will said, reaching for his putter again.

"Don't shoot back," I told him, and he dropped it. "Macy White is one, too. Did you know?" I thought I'd try her before I broke the news about Paolo.

He waited a second, thinking. "I do now."

"So why couldn't you tell me about Stephanie afterward? You know, when Daniel dumped me for his dream?" There. I'd said it.

"A. I didn't know Macy was a dream, and B. I couldn't tell you anything after that. I tried."

"Not hard enough," I said, though I knew I was being unfair. After Daniel dumped me, I was a black hole of self-pity. Whatever came near just got sucked in and converted into my own toxic matter. Will could have said, "By the way, Stephanie Gonzales? I created her, you know," and all I would have thought was, "Life sucks, nobody loves me."

"So Paolo," I began.

"I know," he said.

"You *do*? How long have you known?"

"Day one," Will said. "Though I didn't really know for sure. I just knew I got along with him better than anyone else in this town, present company excepted. That's not exactly the reality I was used to, was it? I asked a lot of questions and some of his answers were from left field. It wasn't too hard to figure out, especially after Stephanie. But I needed—I needed a friend. I wasn't about to look a gift horse in the mouth." He rolled his green golf ball down a ridge in the picnic table and watched it plop to the ground. "That phrase dates back to the fifteen hundreds, by the way."

"Thanks for the history lesson."

"Who dreamed him? You seem to have all of the inside information."

"Serena." I still hadn't been able to reach her.

"Now that I didn't predict. Anyone else we know on your dream list? Ernshaw? Akiko?"

"Masterson," I said.

"That sounds about right." He looked at me sideways. "What if I told you I was one of them?"

"I've known you forever."

"I'm just saying *what if*," he said.

"You're not even funny, Will." My eyes searched his eyes, which were wide open. My voice turned pleading. "You're not…"

There was enough not right with my world. I didn't need that.

He dropped the banter then. "What's going on, Annabelle?"

"You don't want to know," I said.

"You know that's not true." He stood up and balanced the putter on his palm, and waited.

I took a breath and spilled. "That nightmare I told you about? There's a girl in it. It's like she's been following me. Martin thinks she wants to become real, the way dreams become real. She might already be. He thinks," I took a deep breath, "he thinks she's going to come for me." It sounded like a line from a movie, the kind I was never going to watch again.

The putter fell to the ground and Will left it there.

He took a step toward me. His hazel eyes looked green now, and intense. "Tell me you're joking."

"Do I look like I'm joking?"

He cupped my face with his hand. "You look, you look…" and his words fell away. He lowered his head just a bit. We were so close, there was hardly a breath between us. Standing there, I could ignore the birthday party kids. I could ignore the chill that, in the shade, had turned my bare toes to cubes of ice. I could even ignore the incomprehensible urge I felt just then to stretch myself up on those toes a tiny bit more so that I could touch his lips, just to see what they felt like against mine.

But I couldn't ignore what was coming.

Chapter 36

Will left me for a total of seventeen minutes, which was all the time it took him to get ready for homecoming. Then he followed me to my house so I could change. When I came downstairs, he was sitting on the floor, eating a peanut butter sandwich and getting rug lint all over his pants while he played Mega-Minotaur with Nick.

"Don't you have to pick up Talon?" I asked.

"She's meeting us here."

"Did you get her a corsage?" I said. "Because if you didn't you still have time."

"On the table." It was next to his camera. An orchid.

Martin got to my house before Talon did.

"Are you okay?" he asked, leaning down to kiss my cheek.

I gave him a watery smile.

"You look like a dream."

I wasn't sure about his word choice, but I did a little twirl in my frothy pink dress.

"If you dream about cupcakes," Will muttered in a low enough voice that I probably shouldn't have been able to hear it. I looked over, hurt, until I saw his eyes. And then I wanted to laugh, too.

"And Will," Martin said in a flat voice. "You're here."

"Yep," Will said. "I suppose you want me to turn her over to you now?"

"Please," Martin said. He'd somehow found a tie that perfectly matched his eyes and I wondered how he did that—acquired an entire, eye-matching wardrobe.

"Hey," I lowered my voice so Nick wouldn't hear. "You find anything out in town?"

"Not much. The only one who really remembers her is Esther Finch, but she couldn't tell me anything we don't already know. Powerful. Creepy. Acts helpless but isn't. At least they're all on the lookout; they'll call if they see her."

The door opened again and Talon made her grand entrance. She was wearing her black dress. Her dark hair was slicked down and she had a little spit curl on either side of her face. She looked amazing. Not at all like a cupcake.

"Wow," Will said, and I felt a stab of, not jealousy, but something.

"Wow yourself," she said.

She had a big black purse slung over her arm. It wiggled, and a wet nose poked out of the top of it.

"Spice?" I said.

"You don't think I'm going to leave her alone, do you?" Talon looked at Martin and Will in a way that said we all knew what was going on now. "Besides, maybe Spice can help sniff out your psycho nightmare girl."

I wasn't so sure about Spice's hunting abilities, but all I said was: "I don't think they'll let a dog into the dance."

"Duh," she said. "That's why I have the purse."

Will laughed, and picked up his camera, his hand almost steady. "Say bones!"

Spice barked when the flash went off.

Mom came in from the kitchen. "Oh, pictures!" She ran upstairs and came back with her own camera. Then she lined us up: first all four of us; then Martin and me; then Talon and Will; then Talon and me; then Nick and me; and then Martin, Will, and for some reason Nick, again. Spice, of course, was in all the pictures.

With everyone there, my mom looked almost happy, or at least like she was determined to be happy. But she had dark circles under her eyes that matched mine and she was still wearing the sweats she'd slept in. When Will picked up his camera and insisted on getting a shot of me and her together, she plucked Spice up with one hand, gripped me around the waist with the other, and gave an enthusiastic grin. It was pretty convincing, but it didn't fool me. Apparently it didn't fool Will, either.

He drew me aside a minute later when Mom was taking a portrait of Talon and Spice. "Your mom doesn't know, does she?" he whispered.

I shook my head. "She's still upset about my dad, I think."

"Oh, good," he said, and then quickly added. "Not *good*. But better than her worrying about the other stuff."

"Do you think she'd let me out of this house if she had any idea about the other stuff?"

"Good point. Are you sure you need to go to this thing at all? I'd stay here with you."

"Martin says—"

"Martin can say what he wants. I want you safe."

"There is no safe for me, Will. Not while she's around. She'll be at homecoming, I'm pretty sure of it. I need to be there, too."

"But—"

Martin came up behind us and touched me on the shoulder. "We'd better get going."

My mother took one more picture of the entire group and I hoped it wasn't the last picture she'd ever take of me. The one they'd use for my Missing poster. But the fact that I could be forever known as the girl in the fluffy pink dress was the least of my worries. I hugged her good-bye, and she looked pleased. "I love you, Mom," I whispered. Then I walked over to Nick.

"You're not going to hug me, are you?" he asked.

"Of course not." I leaned over and gave him a quick peck.

"Hey!" he said, wiping his cheek.

"Later," I said.

"Later, Fluke Fish," Will called to Nick.

"Nematode," Nick called.

Martin held the door open and the rest of us walked through it:

me, then Talon, and then Will. Martin was a gentleman; he didn't let it slam on Will's foot.

"So," Talon asked, shoving her cell phone in her purse, "do we take one car or two?"

"One," Will said, at the same time Martin said, "Two."

"We may need to split up," Martin said reasonably. I hoped he meant "split up" as in divide and conquer and not "split up" as in dump me.

"Right, chief," Will said. And it felt like that—like we were playing a game of cops and robbers. The dream police. No, not dream: nightmare.

Will held the car door open for Talon, and she and Spice slid into the passenger side. Talon gave me the thumbs-up sign and I gave her one back, even though I didn't mean it.

A few weeks ago, I'd actually sort of wanted to go to home-coming, and then when Martin asked me I'd really wanted to go. Only now I wasn't sure if I was going to be dancing with my boyfriend or with a milk-eyed nightmare. And I didn't know if, after the DJ played the last tune, I'd make it home.

Chapter 37

The bleachers had been pushed back, so the gym seemed larger than usual. Even so, it was packed with bodies. Tables had been set out on one side of the room, with bits of ivy around candles that weren't lit because the powers-that-be didn't trust a bunch of high school kids around fire, even if it was the kind of fire that was kept in bowls. The basketball goals had been pushed up in the air, and the posts were wrapped with ivy, too, as if we wouldn't know they were still posts.

Everyone was there.

Billy with Stephanie, who was not wearing a frothy pink dress, but something green and venomous. Macy White, in cobalt blue. Daniel, grinding with Tami Newton, who could have been Stephanie Gonzales on a bad hair day—if Stephanie ever *had* bad hair days. Paolo, by himself and sporting a camera, like Will's. And Coach Masterson, talking to Ernshaw with the chaperones, which I didn't think was just a coincidence. There was confetti on the floor, like in my dream. But I didn't see the girl.

We had a plan. Not a great plan, but still. Find the girl. Tail her, corner her, but *not alone*. Martin had stressed that part. "Nightmares aren't like us. They can *do* things. She'll be stronger than any one of us alone, but maybe together…" he'd let the thought finish itself. Then we all—Martin, Paolo, Will, Talon, Stephanie, Macy, and I—were going to "contain her" (this is the part that got a bit hazy for me, though Martin had brought ropes) and "transport her" to the tree. ("Like how, in the trunk of Paolo's Impala?" I'd asked, but hadn't gotten an answer.)

I wasn't sure why Stephanie and Macy were willing to risk it. They weren't exactly good Samaritans, despite their membership in Devils Are Angels. When I asked Martin, he said, "They know better than anyone what Chilton could become if nightmares start creeping in. *Nightmares*, Annabelle. They're not nice." But he made "not nice" sound like it burned his throat. "There's this thing they chant, *kill the dream, kill the dreamer; kill the dreamer, kill the dream*." The words clicked in my brain. Familiar, inevitable.

"Well, when you put it that way."

I scanned the room, my eyes jumping every time I caught a snatch of white. Will took his camera and began shooting everything on one side of the gym. Paolo took the other. Talon clutched her purse tightly and occasionally whispered to it.

"Come on," Martin said. "We may as well dance."

"How romantic."

"Let me rephrase it then: my beautiful Annabelle, will you do me the honor of dancing with me?"

Scared or not, my heart flipped. "Of course."

He grabbed my waist and pulled me in. I wanted to put my head on his shoulder and block out everything except the sounds of Harmony Tyler, who was singing a song about slow dancing. I wanted to think, as I would have thought a week ago, how totally meta it was to be dancing to a song about dancing. I wanted to think about how my head felt against Martin's shoulder, and how I might like his sweatshirt better than his suit. But every time I started to think about something normal, I reminded myself that nothing was normal, least of all my dancing partner.

The song stopped and the next one started.

Maybe my dream was wrong. Maybe the girl wasn't at homecoming—or even in Chilton. Maybe she was still in my head.

I saw Will reach out for Talon's hand, and the two of them pressed together, with Spice between them, and Paolo beside them like a sentry. I saw Billy kiss Stephanie on the forehead, and for a moment, I imagined not hating her so much. Then the music stopped and Martin said, "I've got to talk to Steph. Do you mind?"

"Of course not," I said. But when the two of them started dancing and whispering, the hate feelings came back.

"Excuse me, Miss," said a voice behind me. Will, of course. "May I have this dance?"

"Thanks for rescuing me."

He held out his hand and I took it.

"Just seeing them over there makes me—"

"I don't want to talk, Annabelle," he said. "If that's okay?" He gave me a smile to show he wasn't mad or anything.

253

"Okay," I said. Will didn't want to talk? Will *always* wanted to talk. Or maybe he meant he didn't want to listen. To me. Talking about Martin. Or maybe he just wanted to dance. He'd proven himself a decent dancing partner at my cousin Heather's wedding last summer, which he'd been forced to attend when I'd beaten him at poker; he started betting favors after he'd run out of dimes. Just like then, he'd cleaned up nice, even in seventeen minutes. His hair was combed, his tie was straight, and he smelled like a mixture of soap and sea, so I felt like we were swaying together in the sand instead of on the planked floor of the high school gym.

I stole another look at Martin. He and Stephanie were deep in conversation, but he looked up at me and winked.

Where was the girl? I thought about asking Will to take me on a tango through the gym so we could cover more ground. But we stayed in one place as the song played on.

Spinning round in circles
Tried so hard to find
Another girl like you
Someone to read my mind
Hiked through Colorado
Spent a long night in Tibet
I was looking for the perfect love
I hadn't found her yet
'Cause it was you
It was always you

"Seriously," I said to Will, forgetting that I wasn't supposed to talk. "Could this song be any cheesier?"

"I like it."

"And mind reading. Do you think real people can read minds?" As in people who weren't Martin Zirkle.

"It's not a question of reading minds," Will said, resigning himself to conversation. "It's more about reading people, don't you think? You, for example, are a billboard."

"I think I've just been insulted," I said.

"All I'm saying is I don't have to read your mind. I just have to look at your face and I can get a pretty good idea of what's going on in there."

"Such as?" I asked.

"Such as the fact that while you're dancing with me, you're thinking about Martin over there talking with Stephanie." Will's camera hung around his neck, but he had shifted it to the side so it wasn't between us. Now it clunked me in the armpit. "You're jealous and you're dancing with me because you think it might make Martin jealous back. *Now* can we stop talking?"

"I'm not jealous," I blurted.

"Look, Annabelle. It's not rocket science."

"How can you stand there and judge me?"

"I'm not judging," he said. "I'm not standing; I'm dancing. I told you we shouldn't talk."

"I'm not dancing with you because—" I started, but I didn't know how to finish, so I just buried my head in his shoulder.

"It's okay. I don't mind making Martin jealous." His voice had that extra something it had had in it whenever we'd talked lately, like a little piece of flint that wouldn't catch.

We danced for a minute in silence, those insipid lyrics going on and on. And then Will stopped moving. He lifted the camera back to his eye and clicked. His left arm gripped me tighter as he let the camera fall.

"What?" I said. But this time, Will was the billboard. I followed his gaze, just in time to see the swish of a white dress and a wisp of yellow hair disappearing across the dance floor.

Chapter 38

I whipped around to where Stephanie and Martin had been dancing. Had they seen her, too? They must have; their little spot on the dance floor was empty.

Will took my wrist, and together we ran in the direction the girl had gone, squeezing past swaying, sequined bodies. We spotted Paolo with Coach Masterson near the table with punch and snacks. Will changed our course straight for them. "She's here," he said. "The girl." No introduction, no small talk.

Masterson put on that concerned face that adults sometimes get when they talk to confused little kids. "What girl, Will? You know there aren't any children—"

"I saw her, too," Paolo interrupted. And to Masterson, "He knows; it's cool."

"Did anyone else go out there?" I pointed to the hallway beyond the gym.

"Only about half the school," Masterson said, frowning. "You all have bladders the size of peanuts."

"What about Martin?"

"He blew past with Stephanie a minute ago."

"Which way did they head?" I asked.

Masterson gestured toward the end of the hallway, past the locker room, to the gray double doors that led outside. "I didn't see where they ended up, though."

"This is it, then. We need everyone, right?" I looked at Will. "Where's Talon?"

"She went to the bathroom before I came to dance with you," Will said. "Spice needed a drink."

"We'll get her on the way," I said.

Masterson started, "Maybe I should come—"

"No," Paolo barked, like he was the coach. "We stick to the plan. You cover the gym. Text me if anything comes up."

I hustled down the hall, Will and Paolo trailing behind, twin satellites.

"So she's here?" As Macy ran to catch up to us, she stumbled a bit, unsteady on her heels.

"She's here." My throat tightened, like someone was turning the tuning peg on a guitar string. *Sharp. Sharper. Sharpest.* I moved faster, my eyes focused straight ahead, so when a hand reached out from the side and held on to my arm, I gave a small gasp.

"Easy, Annabelle." It was Daniel. "Where's the fire?"

"I don't have time, Daniel," I said. "Macy, talk to him." After all, Daniel had brought her to Chilton. And he'd had that dream. Someone needed to tell him what was going on, that he could be in danger, too, but it didn't have to be me.

"Macy? What are you girls up to?" He seemed suspicious. Like this was the opening scene in *Attack of the Ex-Girlfriends*.

"Just talk to each other," I said. "Or Paolo. Or Masterson. Whoever." He was still holding on to my arm but I pulled it away.

"You look great, by the way," he said, but I kept on walking without even turning around to call him a liar. There was no sign of the girl in the hall. I slipped into the bathroom to grab Talon. Will and Paolo waited on the other side of the door. "You have ninety seconds," Will said.

A couple of senior girls were at the sinks, checking their mascara and talking about how they were going to rock somebody's world later at Pandapas Pond. I saw one of them give my dress the once-over and smirk. I ignored her and bent to look beneath the stalls. A pair of purple sandals and a pair of neon orange pumps. No sign of Talon's spiky silver heels. In fact, there was no indication Talon and Spice had been there at all…except, wait, in the corner beside the sinks, a small Tupperware bowl, half full of water.

"Talon?" No answer.

"Annabelle?" Will half-opened the door, and the mascara girls shrieked.

"She's not here." I went back out into the hallway. "But I found Spice's dish. I'm going to try her cell."

I dug around in the little clutch purse I'd borrowed from my mom. When I pulled out the phone, there was a new message.

"It's from Serena." Will and Paolo looked over my shoulder as I read.

Got your text. Coverage sucks. What's up?

I dialed her back but it went straight to voice mail again.

"Text her," Paolo said.

"I can't explain this in a TEXT." My voice bounced off the lockers in the hall.

"You don't have to explain it all," Will said. "Just find out where she is."

I typed quickly, distracted, hoping I was making sense. As I hit send, Will said, "Oh good. Company."

It was Macy, who was smiling a little, with Daniel, who was not.

"I guess you told him," I said.

"He doesn't like thinking that someone else is in control," Macy said. "Or you know, that a slew of new nightmares might show up in the cafeteria on Monday." At that moment, Macy seemed almost human, like someone I could be friends with.

"No Talon?" she asked.

I shook my head.

"Any sign of Steph? Martin?"

More head shaking as Billy Stubbs came down the hall and headed toward the bathroom.

"You're a girl," he said to Macy. "Go in there and see if Stephanie's inside."

"She isn't," I spoke up. "I was just in there. I think she's some-place with Martin."

Billy's face went from *huh?* to *I'll-rip-his-head-off* in two seconds.

"It's not what you think." I wondered how much Billy knew. Not much, by the looks of it. "I'm going to check outside—"

"If he lays one hand on her, I swear, I'll kick Zirkle's ass."

"He isn't making out with her, you Neanderthal." He'd better not be, anyway.

Billy looked at me like he'd never seen me before. And I guess it was entirely possible he hadn't. "Something's going on," he said.

Will did his sideways Will thing. "You noticed."

"Are we leaving?" Macy asked.

"We are," I said. "We have to get Talon. Maybe she just took Spice for a walk."

"And maybe the Phillies are going to win the series," Macy murmured.

"No way, they're already out of it," Daniel said, a reflex action.

I pushed open the side door to the school and paused. I was ready. I knew the plan. *Get her before she gets us.* My whole body seemed to vibrate as I scanned the darkness for that flash of white.

And here's the thing about being scared: When it's actually happening, and you're not just thinking about how it *might* happen, the fear does something strange. It's almost like it sets you free.

I don't mean it disappears. It's still there, crushing your lungs, tangling your stomach into knots. But you can see it for what it is. You can see how little it matters next to what needs to be done.

I knew they were out there—Talon and Martin. Even Stephanie. That gave me the courage I needed.

Sure, I knew the little girl was out there too. And I wasn't sure I could face her, but I had to try.

Ready or not, I had to put my game face on.

Ready or not, it was time for me to play.

Chapter 39

"We'll split up to cover more ground," I said. "Billy, Daniel, you can run. Hit the practice fields, the—"

"Who are we looking for, again?" Daniel asked.

"Talon Fischer, Stephanie Gonzales, Martin Zirkle," I said. "And a demented little girl in a white dress."

"I know what Macy said and all, but seriously, this is for real?"

It made me feel better to quote Martin. "It appears so."

Daniel nodded, his face uncharacteristically grim. "And Talon Fischer is—?" He tried to remember.

"My *friend*," I said, as if the emphasis would jar something loose in his brain. When it didn't, I added, "Lots of piercings. You thought she had a cute butt." A little something he had shared with me while we were dating. Will was right. Why *had* I gone out with that guy? At any rate, the mention of Talon's butt seemed to do the trick.

"What the hell are you people talking about?" asked Billy.

"Talon Fischer's butt," said Daniel.

"And a crazy girl who's trying to kill Annabelle," Paolo added.

"*All of us*," Macy piped in. "She won't stop with Annabelle. She's a—"

"Psychopathic nightmare," I finished, just so Billy was clear.

"Wait, I know what this is, this is one of your geek games, like Dungeons and Dragons or something?"

Paolo bristled until Will whispered, "You get to be Dungeon Master."

"Yeah," Paolo told Billy. "Stephanie and Martin are playing, too, and it's our job to find them before…"

"Before the other team," Macy concluded.

Daniel gave us a confused look. "So I know what to do if we find Stephanie and Martin and Talon," he said. "But what if we find *her*?"

Run, I thought. I swallowed hard.

"Tell her I'm looking for her," I said, hoping Martin showed up with his ropes in time. Were we seriously basing our plan on a dream and an entry in Wikipedia? "Yeah. Tell her that. Now go."

The rest of us paired off, dreamer and dream. "I'll go with Paolo," I told Will. "You and Macy check the tennis courts."

"But—"

"I'll take care of her," Paolo said, patting me on the head like a puppy. "Don't worry, Dude. I wore my gambeson."

Paolo's shoes were soundless as we walked around the building. Mine clopped. The more softly I walked, the louder they seemed to get.

"So I talked to Ernshaw," Paolo said, his voice quieter than my shoes. "He's tight with Masterson. You know?"

"I didn't." It suddenly dawned on me why Martin had once asked me if I knew anything about the coach's closet and if it was really big enough to live in.

"Ernshaw's a science genius and he still doesn't know what the hell we're supposed to do," Paolo said. "He started muttering, *mind over matter and matter over mind.* Does that mean anything to you?"

"Matter over mind?" I said. "Maybe Will would know. Or Martin." Where *was* Martin? I said a quick prayer that he hadn't turned back into vapor.

"You didn't hear from Serena again, did you?"

"In the last two minutes?" I said. "No."

"Right." He walked a few more steps. "How about now?"

"Paolo. You're hopeless," I said. And it occurred to me that he really was.

"I can't help it. I worry about her," he said. "The nightmares. They're not like us. They have powers you can't even dream of."

That was so *not* what I needed to hear.

We reached the area behind the band room. It was too dark to see much more than the rough-cut version of the universe, but I knew what was there: the rock where Talon had seen Macy kissing Daniel that time, and next to it a low, Japanese maple tree that would have been red had there been enough light to give it color. The leaves made a perfect dome and the inside was like a cave.

A low branch shook, too strong for just wind. Paolo and I froze—body, breath, heartbeat.

The branch trembled again. I waited for the blond hair, the white dress.

I cut my eyes over to Paolo's. He shook his head slightly.

My pulse throbbed in my neck. The night was inky, with just a sliver of moon still low in the eastern sky, but even its slim light was blocked by the flank of the school.

Game face, I reminded myself, and took a few steps toward the tree.

At the edge of the branches, I crouched down low, trying to peer through the leaves. Ever so gently I reached down and raised the bottom of a branch like a veil. A dim form, much too small to be a girl, moved under the maple branches. Then I felt something like damp hair press against my fingertips.

Jerking my hand away, I toppled into Paolo and knocked both of us onto the ground.

As I started to scramble to my feet, I felt a wetness rasping my cheek and smelled an unpleasant, but familiar, stink.

Nothing else in the world could smell quite like that combination of singed tar and coffee pee. Except maybe singed tar and coffee pee.

"Spice?"

In response, the little dog danced onto my chest and gave me a full-tongue kiss on my chin.

"Oh, oh." I sat up and held her in my arms, giving in to that sort of hysterical laughter that only comes when you've been scared out of your mind.

"What is it?" Paolo asked.

"Talon's dog!" I said. I rose to my feet, still holding the wiggly little animal in my arms. Talon had to be close. I started to call for her, when Paolo pointed to something in the grass, just outside the tree's canopy.

I pulled out my cell phone and let its light cast a dim glow toward the ground. It glinted off a spiky, black pump with a silver heel.

And just under the leafy fringe of the tree, a pedicured foot with skull and crossbones painted on the big toe.

Chapter 40

I wanted to scream. I wanted to run. But neither would help.

"Here." I shoved Spice into Paolo's arms and stooped over Talon.

I touched her bare shoulder. She was cold but she didn't feel dead.

"Is she breathing?" Paolo asked, the dog wriggling in his arms.

I lowered my ear. At first I could only hear my own heart pounding in my head, but then I heard hers, as steady as...as steady as Talon.

"She's knocked out. Or maybe she's—"

"Asleep." The way Paolo said it, being knocked out would have been better. "It's your nightmare. Get her up. Now."

I shook Talon, wishing Paolo hadn't called the girl *my* nightmare. Martin had said she wanted control—of everything, of everybody. But no one controlled Talon Fischer.

"TALON!" I shook harder. "Can you hear me?"

Her eyes rolled back in her head for a second like somebody possessed, but then they straightened and focused.

"Talon?" I said.

"You were expecting Snow White?"

I choked out a stale laugh. Talon was awake. She was here. She looked a little shaken, but she was still Talon.

I typed into my phone: "Found her behind the band room," and hit send.

Will reached us first, with Macy not far behind him.

"How is she?" he asked, panting. They must have run.

"I'm right here, you know," Talon said. "You could just ask me."

"Cheeky. That's a good sign." Will took off his suit jacket and wrapped it around Talon's shoulders. He tilted Talon's chin and looked into her eyes. "Really, you're okay?"

Billy had rounded the corner of the school with Daniel a few steps behind. "Where the hell is she?"

"Right here," I said.

"Where?" He'd caught up with us now and was looking around like he expected to see the ghost of Davy Crockett.

"Here!" I pointed to Talon.

"He's not talking about her," Macy said in a stage whisper, "He's talking about Stephanie."

"That's what the text said." Billy waved Daniel's phone around like exhibit A. "Found her.'"

"I guess she meant the other her," said Daniel.

Billy ground his shoe into the dirt and stared in the direction of the football field. "We're at a dance with like a million people and not one of you has seen Stephanie!"

"I saw her," Talon said quietly.

"Martin?" I asked.

She nodded.

"Where?" Billy grabbed Talon by the shoulders and shook her a little.

"Hands off," Will said in that protective way he usually saved for me. "She's not a football."

"It was all white," Talon said. "Everything. Like a coloring sheet that hadn't been colored in yet."

"What the hell is she talking about?" Billy asked.

"A dream, I think," I told him.

"A freaking dream?"

"One person's dream is another person's reality," Paolo said simply. It would have made a good T-shirt. Even I would have worn it.

"Sometimes it gets hard to tell the difference," Macy added.

"Sometimes there *is* no difference," Will said.

Billy looked at us like we'd just beamed down from Pluto. "What is wrong with you people?"

I turned back to Talon. "So what happened?"

"I saw Martin and Stephanie; they were running."

"This is bull," Billy said.

"It's possible Martin and Stephanie are still in the gym and we missed them," Will said in the kind, yet firm voice he generally reserved for his cousin, who was four. "Why don't you go back and check?"

"Maybe I will." Billy turned away from us. Then he froze.

"Found you!" called a little girl's voice. "Want to play again?" She was shrouded in darkness, but the moonlight caught her eyes, turning them iridescent, like opals. She came toward me, sizing me up. I was taller, but even though one of my hands could have easily fit around her slender arm, we both knew she was stronger.

She has powers you can't even dream of. That's what Paolo had said.

"I don't like games," I told her.

"Except football," she said, winding a lock of flaxy hair around her finger. "And poker."

"I don't like *your* games," I said.

Her laughter was bubbly, little-girl laughter that ended in a hiss. "I don't care if you like my games or not. You still have to play. Follow the leader. Catch me if you can!"

She began to skip, her arms out to the side, and I moved to follow, wondering, like Daniel had, what I'd do if I caught her, wondering if she was more dangerous in my head or out of it.

Bottle tree, I thought again. That was the plan my subconscious had dreamed up. My conscious wasn't helping, Martin and his rope were gone, and Will's encyclopedic mind hadn't come up with an ancient Mesopotamian way of getting rid of nightmares. There didn't seem to be another choice.

"How about I be the leader?" I said. Now I was glad Will had driven, since Martin hadn't left me his keys. "Why don't *you* follow *me*?"

"*I'm* the leader," the girl said. She looked like flesh but her voice had the quality of an echo. "Wherever you're going, I'll already be there."

She ran in the direction that she'd come from. I ran after her, but I wasn't surprised to find that when I turned the corner, she'd disappeared.

"Where'd she go?" Billy said.

I let out my breath. *Wherever you're going, I'll already be there.* "Black Beak Mountain, I hope."

Will looked at me, an assessing, I-hope-you-know-what-you're-doing look. "I assume that's where we're going, too."

"Why?" Billy asked.

I put it in terms he would get.

"If we go to the woods, we find the girl. If we find her, we find Stephanie." *And Martin*, I added silently.

"Syllogism," Will said automatically. "I'll drive."

"I've seen that matchbox you call a car," Billy said. "I'll drive. We can all fit."

"What do you drive?" Paolo asked him. "A cruise ship?"

"An Eminence," Billy proclaimed. It says something about the tension of the moment that neither Will nor I cracked a smile.

We piled into Billy's SUV, which really *was* like a cruise ship. We were higher up off the ground than I was used to being. As he pulled out and headed for the highway, the road seemed more open. But the mountains, backlit by the slivered moon, were just as large as ever.

Once we hit the interstate, almost no one spoke. We slipped into our own little pods, all seven of us.

The stereo throbbed. The singer's voice, over a grind of guitars, sounded like a chorus of chainsaws. *"Evasive maneuver! I think I'll remove her!"*

Ugh. "What are we listening to?" I shouted, coming out of my pod, just for a second.

"Steroid," Billy said.

Figures.

The mountains rose, and we rose with them. The engine's drone and the grind of the music merged with the curving landscape; it was hypnotic, and I felt increasingly spacey, like I'd overdosed on cold medicine. I rested my head against the cushioned backseat and shut my eyes.

I was only gone for a second, and not even really gone. It was more like hovering. I sat there in the pulse of the Ecstasy? Enterprise? Prominence? Whatever, *car*. But I was also on the edge of something else, some*place* else. A pale white space, like Talon had described.

"Hello," A voice breaks the still air and a hand touches my cheek.

"Martin?" My lips feel dry. "Where are you?"

It is Martin, but not. An altered version, watery around the edges.

"The bottle tree——" he says.

Then another voice. Stephanie's. Sharp, from a distance. "Hurry."

I watch as Martin takes the almost-Stephanie's hand just before they dive into the whiteness.

Chapter 41

Billy turned off the highway and we wound our way through The Town that Time Forgot. The houses looked worn, dusted with coal from the passing trains. My mom would call it "jerry-rigged," as if everything had been originally intended for something else. The only places still in business were the Dollar General, which looked like it had once been a bank, and the feed store, which looked like it had been a feed store since the days of Billy the Kid. Talon gave directions: Main Street, past the furniture factory—boarded up now—left on the river road.

The streets were bumpy and dark except for the fluorescent glow from a lone convenience store.

"Pull over. We need caffeine," Paolo said. He slid out of the front seat and returned with four cups of coffee, a few cans of a soda-like substance meant for truck drivers and college students, and a bag of chips, which, last time I checked, did not contain an energy-imbuing substance.

"Take your pick," he said.

Will, Macy, and I went for the coffee, which, unlike the Trucker's Delight, contained ingredients I recognized. Talon went for the Trucker's Delight, of course, and pulled out her cell.

"Anything from Serena?" Paolo asked, quickly, like he'd been downing Trucker's Delight himself.

"Nothing."

I checked my phone, too. *New Message.* The accompanying beep must've gotten lost in Billy's chainsaw symphony.

"YES!" I said. "It's from Serena. She wrote one hundred seventeen. And then a bunch of question marks."

"Is that latitude or longitude?" Macy asked.

We all looked at Will. "Don't ask me," he said.

"Do we finally have a question you can't answer?" Talon asked him.

"My people don't camp," he said.

"Mine do," Billy said, turning down the music. "It's her campsite number, Brainiac."

"She's in a cabin," Talon said.

"Then it's her cabin number. Whatever. Let's roll." He pushed the car into hyperdrive. My coffee was still warm when we arrived at the check-in station.

Billy parked and walked straight to the building, which was deserted. He looked in the window, then stared at the map that was posted outside, tracing a route with his finger.

"This way," he said, and we followed. The first turnoff was full of RVs. The one closest to us had a sign that said "The Andersons" hanging next to a geranium that had probably visited fifteen states before it died in the Blue Ridge of Virginia. A clothesline hung from the trees, the laundry flapping like ghosts. We stayed on the main path; pant legs whipped in the wind behind us.

We passed another loop, this one with tents. I could hear the strains of guitar, the static from a radio. Billy took the left loop toward the camping cabins.

The cold pierced through my dress and I hunched my shoulders.

"Yeah," Talon said. "I remember this place."

"Ditto." I started thinking about the ghosts of those tiny gray mice and that incomprehensible tree.

Cabin 106.

Cabin 107.

A campfire burned outside 109.

I started to run, Will behind me, Talon behind him, slowed down by Spice and her own ridiculous shoes.

Cabin 115.

In the darkness ahead, I could see a figure sitting on the porch of what must have been 117.

We thundered toward it and stopped, cold, when the figure stood.

"What the hell is going on?"

Chapter 42

I don't know which was more shocking: the fact that the figure rising like the moon from an ancient rocking chair was Serena, or the fact that Serena, who never cursed, had yelled *hell*.

Her eyes widened as she took us all in.

We must have looked like the kind of stuff you find in the scratch-and-dent sale bin a few weeks after Easter. Me in my flouncy dress, Daniel with his wilted boutonniere. Gangly Will, his tie in a loose knot mid-chest. Talon and Macy, the Virginia clay clinging to their pointy-toed shoes.

And the mere presence of Billy.

"Not to be rude or anything, but what are you guys *doing* here?" Serena said. And then she must have realized who wasn't here, along with who was. "Where's Martin?"

"Where are your parents?" I countered. I thought I'd better check before I started talking.

"They're still at the bluegrass jam," Serena said. "Now what's going on?"

"While you guys catch up, can we come in?" Talon asked. "It's cold as a witch's tit out here."

Serena opened the door, and our version of the Dance Hall Mafia filed inside.

My voice dropped to a whisper—it didn't feel right to say this stuff out loud—and I told Serena everything. Or at least the SparkNotes version of everything.

The more I talked, the more she stared at me, nodding at the appropriate moments and saying "Right." But her eyes said that I'd flown completely off my nut.

"That's...interesting," she said once my verbal diarrhea finally let up.

"You don't believe me?"

She picked at one of her cuticles. "Well, it's a lot to believe, isn't it?"

For a second I'd forgotten about all the others in the room. Macy was sitting beside Daniel on Serena's bunk, and Billy was pacing the far end of the cabin like a caged bear. Serena's eyes locked for a minute with Paolo's and then fell away.

"I know it's a lot to take in," said Will, who was standing with Talon behind me. "You just need to think about—"

"Shit! What are we even still doing here?" Billy barked. He strode over to where Talon was standing and glared at her. "You said you saw Stephanie. So where is she? Where's Zirkle? People don't just disappear!"

"Back off," Will said, putting himself between Billy and Talon.

Billy half growled and returned to his pacing.

"So this is happening," Serena said.

"Wait, you don't believe me but you believe BILLY?" I said. "It's real. Remember that tree with the bottles? We need to get her there, the little nightmare girl. In my dream, she was in that clearing, where we buried the mice. She was sitting in the middle, sewing a little doll and then she—"

"The girl was sewing a doll?" Serena interrupted.

"Yeah, an old rag doll," I said.

She walked over to the built-in box under the window, reached inside and pulled out a small, stained rag doll with tight red stitches at its neck. It had the same limp yarn hair, the same broken button eyes. Only now the doll was wearing a ragged pink dress. At first the gauzy fabric seemed to be embellished with red sequins, but when I looked closer I saw they were flecks of dried blood.

"Where did you get that?"

"It was on my cot when we got here," she said. "I couldn't stand looking at it so I put it in the trunk."

Talon took the doll from Serena. It was no bigger than her palm. She squeezed it. "Freaky," she said.

"She knew I'd come here." My voice started rising to an octave that I'm pretty sure could only be heard by dogs. "She left it here—"

"It's okay," Will said.

"How do you know?" I snapped.

"I'm going to make it okay." He took the doll from Talon and shoved it in his pocket. "It's nothing," he said.

Will never lied to me. I searched his eyes.

"It's nothing," he said again.

"We should look around," Billy said. "There could be something else, maybe. Something from Stephanie. A clue."

"Right-o, Sherlock," Talon piped in a fake British accent. "You and Watson drag the lake, Miss Marple and I will head up to the haunted castle."

"Seriously," Billy said. "Bite me."

"He's right," Macy said. "Maybe there's something we're missing."

She stood and shrugged, then glanced around the corners of the cabin. There wasn't much to see. Bare walls, a few bunks, the Mendezes' bags, two windows, empty windowsills.

Billy walked over to the box where the doll had been and wrenched it open. He pulled out a wadded-up blanket and a rumpled plastic grocery bag. He dug his big hand inside the bag, then grinned. "Jackpot!"

"You found something?" Will asked.

Billy nodded and pulled out a six-pack, the cardboard carrier splotched with mold. "Sealed," he said. "They're safe." He grabbed a bottle and set the carton with the rest in the middle of the room. "Any takers?"

"It's not a good idea," Macy said. "For any of us. We need to stay sharp."

"I'm sharper when I drink." Billy rested the bottle against the edge of the bed, then came down hard on it with his right hand. The top rattled on the ground. "A little skunky, but what the hell."

He took a gulp, then picked up a second bottle and threw it to Daniel. The remaining four beers, he jammed into his coat pockets, two on each side.

"So, you guys ready? We should head out," I said to everyone, and then turned to Talon and Serena. "Remember the way?"

Serena nodded. "I can find it again."

Will bristled beside me. He put his hand on my back and tapped out "N-O-T-Y-E-T."

Aloud, he said, "Annabelle, could I talk to you, alone?" as he opened the door. "I'll be quick."

"Stay close," Serena called. "Keep one hand on the cabin."

Will pointed. "We'll be right by that tree. Five minutes. I swear." He walked and I followed, the air sharp on my bare arms.

Chapter 43

"What the hell are you thinking? Running after a sociopath in the middle of the night? It's crazy. You don't have to do it." He stopped short. "I can't lose you."

"What choice do I have? And besides—"

"You don't get it." His voice seemed to have grown moss. "I *can't lose you.*"

We were silent for a second, looking at one another across the darkness. Unexpectedly, the lines of his face were easier to read in the dim light, like the chiaroscuro paintings Ms. Sage had shown us in class. She'd said the dark helps us notice the light, and it's true. In the brim of night, the slight uneven cast of Will's cheekbones blurred into shadow, while his eyes almost gleamed.

"It's like that for me, too," I finally said.

"I doubt it." His voice was so quiet that I felt his words more than heard them.

"What do you mean? Of course it is."

"I mean—" But he never finished. Instead he leaned down and

pressed his lips, his breath, against mine. The shock of it filled my lungs. This was Will. *My* Will. Kissing me.

But when he wrapped his arms around me, I couldn't help it; I leaned against him, kissing him back. At first it was like drawing nectar from honeysuckle, light and unbelievably sweet. I felt a trill of warmth, the green of willow, even though as we shifted, I could hear the crunch of dead leaves below our feet. He pressed deeper, with more insistence, and I pressed back. Something clicked inside me, a key opening a door.

I pulled away, struggling to calm my breath, to find my voice, but all I found was a whisper. "My God, Will. You like me?"

He shook his head.

"You don't?" It didn't make sense. Not after a kiss like that.

He shook his head again.

And then it hit. My throat was full of dust. "You—?"

I couldn't say the word out loud, but he knew what I was thinking.

He nodded, and lowered his lips again to mine.

All the comfort that Will had ever given me was in his kiss, but there was this new thing, too, unfathomable, undeniable, true. There, as if it had always been. I loved him back.

I loved him as if—I don't know how else to explain it—as if he *were* me. Like in my mom's romance novels, which had always seemed totally bogus before. It was bone-deep, soul-deep. But this was *Will*, not some bare-chested stud in cowboy boots. Best. Friend. *Slow down*, I told myself. *Breathe.*

I pulled my face away, but his arms still encircled me. "So, that was…" I trailed off, looking into his chest, feeling something I never felt with Will—shy.

"What?" he asked, his voice as soft as his lips. "What was it?"

"I don't know," I said, which was of course a lie.

"Are you okay?"

"I don't know," I said, and this time it was the truth. "What about you?"

He nodded, and grinned his crooked grin.

I cleared my throat. "It's just a little…"

"…weird." He finished for me.

"Seriously weird," I said. "How…? When did this…?" I knew I wasn't making sense, but I also knew he'd understand.

He shrugged. "When *didn't* it?" he said. "I'm sorry, Annabelle. I know this probably isn't the time. I just couldn't keep acting like it wasn't there."

All those times, in the darkroom, in the car, at my cousin's wedding even, there had been something running between us, a pulse. I had pretended not to feel it. I didn't know how to act, now that I'd stopped pretending.

"So, what happens—?"

But he was kissing me again, shutting off the question I was bound to ask. He didn't care what came next, he wanted now, and I couldn't blame him. With the nightmare out there, now might be all we could have.

I shut my eyes this time, giving in to the space inside me that had always loved Will. But what I saw when I closed my eyes was not darkness, but light. The same pale light I'd seen in Billy's car when I'd slipped away for that moment. The white space.

"Martin?" I thought, and Will's kiss felt muted, distant, like I was truly a million miles away, at some border between dreams.

Martin is there in the whiteness, standing in his dark suit, the boutonniere I'd given him still crisp on his lapel.

"You shouldn't be here," he says.

"Neither should you," I say. "Where are we?"

"I'm in the locker room at school. My body, anyway. She got us. Me and Steph, both. She put us under."

I imagine their bodies, long and beautiful, lying side by side on the cold floor.

"We'll go back," I say. "We'll wake you up."

"You have to finish her first. Before she gets you, too. Go to the tree." *His voice is firm. "You have to——"*

An earsplitting screech blocks his words.

I focus on Martin's lips, trying to read in them what I can't hear. I remember learning once that on TV, the extras mouth the words "peas and carrots" in the background to look like they are talking when they aren't. That's all I am getting from Martin. Peas and carrots. The screeching intensifies. Martin's expression is eager, desperate—and gorgeous, even more gorgeous than before he disappeared. Inside the space that is not space, Martin is luminous. The Prince of Nowhere.

Dream Martin takes me by the shoulders, but instead of drawing me to him, he shoves me away.

I feel myself stumbling backward. Tumbling, tumbling down and down, I hear the screeching fall away and what sounds like Ernshaw's voice, distant, as if it were coming from a tunnel, "matter over mind, matter over mind..."

Then I hit land again. My eyes jolted open. Awake.

———————

Will wasn't kissing me anymore; he was staring at me.

"You left," he said, his voice accusing.

"We have to go," I said.

I looked down at my hand—my hand in Will's hand—and then up into his eyes. There was something there, not fear, not resignation...but something hard. Determined.

"Will, I want you to know..." But I couldn't finish. Instead I stood on my toes and kissed him quickly on the lips.

The leaves rustled. Will tightened his grip on my hand. Together, we turned to face the night.

Chapter 44

Serena left a note for her parents. ("What am I supposed to say?" she'd asked. "That I went looking for owls with friends?" "Close enough," Talon had answered. "Write it.")

We hurried along single file, like dwarves headed for the mines. Serena took the lead, followed by me and Macy, blundering through in our dresses and heels; then Will; Paolo; Billy, bearlike, bottles clanking in his pocket; Talon, with Spice straining at the leash; and at the rear, Daniel.

The woods were quiet except for the rumble of our footfalls; Serena led us to a side trail, and then to another until the way began to narrow. As the trees arched over to make a dark tunnel, I knew where I was. It was the path where we'd stumbled upon the clearing. The path from my dream.

"Hold up," I whispered. "It's just ahead." Serena stopped and I nosed in front of her.

When I looked up, though, it was not the opening I saw.

It was the girl.

The pinpricks in her blank eyes glistened like drops of blood, and her mouth was smeared with something dark and rusty.

"I won." Her voice came out high, like those old baby dolls that talk when you pull their strings. "I told you I'd already be here!" A snake wove a path between her feet as it crossed the trail.

I stood before her—like a birthday present, all wrapped up in a fluffy, pink bow. Knowing she was stronger, knowing she'd buried me once, here at the edge of the clearing. Swearing she wouldn't do it again. This was my world, not hers.

A few more steps and the forest would open into that large circle of matted grass, edged by trees, with—I hoped—that one colossal tree still standing in the middle. I imagined it as a painting, a wish—gnarled, mystical, magnificent, its bottles glinting like colored promises.

"What do you want?" I kept my voice low, reined in.

"Play with me!" She turned her moon-blanched eyes toward my face.

I pushed ahead, past the girl until I stood below on the cusp of the opening, hoping to see branches and bottles and not the truncated stump. In the glow of night, the space yawned before me, just as I remembered it—and in the center, the enormous tree.

I went over what I'd learned. Spirits. Corks. River. And then I looked back to where the girl was standing, a few feet back on the path. If the bottle tree had power, it was inside the grass circle. I could feel it. I knew the girl could, too.

Then I felt something else. Hands on my neck, strangling. The girl's fists were clenched by her side. Like in my nightmare, an invisible vise gripped me, cutting off air. But this time it was my breath, my body—real, alive. If I died this time, there'd be no waking up.

"Stop!" I tried to scream, but my open mouth was dry and soundless.

The girl's body began to tremor, her smile stretched wide and thin brown liquid trickled from the corner of her lips. She answered my unspoken question in a grim whisper. "You're special, but it's not going to be you, it's going to be *me*. I'm going to be the mommy, and you'll be nothing…not even a dream."

My eyes flashed to Will…Serena…Paolo…Macy…Daniel…Talon…Spice…They were all stiff, gripped by whatever held me. Even Billy, huge as he was, couldn't move anything but his panic-stricken eyes.

A thick red-skinned snake rippled in the branches near the girl. Piercing the canopy, it stretched its long body toward her and slinked around her neck. A jewel that shimmered as it moved.

"I'm going to be like you," the nightmare went on. "I'll be the Dreamer. I'll make the dreams."

"You're wrong!" I said it in my mind, loud enough that she'd be sure to hear me. "I'm nobody. I didn't—"

"Did too! You brought us here. All of us. Even me." The girl got on her tiptoes and put her lips inches away from my face. Her pupils throbbed and I could smell her ripe breath. The red snake raised its head, too, staring and nodding as it stretched toward my cheek. "You're the Dreamer," she hissed.

She placed her palm on my forehead like a faith healer. For a moment, I felt her fingers sear inside my head, rummaging around, rearranging. "Here," she said, pressing her palm flat again. "Here. Here. Here."

I closed my eyes in pain, but in my mind I could see. It was like I was opening the lid of a little box. And then another. And inside each was a frozen dream.

I stand in the open doorway to Will's bedroom. I have come there to ask him something about gravity. But when I find him, he is with a girl. She is beautiful, glossy, perfect—everything I am not—and she is unmistakably Stephanie. She sits on the edge of his bed, a long string of neon green gum trailing from her mouth to the tip of her pinky. It hovers there, a swing bridge between her lips and finger. Will lies back, his eyes opening to the sight of me.

I hold the hand of a frail old lady at the nursing home where my mom works. Jared Wales, my mom's divorce lawyer, stands in the corner of the room, taking notes on a large yellow pad. I have just told Mrs. Finch that for Christmas I want a cup that will always be full of whatever I want to drink.

Talon, Robert the library guy, Will, and Stephanie sit at a table in the food court with cups, wadded napkins, and French fries spread out before them. I stand near the table, holding a little dog. The fur of the dog is short, spotted brown, black, and white—just like Talon's Spice. The dog's mouth opens and I pull out a large white bone.

———

On the train I sit, pimpled and awkward, on a torn vinyl seat—a backpack beside me, my Miss Piggy toothbrush poking out the front pocket. In the flat frame of the windows, trees and hills have blurred to green. The train is almost full. The me in the picture looks down at my lap, but the me in my mind scans the seats. And there, a few rows back, Martin sits with his arm around Macy. But it isn't exactly Macy. The hair is all wrong. And Martin is a duller, colorless version of himself. He looks a lot like Daniel. They could be cousins.

———

"Stop," my mind screamed. "Stop it!"

The girl's grip loosened for a second and I jerked myself free. "You put that there!" I yelled. "Those things weren't real. You put that stuff in my head!"

"I didn't say they were real," the girl said. "I said they were dreams. Your dreams."

"They aren't mine!"

But as I said it, I knew I was the one lying. It had all been there already. But how? I'd read about Spice and the bone in Talon's dream journal. And Will knew he'd dreamed Stephanie; he'd admitted it. Those were *their* dreams. But they'd been there in my head— Stephanie, Spice, Mrs. Finch, Macy—a parade of Chilton's dreams.

Martin had matched us up like chess pieces, a different dreamer for each dream. But I knew the girl really only wanted me.

And I knew why. Because somehow, she thought it all came down to this: I was the one true dreamer. The chosen one, like

Harry Potter or Buffy the effing Vampire Slayer. I was the one she had to take down.

I wanted to convince her that she was wrong, that she'd made a terrible mistake. I sat at the nobody table, for crying out loud. But there's no arguing with a nightmare. And even if I won, if I could convince her I really was a nobody, then what? Would she turn on one of my friends instead?

My stomach seized, and I doubled over.

The girl reached out and grabbed my wrist. "I'm supposed to be the Dreamer," she pouted. "Not you. Me!"

I jerked my hand away and stumbled backward into the opening.

As my shoe touched down on the ground in the clearing, I felt a shudder below my feet. Thunder rumbled. The air ripped in two. Out of nowhere, a tempest. It was like a dam had broken, only instead of water gushing out, it was wind.

The girl scrambled back, deeper into the cavernous pathway, away from the draw of wind, disappearing in the dark. From the distance, I could make out the glint of her eyes.

Will teetered, as if suddenly released from the nightmare's grip. Talon crouched down and clutched Spice to her chest. They were free of the girl.

But now it was the wind that had them, had all of us.

With a trumpeting blast, the wind shoved us toward the orbit of the tree. We wobbled like drunks as the air bellowed around our heads, sucking us into the clearing.

The bottles tied to the branches pitched violently, some knocking into each other and smashing into bits. More thunder. Dead leaves swirled about our heads.

Macy stumbled closer toward the center of the clearing as if pushed by a giant hand.

"Hold on!" I shouted, but my voice was lost in the air that blustered around us.

Daniel, who was farthest away from the clearing, fought his way back down the path, until he was clear of the wind. He stood, watching us, his hands helpless at his sides.

Macy tried to run. I watched as her feet slipped out from under her and she hurtled toward the tree. Her body lifted off the ground, suspended for a moment in the air. It was as if the force of gravity was canceled out; her body slanted toward the tree, rising.

I ran toward her.

From the side, Billy lunged. He grabbed Macy by the ankle. For a moment, he just stood there, flying his awkward kite. Then he yanked her downward, trying to reel her in.

As I stumbled forward, I saw Paolo's feet starting to slip from the grass, but Serena, small as she was, tackled him, pinning him down.

The tree was like a huge magnet. A magnet for dreams. All of us were wind-battered, but the dreams were pulled in by something much more powerful.

I turned back toward Billy; he had his arms wrapped around Macy now, but her entire body jerked and wrenched, as if trying to tug itself free. Talon started to lurch toward them on her ridiculous shoes. Her heel hit something hard and she fell, her arms opening to brace her fall; in a flash of lightning, I saw Spice ripped away by the wind.

"No!"

The little dog flew upward, twisting. Before I could stretch out to grab her, she was out of my reach. Her leash whipped past my fingers, beyond me.

Will, who had been a few feet behind, ran past me and jumped in a wide arc, impossibly high. He caught Spice by her waist with both hands and pulled the dog to his chest, but instead of dropping to the ground, they both kept rising.

"WILL!" I jumped up, but he was far above my head, his body twisting. Then, in a single hellish moment, he slammed into a web of branches; I felt my throat go raw. Thunder.

Bottles smashed. A bolt of lightning crashed down from the sky, splitting the tree with a tremendous crack.

Will's body contorted in midair…then *he* was wind. Vanished.

The air scorched with sulfur. Where Will had been, a bottle shattered into chunks of glass, spraying blue dust.

Chapter 45

The wind died with a long exhale. The leaves, which had been whirling about, drifted back to the ground. Stillness descended. The two halves of the tree lay ruined, charred, smoke rising from them in plumes.

In the absence of the wind, I crumpled to the ground. I looked to Talon, but her eyes, lined in black, didn't say anything I could read.

A hand on my shoulder. "Annabelle?" Serena kneeled beside me and wrapped me in her arms. I leaned into her, too dazed to speak. The only sound was our ragged breathing, and in the distance, the wind-chime laughter of the little girl.

The girl. She knew to run away before the wind really started blowing. She would know where Will had gone, how to find him.

I disentangled myself from Serena's arms. "I've got to—" But I couldn't explain it. I needed to run, to get to the girl, to get Will back. I must have looked wild-eyed, half crazy in the dark, as I shook my head and started to sprint across the clearing to the path.

"Where are you—?" Paolo started.

"Come on!" I yelled, not looking back.

I could hear Macy call, "Wait! Annabelle, wait!" But I didn't wait. I kept running in the direction of the laugh.

Before I'd gotten far down the path, the girl's wind-up voice called from the thickest part of the woods. "Hide-and-seek! I'll hide!"

I went straight for the voice, clambering over dying ferns and ducking under low branches of scrubby trees. At the base of a tree, three brown snakes, curled in a heap, pulled apart and scattered. Two slithered toward my feet. Swallowing, I hopped over the length of them and plunged forward through the brush. The skirt of my dress snagged on briars, but I ripped it free, charging on until I arrived at the place where the girl's voice had seemed to come from. I was standing on the edge of a ravine. I heard her again, calling me over the edge.

This time I stayed put. "Where's Will?" I shouted. "Where is he? I bet you can't tell me." My voice echoed in the night.

"Who?" She was in the branches now, closer.

"Will," I said. "*Will*. I bet you don't even know where he is. Not much of a dreamer, if you don't know that."

"Am too!" Closer.

"Prove it," I said.

She sprung out from behind the tree I was leaning against. "Found you!"

I stepped back, teetering. One step more and I would have fallen fifty feet. Fixing a smile on my face, I edged away from the ravine. "*I* found you," I said. "You lose."

Her pale face contorted. "Liar!"

I could feel her invisible hands against my shoulders, forcing me down to my knees. I started to bend.

"No!" I shoved the hands away in my mind, and stood. I imagined a wall between us, made of something strong and clear, something she'd have to bang against with her fists. *My* world, I reminded myself. I was in control.

She pressed against the barrier, but it held.

A scrunching sound came from the woods and I waited for my friends to emerge from the brush. They didn't. I flexed my fingers, anxious. "Where did Will go?" I repeated.

"He didn't go anywhere, silly. He's gone." She twisted her hair around her finger again. She was toying with me now—a cat who first played with the cricket it intended to eat. "He doesn't matter."

"You're wrong," I said. Will Connor mattered. He always had. I turned Ernshaw's phrase over in my head. *Mind over matter. Matter over mind.*

"Where is he?" I asked her.

"He isn't!" From the nest of her hair, a shimmer of emerald—a beetle scuttled down her cheek. It looked like scarabs we'd studied during our unit on Ancient Egypt. The bug darted down her shoulder, zigzagging along her arm until it reached her hand, where it perched on her pinky like a ring.

"You're wrong," I said. "It was a mistake. The tree only wanted... It only wanted..."

She laughed. "It wanted your *dreams!*"

I looked into the girl's sour-milk eyes.

"You didn't know, you didn't know!" she squealed. "*He* was your dream, too!"

"It was the dog," I said. "The *dog* was a dream. Will just got caught."

But the conversation at the golf course came back to me—a passage that, as I read it in my mind, was highlighted in yellow: *"What if I told you I was one of them?"*

Was Will a dream?

No, that was cracked. *She* was cracked.

"Tell me where he went," I repeated.

"Why do you care?" She raised her hand and brought the beetle to her lips. Tenderly, she opened her mouth and the bug crawled inside, then out again, wandering down her chin and settling at the base of her throat. The red snake pulled back its head, curled like a question mark, and snapped at the beetle, swallowing it in a single seamless motion. "He's just a dream. Your very first dream come true."

"That's not right!"

I had to focus—on something other than the beetle-eating snake and the girl's lies. If there was any chance of getting Will back, and Spice—if there was any chance of waking Martin and Stephanie—I had to act now. I wanted my friends. Talon's boldness, Serena's unshakable loyalty. But they hadn't found me. Here, when it mattered most, it was just me. *The chosen one.* Yeah, well.

I stepped toward the girl, reminding myself I was bigger. Sure, she was crazy strong, not to mention just crazy. And she had those nasty eyes, and the snakes, and the whole mind-invasion thing going for her. But I had something, too—I had to, right? I wasn't going to let her puff us away like dandelion fuzz.

"Listen, you little snake." All the panic I'd felt—all the fear she'd sparked, all the confusion—burned away. What was left was incandescent rage. I harnessed that anger, controlled it, funneled it into a power I wasn't sure I had. *"Tell me where he is."*

For a second, the girl looked small and confused, like a real little girl lost in the woods. Then she straightened and put her hands on her hips, a sassy poltergeist.

"He's nowhere," she said. "And so are you. Both of you, you're nothing." She opened her hand and I saw she was holding the stained rag doll with the stitched neck and pink dress.

"Where did you get that?" An image: Will stuffing the doll in his pocket. *It's nothing*, he had said.

"Nothing," the girl echoed.

My wall shattered, and invisible hands pushed me, hard, toward the edge of the ravine. The girl hadn't moved from where she was standing, but she grinned, wildly, tilting her head as if listening to some unearthly music.

As I felt myself being shoved back, I grabbed the trunk of a tree, a slender maple that had already surrendered most of its leaves. It was all that stood between me and a fifty-foot drop.

Then I saw them—all six of them: Talon, Serena, Paolo, Macy, Daniel, and Billy. They emerged from the woods with barely a sound, like they'd been there all along.

The girl saw them, too. Pleased with the idea of an audience, she gave an awkward curtsy, and I took that second to push against the invisible hands. The pressure slackened, the barest sliver.

Paolo and Billy made a move to tackle her, but Macy held them back with an outstretched arm and a firm headshake. Billy tapped an empty beer bottled against his leg. Serena crouched, her curly hair savagely haloing her head. Beside her, Talon stood tall in her ridiculous spiked heels.

The girl squeezed her eyes, tightening her grip on me, and I felt the maple's bark dig against my back. Then it struck me...where we were, what we had.

I pushed the hands away in my mind. "The tree," I wheezed as the others neared, jetting my eyes back at Talon, then down at her stilettos. "Bottle." Like Will said, my face must have been a billboard, because after a second, Talon's eyes sharpened. The bottle tree that had taken Will was ruined, but we had the makings for a tree of our own.

There was a hot spot in my brain that pulsed, and I focused on that, willing the girl's hands away. The throb in my head grew brighter, more intense, and I directed it toward the girl. Her invisible grip slipped and I felt myself break free. "The bottle!" I yelled at Billy, then nodded to Talon.

The nightmare screamed, her voice a dark pit. She could read me, too, and she knew what I was thinking. But she couldn't fight me, not now that I'd finally found my strength. "It's not fair!" she screamed. "I'm the Dreamer! It's supposed to be me!"

She lunged at me, but I sidestepped her, just as Talon peeled off her shoe and slammed the spiky heel hard into the maple's smooth trunk. It stuck there. Talon twisted the shoe and the heel snapped off—leaving the spike behind.

"Get back!" I yelled to Paolo and Macy. They bolted into the brush like startled deer.

"ME!" The girl shrieked.

I held up my hands, as if I was playing football, and turned to Billy, who was a dozen feet away, confused, holding on to his empty beer bottle like a toddler.

"Pass!" I called.

Instinct took over. He drew the bottle up beside his ear and fired it straight to me. I caught it and then rammed it down on Talon's spike.

It seemed impossible that it could work, that a shoe heel and a beer bottle could have even a fraction of the power of the tree in the clearing—or any power at all. But then the wind came. It wasn't as harsh as before, more a groan than a howl.

The girl balled her fists and opened her mouth as if she was about to throw a tantrum. But before she could utter the first, bloodcurdling scream, her white eyes yellowed and her hair dulled to gray.

Rising, she faded to fog, a wisp of smoke that swirled into the bottle's mouth, and she was gone.

Chapter 46

"Dude." A hoarse whisper. Billy.

Everyone talked at once.

"Is she…?"

"Damn."

"But I thought…"

I tuned them out.

Whatever had been holding me up—fear? adrenaline?—drained from my body, and I sank to the ground in a tattered, pink heap.

It was over, I thought. She was gone…

But it wasn't over.

Because Will was gone, too.

And Spice.

I looked up at the pocked bark of the maple. The brown beer bottle pegged to the tree seemed dull, ordinary, like something left by drunk college kids.

The others kept talking in funeral voices. There were words, but all I heard was static. Now that the threat was gone, I could only think of what I'd lost. I pictured Will bounding past me, the little dog in his arms, careening toward the branches, out of reach. Will's face. Blue ash.

I became aware of a pressure at my elbow. Talon. "You in there?"

Was I?

If I spoke, I'd start crying. If I started, I wouldn't stop.

"It's safe now," Serena said. "Come on. Before my parents call out the rangers."

I thought about my mother, awake by the phone. I thought about the Connors, waiting for a call that Will would never make.

Billy plunked down beside me. "What just happened?"

"Crap if I know," I said. Then I realized that in the chaos, I had forgotten. "Stephanie should be okay. I'll bet you can find her now. Back home."

"Then I'm heading out. Come on." He stood and reached down to help me up.

I gave him points for loyalty.

"I'll meet you back at the car," I said. "Ten minutes, I swear."

Talon, who looked a little like the Leaning Tower of Pisa with her one broken shoe and one spike, snapped off her remaining heel. She tossed it into the undergrowth and came back toward me. She looked wrong somehow, incomplete, and I realized it wasn't just her mangled shoes; it was the fact that her hands were empty, that there was no leash, no little dog scampering by her feet.

"We'll both catch up," she said.

Paolo nodded. "Let's find your parents," he said to Serena. His voice was flat, without the wink of humor it always had when Will was around. In the background, Billy hummed like a power tool. It was the Evasive Maneuver song that had been playing in the car.

———

How normal, I thought. I tried to be normal, too. I put my body on autopilot, my brain on mute. But my heart felt like a clump of tinfoil in my chest. If a word from me could have made it stop taking in blood, I would have said it.

Together, Talon and I walked back toward the clearing, without even saying out loud where we were going.

"He's coming back," I said. "And Spice, too. They'll be back now, right?"

Talon shrugged.

"Will?" I shouted. "Here, Spice! Will?"

Talon's voice joined mine.

We yelled the whole way back to the clearing. Occasionally, Talon whistled, piercing the night.

There was no movement, except the wind, soft now in the trees. I marched to the center of the clearing. "WILL CONNOR, GET YOUR SKINNY ASS BACK HERE!" I screamed. Talon almost smiled. Except she didn't.

"WILL!" I shouted. My voice broke like the bottles. The moonlit grass was sprinkled with shards of green, brown, and clear glass—plus a splash of blue. The luster of it triggered something, a half-formed idea.

At the base of the tree, I crouched down and picked up a sharp edge, cobalt, almost the color of Martin's eyes. It sliced into my palm, drawing a thin line of crimson across my fate line. The sight of my own blood, the prick of pain, gave me a weird sort of relief, and I thought maybe I should just keep digging in.

"Annabelle, what are you doing?" Talon asked.

"Picking up the pieces," I said. Isn't that what people did when their lives fell apart?

I spied another hunk of blue glass, a perfect triangle, and picked it up, too. Will's bottle, the only blue, flashed in the dirt. I crouched down and pried up a few more pieces. Talon helped, and soon all the shards were gathered in the folds of my dress.

Talon stood and brushed herself off.

I stood, too. We weren't yelling anymore. We knew no one would answer. Holding the skirt of my dress like a sack, I lumbered after Talon toward Billy's car, where our friends—the ones who weren't vapor—waited.

Chapter 47

My phone chirped as soon as we were back in range. Seven voice mails from my mother.

Paolo dialed the coach and told him to check the locker room.

"What about the Connors?" Talon asked. "Who's going to tell them?"

Paolo half raised his hand, like he was in class. "I'll do it."

"I will." It came out harsher than I meant. "Please, let me?"

"What are you going to tell them?" Macy asked.

"Maybe that he's lost?" My throat ached when I said it.

"Agreed. We should keep our story simple," Macy said. "Will's lost in the woods. He took off after Talon's dog and neither came back. That's it."

My phone chirped again. A text from Martin.

Steph and I are okay, it said. Are you?

I was a million miles from okay. On way home, I texted back.

Meet at your house? he wrote.

In the morning, I said. But it was morning already.

When Billy dropped me off, I barely had time to say good-bye before he peeled away, gunning to get to Stephanie.

My mother, who had seen our headlights, ran across the yard to meet me, phone in hand. She gave me a long hug, then looked at my ripped dress, the mud and blood. "I'm calling the cops."

"Don't," I said. "I'm fine." Then the tears came, so hard and fast I gagged over the words I had practiced in the car. "Will's lost. I looked and looked."

"Dear God."

She held me again.

My mother went with me to tell the Connors. Nick came, too, his eyes wide and his mouth, for once, silent. Then we did call the cops, though I knew they wouldn't find anything.

At home, my mother tucked me in like I was a baby, adjusting the quilt and then readjusting it. "They'll find Will, Annabelle. I'm sure of it."

"How do you know?"

"It's *Will*," my mother said. "Twenty bucks says he'll find us. Will and Spice, both. That dog's as smart as she is ugly." Finally, she forced herself to stand. "Get some sleep, sweetheart."

I wanted to believe her. I wanted to believe Nick, who, on the way back from the Connors', shared his vision of Will building a compass out of a shoelace and a sharpened stick. I wanted...What did I want? For everything to be back to the way it was before? For none of this to have happened? For none of us to have ever dreamed?

But that didn't seem right, either. Martin, Macy, Stephanie, Paolo, and all of the rest of them. They were here now. They were real.

Will.

I wanted Will.

I had my own vision of him—when we were four, clutching a worn copy of *The Velveteen Rabbit*, which had always made me cry. *"Real isn't how you are made," said the Skin Horse. "It's a thing that happens to you. When a child loves you for a long, long time…"*

My chest tightened on nothing, a fist gripping empty air.

I could hear my mom down the hall, starting to scrub the bathroom floor, which she hardly ever did, and never at three in the morning.

I didn't know what to do with my brain. I dug out a sketchbook from under my bed and began to draw, letting the lines and curves form their own design.

The strokes of my pencil became Will's hair, Will's face as it appeared to me outside the cabin—shadows and light. I touched his face with my finger, and put the sketchbook down.

Billy had given me a bag from under his seat for the pieces of glass. I untied the knot and emptied the contents on my desk. I still had some superglue in a drawer from when I knocked over a lamp. Starting with the triangular piece of glass, I puzzled the bottle back together, bit by bit. When I was done, I tore out the sketch. I would have let Will see it, if he'd asked.

Will, I wrote at the bottom of the paper. *I can't lose you, either. Come back. —Annabelle*

I scrolled up the note, stuffed it in the bottle, and sealed it with a cork from the junk drawer. Then I sneaked out the back door. The light was silver now, not yet dawn, though the birds had already started singing. I listened to them as I ran all the way to the river.

Tears came again—the world, a blur of burnt orange and gray.

When I got to the water's edge, I tossed the bottle into the current. It went under but then a few yards down, it bobbed back to the surface.

In the rising light, I watched it float away.

Chapter 48

I am standing barefoot in a long, blank hallway. All around me is white, like the space that surrounded Martin and Stephanie when they last tried to reach me. At the end of the hallway is a door. I open it to find a small, tidy den. The paneling is wood, the white space is gone. I am in.

In the corner, a gray-haired man is collecting a fishing rod and tackle from a trunk. He doesn't look up when I enter the room. As if I am not here.

I follow him out the back door, across the yard, to a spot where grass turns to rock, and the rock slopes to sand and a wide expanse of water. The early morning light casts fragile shadows. The air smells of salt and rot.

The man sits on a large flat rock, selects a hook and lure, and knots them to the end of his line. He looks across the water and his eyes narrow.

I follow his gaze to the other bank. A tiny, spotted dog scampers along the edge. She runs back toward the river, barking, but then she stops. A body is sprawled in the sand. Will's body.

Motionless, bent, one bare foot still submerged in the moving water.

Chapter 49

Martin was still beautiful, his face unscathed as he stood on my porch in the late morning sun.

My own face was etched with scratches. He reached out, like this time he wanted to make sure that *I* was real. Then he held me in his arms. I stood there, stiff, not able to exhale.

"I needed to be with you last night," he said. "After."

"I couldn't." My eyes misted. "But I'm glad you're back."

"I'm glad *you're* back," he echoed when he released me. "Should we walk?"

I told my mother where we were going and she let us leave, though I could tell she was fighting the instinct to lock me in a tower like Rapunzel.

Our feet took us again to the river, but I turned us left instead of right, away from the pump house. The river didn't seem to mind. Before I turned to Martin, I scanned the bank, but it was empty.

"Did Paolo tell you everything?" I asked.

"I think so."

"Then maybe you can tell me," I said. "Because I don't understand. Why Will?"

He shrugged. "From what Paolo said, it could have been anyone. Or not *anyone*, just…"

"Just what?" I asked, not wanting him to say it.

"Dreams."

I held his gaze. "You knew all along, didn't you?"

Martin nodded. "He had the mark—the tattoo, like mine. It was faint, almost the color of his skin."

"The mark," I murmured. "I'm an idiot." Of course the lines on the back of Martin's neck had looked familiar; I had seen them before—not on Stephanie, but on Will. He usually wore his hair longish, but I remembered seeing those same waves on his neck years ago, when his mother still cut his hair. He'd said it was a birthmark, and I'd shown him mine, shaped like a little fish on the back of my leg. "Why didn't you tell me?"

"Would you have believed it?" he asked. "I'm not sure *he* even knew what he was." His pace slowed and he kicked a pinecone out of his path. "You didn't know what you were, either, right?"

What? In love with Will?

"That you're the Dreamer," he said.

He waved away my protest before I could voice it.

"The nightmare knew. That's why she targeted you. She wanted you at the edge of the wood. Where she became real. An intersection. So she could force you back into the gray and take your place."

"She was insane."

"That, too," he said. "But she was also right. You're her. The Dreamer. Capital D."

"I'm not a 'capital' anything."

"But it makes sense. You asked me yourself: Why Chilton? Why here? But it wasn't the town. It was *you*. You brought me here. And Paolo says—"

"Look, I *know* Talon dreamed Spice, and Will dreamed Stephanie. That's more than one dreamer by my count and—"

"But you were there, too, in those dreams?"

"They weren't mine—"

"You *made* them yours. Remember I told you about the first dreamer? That she walked among the dreams. That's what you've been doing. It's the only explanation. It's like," and here he took my hands in his, "it's like you're Eve."

"Okay, what kind of drugs are you even on?"

"You're the one," he said again.

"Yay, me."

"You *are*. The sooner you accept it, the sooner you have a chance of finding Will."

A chance.

I looked back at him; his eyes were bright with, I don't know, sincerity? Reverence? And maybe a little regret, too. He dropped my hands.

I know Paolo hadn't told him about me and Will in the woods, because Paolo hadn't seen. But I had the feeling that somehow, Martin had. That he knew.

I didn't want to lie and tell him I wished I could feel differently. Because I wanted my feelings for Will, as much as they hurt. They were real, and they were mine. They told me what I needed to know: that Will was never just my friend; he was always more. The mirror that saw me as I really was. The boy who loved me anyway.

And Martin? I guess Martin was everything I thought I wanted. Everything I dreamed of. The perfect boy. Imperfect for me.

"What if—" My words rushed along with the river. "What if I did find him? Will. What if I found him and he was—" I didn't want to say it. But I did. "Dead?" I forced myself to look in Martin's eyes. "What if this Dreamer touches a person who is dead, in a dream, I mean. Does the person come to this world dead?"

Martin shook his head. "I'm sorry. I don't know."

My face twisted in a way even Martin, with his rose-colored glasses, could not have thought was pretty. But he leaned in anyway, to kiss me. I turned my head so that he hit my cheek. It was still warm, his kiss. Part of me wanted to turn to him, to lose myself and forget everything. But my mind was full. Will's being gone didn't leave me free to love Martin; it took up all the space I had. Will was nowhere, and his being nowhere was *everywhere*. I couldn't let him go.

"So it's like that, then," Martin said.

"I'm still trying to figure things out."

"Looks to me like you've figured them out already."

"Some of them," I said.

And I had. I knew what I wasn't willing to lose. Who I wasn't willing to lose. And I was beginning to understand what I might have to risk to get him again. I would have to believe the unbelievable. That I *was* the Dreamer, capital D. That I could find him and bring him back alive.

The thought of it went against everything I'd ever believed about my life and about myself. I had power? I had control? It didn't seem possible, but it needed to be.

Martin stared out over the river, but his eyes were glazed. I'm not sure he was seeing anything. Then he turned and retraced his steps without waiting for me to follow.

"He was my *best friend*," I called after him.

Martin didn't answer, and he didn't look back.

Chapter 50

The newspaper ran an article: "Boy, 17, Lost on Mountain," so by Monday morning everyone knew Will was gone. The article made him sound like some sort of hero, off in the woods, searching for his date's runaway dog. It mentioned the possibility of foul play and hypothermia. It did not blame me. I did that.

I skipped early morning classes on Monday. My mother said I could stay home all week, but there were things I had to face, and people I had to see. I wandered through the halls of Chilton High, using my pass to collect Talon and Serena. Paolo, who had pre calc with them, tagged along.

We headed to the girls' bathroom on the second floor, which hardly anyone ever used because it had ventilation problems and smelled like dishrags. Paolo hesitated a minute, then followed us inside.

The four of us dissected my dream, the fishing gear, Will in the sand, and Spice barking, which made Talon have to take a private minute in a stall.

"I still don't think it was the white space," I said. "It was just a white hallway. But it wasn't a normal dream, either. The guy didn't see me. It was like I was watching TV."

"Are you sure the person on the bank was Will?" Serena asked for the twenty-fifth time. I knew she was avoiding saying "body." The *body* on the bank...

"I only saw him for a second."

"You need to go there again," Talon said.

"But if I touch him and he's dead, does his body wash up on the shore of the Roanoke River?"

"Uncharted territory," Paolo said.

"What about the girl," I asked. "Is she out there, too?"

He shrugged.

The bell rang, so we filed down to the cafeteria for lunch, which I didn't plan on eating. Serena sat down on my side of the table next to Paolo, trying to fill Will's empty space for both of us. Daniel had moved over from the second-tier jock table to sit next to Billy. I guess if you spend homecoming in the woods chasing someone else's nightmare, it forms some type of bond. Martin was there, too, across from Stephanie. But when he saw me come in, he switched tables.

"How's it going?" It was more than a casual question. I shrugged.

He nodded and paused for a second. "You'll find him again."

"Wish I had your confidence." But when I looked at Martin, really looked at him, he didn't look confident at all. His blue eyes were sad.

"Martin—"

"You find someone, you lose someone," he said. I knew that by losing someone, he wasn't talking about Will. He was talking about me. "Good luck, though."

"Why are you even wishing me that?"

"I want you to be happy," he said. "Is that so hard to believe?"

"Everything is hard to believe," I said.

He smiled a little and then glanced over at Talon to see if he'd said the right thing. She tossed a potato chip at him and he turned back to me.

"But just to be clear, Annabelle," he added. "I'm not going anywhere. I'll be right here, waiting. Maybe when you find Will, the three of us can have breakfast."

I cringed, remembering the French Toast Incident, as he leaned in and kissed my cheek. It was a gentle kiss, demanding nothing, more of a punctuation mark than anything else. "I'll be here."

He rubbed his arms and I saw goose bumps.

"Are you okay?" I asked.

"Just cold," he said.

"But you don't get—"

"So I've heard a rumor," Stephanie said, stopping by our table as she carried her tray. "The Dreamer, huh?" She leaned down so her full lips were right near my ear. Her lip gloss smelled like fresh strawberries. "Personally, I think it's bullshit," she said. "But even if you are her, it doesn't mean I have to like you."

She stood up again to her full height, staring at me with those Cleopatra eyes. After all we'd been through, Stephanie Gonzales still hated me. Most of me hated her back, but a sliver of me was grateful; at least this part of my life was still normal.

"Will's pretty cute for a total reject," she said. "I hope you find him." Her words were biting, but her eyes weren't. Maybe things with Stephanie weren't so normal after all, because all of a sudden, I wanted to hug her. I sat on my hands, just in case, and she walked away to empty her tray in the trash.

Across the cafeteria, I spotted the one person (other than Will) that I really wanted to see: Mr. Ernshaw.

He must have drawn the short straw, which I'm pretty sure is how they pick high school lunchroom monitors. His shirt was rumpled and his hair looked as if he'd taken grooming lessons from a sheepdog. I walked over to him.

"Matter over mind," I said, like I was double-checking my homework. "What does it mean?"

"It's an idea Jim—Coach Masterson and I—were playing around with," he said. He took off his glasses and wiped them, then put them back on his face. "I suppose I keep trying to find a scientific explanation."

"Did you?" I asked.

"Are you taking notes?" he asked, but his eyes were kind. "Okay, how about this," he began. "What if a dream—or some dreams— exist beyond the confines of our minds? What if they're matter? *Real* matter. Solid, liquid, gas, and then a fourth state, if you will."

"Not nothing," I whispered.

"Exactly. Not nothing."

"And the fourth state, if there was a fourth state, might be something else and even exist somewhere else, in another realm." Now he was combining science with fiction. But he was on a roll. "What if dreams exist in that fourth state?"

I looked over and his eyes locked into mine. "Nothing is lost, Miss Manning," he whispered. "Because nothing ever entirely disappears."

Mr. Ernshaw concluded in a normal voice, "My theory is that Mr. Connor has changed states. He simply needs a catalyst to help him change states once more. You may be that catalyst, Miss Manning. It's a stretch to call any of this remotely scientific, but it puts it into a context that makes me feel a little more comfortable. And it has the added benefit of providing hope."

"So what we need to do is…"

"Change one form into another." He gave me a weak smile, then shrugged. "Of course, that's just my hypothesis. It's up to you to test it."

"Test it how?" I asked.

But I knew that answer myself.

Like the song goes, all you have to do is dream.

Chapter 51

That night, I closed my eyes and tried to cast myself into the white space. I knew my chances; I had read somewhere that more than 1.5 billion dreams are produced on a single night in America alone. With all those dreams pinging off the stratosphere, how likely was it I could find my way back to that hallway, though the door, and across that river. To Will's body.

No. I chased the thought away. *To Will.*

If I'm the chosen one, then I get to choose, too. And I choose to find Will, to bring him home.

White space. White. I thought about snow and milk and pillow-cases and the mysterious bleached spots on fingernails. I thought about gym socks and the porcelain figurines of sheep my grandma had kept on her living room mantel. I thought about feathers and bare museum walls. *White,* I sang to myself, *white white white.*

But sleep didn't come. Maybe there was too much pressure. My dad always said I had a stubborn streak, and he was right. It was hard for me to do anything on command.

The clock by my bed flashed 9:30, 12:30, 2:00 a.m. I thought I drifted off for awhile, but when I looked at the clock again, only seven minutes had passed.

Finally, I slept. I woke at 4:23 a.m. to find that I'd dreamed about my father, who was with me and Nick on a fishing boat with a talking salmon. It was the closest to Alaska I'd ever been, and for a moment I saw what my dad saw: huge mountains, untouched water, beauty. Until one of my dad's shipmates cut the salmon's head off.

Then I was somewhere else, a playground. I was a child, still in preschool, and I wore a flowered sundress and sat alone in the sandbox, banging a red shovel against the flat bottom of a blue bucket. And then I wasn't alone. There was a small boy a few feet away. He had messy hair and a grim, determined look on his face as he tried to poke a straw in his juice box. He kept missing the hole.

I woke again, but if I dreamed, I wasn't aware of it. It was after 5:00, nearly morning.

I checked my phone and saw texts from Talon and Serena, and one from Martin that said simply, I'm here. I didn't write any of them back. I texted Will instead. In bed, I wrote. Where are you? I waited for an answer, and slipped the phone under my pillow so I would hear the beep if there was one. But there was no beep, just a faded drone as headlights from a passing car cast long shadows across my wall. And eventually, the door slam and grind of the street waking up. I buried my face in my pillow.

I thought about the white space. I thought about Will.

If he was a dream, like Martin said, I should be able to find him, to dream him. But the thing was, with Will, it wasn't dolphins and sunlit waters. To me he was *real*. If Will was my dream, he was my first, my purest, my truest and best.

I shut my eyes and tried again to retrace my steps, wind my way back into the white hallway of last night's dream. I tried to visualize my bare feet on the floor. If I concentrated, I could feel the floor, too, the coldness of it. At the end of the hall was a door, and I opened it.

Chapter 52

I am in the same den, watching the same fisherman rifle through his closet. I look down at my T-shirt, and find that it has been replaced by my homecoming dress. Not the one Martin bought me, the one I bought myself—periwinkle blue, so I look as if I've stepped out of a jazz club from the 1960s. I follow the fisherman out of the house, and feel the rocky gravel of his driveway under my feet, then the smoothness of the red, clay path that leads to the river. I will him to hurry, but he takes his time, whistling a little.

We hear the barking at the same time. The fisherman swears under his breath, then swears again when he sees what is near the dog. He puts down his fishing gear and runs back toward the house. I force myself to continue forward, toward Will's body where it lies on the bank across the river. The water is cold, the rapids moving faster than I'd imagined. My dress swirls like seaweed around my legs. The rocks are slippery under my feet.

I call his name. "WILL." He doesn't move.

When I reach the other side, he is still on his back, his eyes shut, a slight stubble of beard on his face, his hair coated in grit and his lips baked by the sun. A handful of broken glass is scattered next to him. The blue of the bottle, shattered again, shines in the early light.

Spice scuttles around my ankles, whimpering now instead of barking. I bend down close to Will and reach out one tentative finger, until I almost touch his face. Just inches away, I stop, afraid. There is no movement, no sign of breath. If I touch him now, do I send him back, dead, to the land of the living? My fault. My fault. My fault.

"You're not—" My throat is raw. "Tell me you're not—"

I kneel on the ground, my hands pressing into the sandy earth beside him. My fingers hit on a small river rock, like the one I keep at my bedside. I pick it up, rubbing my thumb against the smooth surface. I think of what Martin said, that at any moment a dream pebble can turn into a feather or a chunk of ice.

I close my hands around it, making a fist. It feels cold and wet in my palm, and when I open my hand again, it glistens. Not a rock anymore, but ice, melting into the warmth of my skin.

I look toward the river and think of Will. Not as he is now, but as I really know him: his crooked smile, the gleam of his green-gold eyes. I see the real Will, the one who teases my brother and listens to strange music and tells me things I've never heard before. The one who says he can't lose me. The one I cannot lose.

"Please," I whisper to the air.

In my periphery, I see something. Movement? A slight rising of his chest?

"Will!"

His eyelids waver. I am sure of it. And then slowly, slowly they open. Will, the Will I have known almost my whole life, squints up at me. His cracked lips spread into a smile. His voice is dusty, and I can barely hear it over the rush of the river. "Annabelle Manning, as I live and breathe."

Spice licks my feet and her whimpering ceases.

"Is this a dream?" Will asks, trusting me to have the answers for a change.

My eyes stare into his eyes, my smile melts into his smile. I tell him the truth. "For now," I say.

Then I grab his hand, and lead him away from the river.

BOY FOUND AFTER THREE DAYS IN WOODS

CHILTON—A Chilton boy was found dehydrated but essentially unharmed early Tuesday when a fisherman spotted him near the shallows of the Roanoke River. The boy, William Connor, 17, of Lorcum Lane, told rescuers he wasn't sure how he'd ended up on the river's north bank, still dressed in a suit and tie from the Chilton High Homecoming Dance. Connor's parents last saw him before the dance Saturday evening, but friends said he disappeared from Black Beak Mountain, 90 miles away from where he was found.

He was disoriented Tuesday, and in serious but stable condition at Chilton Community Hospital.

The fisherman said he was alerted to the boy's presence by a small dog.

"She was running in circles, just howling and a' yipping," said Ray Dalton of Pulaski, Virginia. "She was scaring the fish so I waded upstream to see if I could shut her up. That boy was the last thing I expected to find."

The dog, also missing since Saturday, was treated by Osbourne Veterinary Hospital and released to its owner, Talon Fischer. Fischer was Connor's date to the homecoming dance, which celebrated Chilton's 42–17 victory over Cave Spring.

Friends kept vigil outside Connor's hospital room for much of the day Tuesday, though none of them spoke to the media. Connor's parents also refrained from comment, saying only that they were grateful to have their son returned to them, and that he was sleeping peacefully.

Acknowledgments

Thanks to Aubrey Poole, our dream of an editor, and all the fine folks at Sourcebooks. Thanks to Susan Cohen and Brianne Johnson, who helped us find our way out of the woods. And thank you Eileen Carey, Shane Rebenschied, and Adrienne Krogh for making us think it might be perfectly fine if people judge a book by its cover.

A champagne toast to Mike Van Haelewyn and Lisa Applegate, who, according to Madelyn's recollections, first introduced the two of us seventeen years ago when we co-taught a teen writing workshop at the Salem YMCA. The same goes out to Tom Angleberger and Cece Bell, who according to Mary's much less reliable recollections, first introduced the two of us a week earlier at one of their famous Ellett Valley porch-pickings.

Dream Boy would be a lot less dreamy without our generous beta readers: David Butler and the Salem Public Library Teen Book Club, Ashley Dabbraccio, Kylee Lambert, and Wendy Shang. Thanks to Melody Veron Irby and Jenny Bitner for helping Mary think through ideas, and to Mary Norris Ferrate for having Mary's back whenever she was getting freaked by life in general.

Big love to the writers of The BookYArd, to Mad's Wednesday Morning Writing Crew, and to the A-Team.

To our families—the Crocketts, Deemers, Hills, Lazorchaks, and Rosenbergs—thank you, especially Butch, Graham, Karina, Stewart, Isabelle, Samson, Crockett, and Gabriel: you have our eternal gratitude for putting up with us through marathon phone-meetings and late-night contemplations of the em dash. A special shout-out to Mary's mother-in-law (also named Mary) who cooked far, far, far more than her share and wiped bottoms and noses while the other Mary was working on this book.

We are also thankful for support—moral and otherwise—from the Hemphills, the Briers and Striers, Andy Bechtel, Natalie Blitt, Laurel Snyder, Joe Corey, Jillian Bergsma, Kristi Stultz, Melanie Almeder, Channing Johnson, the Roanoke College English Department, the Salem Museum, and *The Roanoke Times*.

Thanks to Blacksburg and Salem High Schools for their gold-mines of angst. Thanks to Ginger Rogers (yes, *that* Ginger Rogers) and Mary Shelley (yes, *that* Mary Shelley). Thanks to readers and writers, bloggers, dreamers, and long-distance carriers. To the guy at Mill Mountain Coffee Shop who serves tea with his advice. To whoever makes those cranberry-orange scones.

Thank you Arlington, Brooklyn, and Raleigh. Thank you Blacksburg, Elliston, and Salem. And if you're reading this book, thank you for your kind attention and for your willingness to dream.

About the Authors

Mary Crockett likes turtles, licorice, and the Yankees. Madelyn Rosenberg likes cats, avocados, and the Red Sox. Luckily they both like the weirdness of dreams (and each other) enough to write novels together. Their friendship has survived three moves, six kids, and countless manuscript revisions. Madelyn (*Canary in the Coal Mine*) lives in Arlington, Virginia, just outside D.C. Mary (*A Theory of Everything: Poems*) remains in the mountains near Salem, Virginia. Visit them online at www.marycrockett.com and www.madelynrosenberg.com.